"That's where I
she said, seeing that he was still looking at the beach below.

"I was wondering if that was where it was," Christian answered in a soft, reflective tone.

Erin looked at him curiously. "Do you remember it?"

He slanted her a wry look. "All I remember is freezing to death, literally." And you, he added silently. He remembered nothing of the beach. He had been dying, his awareness almost gone . . . yet his memory of her was perfect. How could that be? he wondered as he studied her upturned face. Perhaps because he had wanted to take the vision of her with him into eternity.

Dear Reader,

Welcome to summer, and welcome to another fine month of reading from Silhouette Intimate Moments. We have some exciting books in store for you, not just this month, but all summer long. Let me start with our June titles, then give you a peek at what's coming up in the future.

First, there's *That McKenna Woman*, the first book in Parris Afton Bonds' Mescalero Trilogy. Parris used her home state of New Mexico as the location of the Mescalero Cattle Company, then peopled the ranch with some of the most charismatic characters you'll ever find. Tom Malcolm and Marianna McKenna couldn't be less alike, but that doesn't stop them from discovering a love as big as the West. And the family created by their marriage provides the basis for the other two books in the series, books we know you'll look forward to reading.

Another special book for June is Kathleen Eagle's *More Than a Miracle*, a follow-up to *Candles in the Night* (Silhouette Special Edition #437). This is the story of a woman who, forced to give up her child, now embarks on a desperate mission to find her son. Her only help comes from the man they call McQuade, and even then, it may take more than a miracle to make her dream come true.

During the rest of the summer, look for books by old favorites like Lucy Hamilton (whose Dodd Memorial Hospital Trilogy ends in July with *Heartbeats*), Heather Graham Pozzessere and Emilie Richards. They're just a few of the writers whose work will be waiting for you— only in the pages of Silhouette Intimate Moments.

Sincerely,

Leslie J. Wainger
Senior Editor, Silhouette Books

Patricia Gardner Evans

Summer of the Wolf

Silhouette Intimate Moments

Published by Silhouette Books New York

America's Publisher of Contemporary Romance

SILHOUETTE BOOKS
300 East 42nd St., New York, N.Y. 10017

ISBN: 0-373-07243-0

First Silhouette Books printing June 1988

Printed in the U.S.A.

Books by Patricia Gardner Evans

Silhouette Intimate Moments

Flashpoint #151
Whatever It Takes #228
Summer of the Wolf #243

PATRICIA GARDNER EVANS

has lived in New Mexico all her life and has traveled extensively throughout the West, exploring old ghost towns, Indian ruins and abandoned homesteads. She avoids housework by spending much of her free time outdoors fishing and raising her own fruits and vegetables. She gets inspiration for her plots and characters from the land and people around her.

Chapter 1

The man staggered out of the heavy surf onto the rocky beach. He stumbled drunkenly up the shore a few paces, just beyond the reach of the freezing water, and fell to his knees. The sharp gravel dug through the thin fabric of his pants, but he didn't feel it. His arms windmilled as he tried to regain his feet. He couldn't, and he pitched forward onto the rocks. The blood welling from a cut on his cheek caused by a razor-sharp slice of stone froze into a scab almost instantly.

The sea sucked at his feet, trying to pull him back into its frigid embrace. Instinctively, he drew his knees to his chest and hugged them with arms that didn't want to obey. Warmth was only a dim dream. His sodden black pants and sweater gave him no heat, and he'd lost his shoes to the sea. His muscles were too exhausted, his strength too depleted, for him even to shiver and generate a little heat of his own. He lay on the wet, cold, black shore and felt himself slipping into final oblivion.

He waited for it impatiently. As his brain cataloged the process with a kind of cynical detachment, his internal systems began shutting down one by one. He lost the feeling in his fingers and toes, then his hands and feet, his arms and legs. The absolute cold spread remorselessly to the core of his body. Sight seemed to be gone, along with smell and touch; if he remembered correctly, hearing would be the last to go. One last bleakly humorous thought tugged up a corner of his almost rigid mouth. He was sure that where he was going, he would at least be warm.

He almost made it. A mechanical howl disturbed him, and his subconscious was annoyed, wishing it would go away. The racket ceased abruptly and, gratefully, he again started that final slide into blessed warmth and forgetfulness.

Someone wearing heavy boots ran and skidded over the slippery rocks. He didn't hear, but the soft curse that followed the footsteps, a human sound in an inhuman environment, penetrated his stupor. Something inside forced him back up several levels of consciousness; he fought it, wanting the promised oblivion to come back. In spite of himself, he listened, finally, reluctantly, struggling to open his eyes. Only his left eye would open; the lashes of the right were frozen shut. He blinked and slowly focused through the arctic twilight on the white bear advancing on its hind legs.

He giggled foolishly. A polar bear wasn't right for the locale. It should be a massive Kodiak, a great brown bear, maybe with a little red cap, like the bears wore in the Moscow circus. The bear squatted down beside him. Instead of the rank smell of rotten fish and rancid seal blubber that he'd expected, there was a sweet smell, a smell of fresh spring breezes and summer flowers. His half-frozen brain accepted that, just as it accepted that it would be the bear, not the cold, that killed him.

The bear seemed to be touching him, patting his face, but he couldn't feel it. One furry paw reached up to push at its head. Inexplicably, the bear took off its head, and he could see that the wicked bear had eaten an angel, gulped her down whole. The warm, salty tears of his grief at such an unbearable sadness melted the frozen snow in his right eye, and he opened it to look into the angel's face.

The angel's eyes were sea green, flecked with golden bits of foam. Long, golden angel hair floated free on a sudden breeze. She was so very beautiful. He wished he could kill the bad bear for eating her. Two tears rolled down his cheeks and froze at the corners of his mouth.

The angel was frowning at him, chewing on her soft rosy bottom lip. He tried to open his mouth, tried to make his thick tongue work and his frozen lips move, to beg her not to be angry with him. He would have saved her from the bear if he could have. He saw the bear reach out a furry arm once more and was bracing for the ripping of its claws when he slid down at last into the lovely warmth of hell.

Without thinking, Erin Mathias pushed the hood of her parka back onto her head as she stared in disbelief at the big man huddled on the beach. Why he wasn't dead defied all the laws of this harsh, unforgiving land. Yet his eyes had blinked open and stared back at her, a startling ice blue that had burned with the fierce will to survive that must be all that was keeping him alive. He had to be very near death; before those incredible eyes had shut, they'd filled with a silent plea that begged her to...to what? Save him, no doubt.

She tugged off a mitten with her teeth and laid her bare hand on his neck just under his jaw, feeling for his pulse. His death-white skin felt colder than the forty-degree water he'd come from, as cold as the chunks of ice littering the shore, but his heart was still beating. Not strongly, but the pulse of life was still moving within him. Standing, Erin rapidly tugged off her other mitten and unfastened her parka. Never had she been more grateful for its warmth than now. She knew that, realistically, the man's chance of survival was poor, but if the polar-bear-fur snowsuit would only keep him alive until she got him back to her hut, she was sure she could save him.

Within seconds her body was racked by almost uncontrollable shivering. An arctic breeze cut through the silk long-underwear top that was all she'd been wearing when she'd thrown on the parka. Her nipples tightened in the cold air and pushed hard against the thin silk. Erin ignored her body's complaints as her stiff fingers worked on the sinew laces of her boots. After yanking off the boots, she shed her pants, then jerked the boots back on, not bothering to retie them. He couldn't afford the time it would take her to go back for extra clothing for him; he couldn't even afford the time it would take her to lace up her boots.

The wind sliced through the silk long-underwear bottoms like frozen razor blades, and every muscle in her body clenched in one never-ending spasm of shivering. She had probably already turned as blue as her navy underwear, she thought wryly as she rolled the stranger over onto his stomach and straightened his limbs. After stuffing his long, limp arms into the sleeves of her parka, she pushed him onto his back and pulled the hood over his head. His wet hair was cut short and plastered to his skull, and it was the color of white gold. She managed to tie the hood under his chin, but there was no hope of closing the parka over his broad chest and even broader shoulders. "Damn, why couldn't you have been a little smaller?" she muttered as she crammed his hands into the ends of the opposite sleeves to protect them. At five feet eight, she was no midget, but he dwarfed her. He had to be at least six three and two hundred pounds. She fed his legs into the fur pants, panting with the effort it took to work them over his own wet pants. She certainly hoped he appreciated that she was risking double pneumonia, not to mention frostbite to delicate portions of her anatomy, to save him, she thought tartly.

The pants would only reach halfway up his lean hips, and there was a six-inch gap between his feet and the cuffs. Jamming his feet into her mittens, she shoved hard to get the long cuffs over his heels. At the very least, she tried to tell herself unemotionally, he'd lose his toes. Sitting back on her heels, she drew a deep breath of the piercingly cold pure air, then exhaled a huge steamy puff as she prepared for the task of getting him up off the beach and over to the small, four-wheeled, all-terrain vehicle parked a couple of feet away. Despite the wind chill lowering the temperature below the freezing point, her underwear top was soaked with perspiration, and sticking to her chest and back. The breeze freeze-dried the silk into a second skin of ice, and she shivered so hard that even grinding her teeth together couldn't stop their chattering.

Erin stepped over him and knelt down, straddling his hips as she reached her hands under his arms. She tried to reach all the way around and clasp her hands across his back, but her arms wouldn't stretch that far. She finally had to settle for anchoring her shoulders in his armpits and locking her arms up and over his shoulders to get a good grip. Caught intimately against her, his head wobbled forward, and his chin settled firmly into the hollow between her shoulder and neck. His breath tickled almost unbearably. At least he's still breathing, she thought as she heaved him upright and staggered backward, weaving like a drunk under his dead weight. Abruptly, she collapsed, landing on her fanny on the sharp rocks and nearly toppling over flat on her back as he sprawled on top of her. His weight on her chest knocked the wind out of her, and for a few moments she could only sit, unconsciously hugging him closer for warmth as she tried to catch her breath. Suddenly she began to laugh helplessly. With him looking like a bear whose fur had shrunk, and her in nothing but her clunky boots and underwear, they could give somebody a good laugh as they stumblebummed around. Too bad their only audience was a couple of sea gulls who didn't look much impressed by their antics.

Her laughter turned grim as she realized that any humor in the situation was black. Working her legs under her, Erin levered herself up to her knees. As the sharp stones jabbed through the silk long johns into the tender flesh of her knees, she swore liberally. "D-damn d-drunk R-russians," she said in a shivering stutter. With a superwoman-style heave, she made it to her feet and did a quick, boozy little two-step to keep her balance, then turned and flopped her partner over the saddle of the vehicle. Sam Akiachak, the bush pilot who'd dropped her off last month, had warned her about the Russians just as he had the year before when he'd flown Daniel and her out to the tiny Aleutian island. The Coast Guardsmen who stopped by on patrol had given her the same warning. The Russians laid in half as much food and four times as much liquor as their American counterparts. Then, invariably, they ran out of liquor halfway through the whale-watching season. With their fast little cutters, they would come across the Bering Sea, sneaking past the coast station on Attu, to trade jars of caviar and other Soviet delicacies for whatever alcohol the Americans might have. Sam had also warned her not to let the Russians know she was alone. They didn't lay in any women as part of their supplies.

She snorted as she swung one of the man's legs over the gas tank and climbed on behind him, hitching him up and dragging him back against her chest. Boy, these guys must be a bunch of real boozers to have run out after only a month, but he'd risked his life for nothing. She'd never developed a taste for caviar and, even if she had, he wasn't getting the four bottles of Molson Golden beer that made up her entire liquor supply. Daniel had brought several six-packs last year and had never gotten around to drinking the last few bottles. She was selfishly hoarding them for her birthday in a few days. She was going to eat the entire Sara Lee double-chocolate, three-layer cake stashed in the freezer, put Harry Chapin on the tape player, swill beer and luxuriate in self-pity all evening.

Sagging against his back, she breathed a long, relieved sigh before she reached for the starter switch—and discovered a new problem. His blasted legs were so long that they were going to be dragging on the ground once they got going. Clamping one arm across his chest and hugging his hips with her thighs to keep his boneless body from oozing off the four-wheeler, she fought with first one of his legs and then the other until she had them both draped over the handlebars. It was an extremely undignified position; too bad he was unconscious and didn't know it, she decided meanly.

She jabbed the starter switch, and the vehicle's engine drowned out the thundering surf. With his legs dangling over the handlebars, swinging back and forth and making it nearly impossible to steer, Erin guided the machine slowly up the rocky beach. The four-wheeler crawled from behind the shelter of a small hummock, and a blast of air straight from the North Pole stunned Erin like a body blow. The gale robbed her lungs of air, and the lack of oxygen seared a fiery pain along her ribs. It stole what little body heat she had left, putting her in danger of developing the deadly hypothermia she knew her passenger was already suffering from, yet her instinctive reaction was to protect the man before herself. Risking her precarious control of the vehicle, she raised one hand to his face to pull the parka hood over it more completely. His chin had sunk onto his chest, so that the top of his head, protected by the thick polar-bear fur, took the brunt of the gale.

Making herself as small as possible, she used his big body for a windbreak. The merciless wind whipped across the barren headland, burning her eyes like acid. Countless times she buried her face in the long white fur of the parka to scrub away tears that congealed almost instantly into solid ice. Her unprotected face felt raw, and it burned, too, until it went numb.

The trip was little more than a mile in distance but an endless torment in time. Finally, through her frozen tears, she saw the rusting hulk of her World War Two Quonset hut. Erin drove right up to the door. As she hauled him off the ATV, she realized that her own strength was gone; only adrenaline was pushing her now. Her body slow and clumsy, she managed the few steps through the air lock, then dropped him. After slamming the outer airtight steel door against the gale, she stumbled down the short tunnel-like passage to the inner door and threw it open on bright light and lush warmth. Her body wanted nothing more than to collapse, but she forced her exhausted, protesting muscles to take her back down the tunnel and drag him into the haven of light and heat.

The warmth inside was as much of a shock to her half-frozen body as the vicious cold outside had been. For long minutes all Erin could do was lie on the floor beside him, her body soaking up warmth like a sponge as heat seeped into every pore. Reaching out, her hand sought his, her fingers light on his cold wrist to find his pulse. It was thready and very faint, but he was still alive. On its own, her hand slipped down and clasped his tightly, as if trying to strengthen his fragile life force with her own.

Gradually the heat revived her, until she was able to push him onto the edge of a thick rug and roll him up inside it. It wouldn't warm him appreciably, but at least it should keep him from losing any more body heat.

She sprinted across the large main room, kicking off her heavy boots as she ran. Two doors were set in the partition across the back third of the hut. She opened the right-hand one on a bathroom whose main feature was a six-foot, circular Jacuzzi. After opening the taps to full pressure, she turned on the jets to mix the incoming streams of ice-cold and steam-hot water, crossing her fingers that the cold-water pump wouldn't choose this moment to be stubborn. While the tub filled, she hurriedly searched her face and ears for signs of frostbite in the mirror over the sink. There were no white, numb patches. She checked her hands and fingers as a matter of course, but the pins and needles prickling in them as warmth returned had already told her that she had nothing to worry about.

She ran water until the tub was almost full before shutting off the taps. She tested the heat of the water with her elbow and discovered that the water was above normal body temperature, but not hot enough to scald him. Thankfully, she had an endless supply of hot water and electricity. The strong current that flowed past the island powered a hydroelectric generator to provide her with more than enough electricity for her Spartan needs, and a previous occupant had ingeniously tapped into a nearby geyser and piped in the superheated water for washing purposes and heat. Ironically, in a land of months-long ice and snow, the only thing she had a shortage of was cold water. Water from the geyser was drawn off into a small storage tank, then allowed to cool naturally. She'd just drained it by filling the tub, and it would be morning before she had cold water again.

She hurried back into the main room, pausing long enough to adjust a thermostat on the rough-paneled wall. Now more of the boiling water from the geyser would run through the radiators and make the already warm room even hotter. A large black, tan and cream cat was sniffing at the stranger wrapped in the rug. As Erin knelt down beside him, the cat looked up at her inquiringly. "Scoot, Oscar." When he refused to move, she nudged him aside and began unrolling the rug. The cat leaped onto a shabby overstuffed sofa to watch her with an offended stare.

Erin paid no attention to the animal. The man was lying ominously still, like a wet bag of rags. Efficiently, she began to strip him, making short work of the snowsuit and mittens. His sweater took precious seconds, the wet wool stubbornly stretching instead of coming off. It made a sodden thump on the plank floor as she threw it aside. His breath caught, and hers did, too, and she unconsciously held it until she saw his chest fall as his breath shuddered out in a ragged gasp. His breathing was getting shallower, the rhythm more uneven. "You aren't going to die!" She didn't hear the fierceness in her whisper or recognize the sudden determination that infused her with fresh strength. "I won't let you."

Despite her haste to undress him, she treated his body gently. Frozen tissue damaged very easily. She spent a few more precious seconds swiftly but meticulously examining his face, chest and hands for frostbite. Calling in a med-evac helicopter from the U.S. Navy base at Adak wouldn't be possible in this gale, but she'd had an intensive first-aid course in the treatment of hypothermia and other cold-related illnesses, and there was nothing that could be done for him in the small clinic on Adak that she couldn't do right here.

She checked the temperature of a suspicious-looking patch of yellowish-white skin on his left cheek. It was even colder than the rest of him. The cut on his other cheek was unimportant now. The frozen scab on the cut was thawing and beginning to ooze, but the cut looked shallow. After tucking the fur parka back around his chest and arms, she moved down to the button on the waistband of his pants. Like his sweater, the pants were black, but the damp material felt like denim, not wool. She unfastened them and then, to her amazement, she found her fingers faltering over the zipper. "Come now, Erin," she chided herself, "this is no time for maidenly embarrassment." She grasped the brass tab and pulled down firmly. She tugged off the pants, then reached up for the plain white briefs he wore underneath. "You've seen a naked man before," she reminded herself dryly as her fingers hesitated again. Hooking her fingers in the waistband, she dragged the white cotton down quickly, trying to keep her eyes on his knees. "Oh, but not like this,'' she whispered faintly before she caught herself staring and forced her gaze to his knees again. She examined his toes and feet, large and strong and well-shaped like his hands, automatically noting the ridges of callus at the outer edges of the soles, similar to the ones on his palms. She found two more worrisome spots of probable frostbite, one on his left heel and another on one of his right toes. Forcing her touch to be impersonally brisk, she checked his calves, knees and thighs. His legs were long, like his arms, and just as strongly roped with muscle.

Carefully she turned him onto his stomach to check his back. His buttocks were as tightly muscled as the rest of him. A small round scar, almost like a dimple, marred the smooth skin of his back. It was a finger's width from his spine and down low, where his broad back tapered into lean hips.

Dismissing it, she rolled him face-up again. Her hands froze on his hips. She had been so intent before on checking his face and arms and legs that she hadn't seen the scar on his belly. As pale as his skin was, the scar was even whiter, like the underbelly of something that would live in the dark slime under a damp rock. The scar was old and roughly circular, like an obscene puckered mouth, extending from his hip bone to his navel.

She realized that her brain must still be chilled, because it took almost a full minute before she understood the connection between the innocuous dimple on his back and the ugly scar on his stomach. Erin felt a chill deeper and more paralyzing than the killing cold of the storm raging outside. Someone had shot him—in the back. Who or why she couldn't guess, but instinctively she knew it hadn't been by accident. Although the shot had missed his spinal cord, which would have killed or paralyzed him, the size of the scar left by the exit wound in his belly showed how the bullet had ripped and torn its way through his body. He should have died from a wound like that, she thought starkly.

Taking a deep breath, she began the last stage of her examination. A heat that didn't come from the radiators flushed the chilling shock of his scars from her body. It had to be done, she reminded herself. He would never forgive her if he suffered frostbite on such an important part of his anatomy and she left it untreated. Her knuckles brushed a dense patch of tawny hair, and she prayed that he wouldn't suddenly wake up and accuse her of committing perverted acts on his helpless body. Although, she thought, shaking her head wryly, she couldn't imagine a less helpless-looking man, even unconscious.

At last she was satisfied that there were only the three patches of frostbite to worry about. "You're very lucky, comrade," she murmured as she began dragging the rug, with him on it, across the floor and into the bathroom. *Very* lucky, agreed an impish little voice inside her. She was no connoisseur, certainly, but he was quite nicely endowed. Suddenly she felt embarrassed. The examination of his entire body had been necessary, but she was ashamed of herself for ogling him like a teenybopper who'd sneaked into an X-rated movie.

At the base of the steps leading to the Jacuzzi, she crouched behind his head and hooked her arms under his. Then she stood slowly, bringing him up with her. Backing up the carpeted steps carefully, she pulled his limp body along. On the top step, she balanced him between her knees with an arm around his neck as she felt on the edge of the tub for one of the rubber bands she always left there. After gathering her hair quickly into a ponytail, she shifted his weight until she could grab one of his knees and slide his leg into the pool. His other leg followed of its own accord, and she eased his body into the tub. He slid down along the smooth fiberglass side, and she scrambled in after him.

Relaxing back against the side, Erin pulled him to her, locking her arms across his chest to keep him upright. She'd already been soaked with perspiration anyway, she thought ruefully, as she felt the warm water soaking through her silk underwear. The job of getting him into the tub had exhausted her. She didn't want to think about how she was going to get him out of it. Still, she was very glad she had the Jacuzzi. She laughed softly to herself. The recommended alternative to using a warm bath for combatting hypothermia was stripping down and climbing into bed with the victim to share body heat.

She rubbed her hands over his chest, trying to warm his cold body faster. Her hands smoothed down his arms, then up, then down again, over his ribs and along his flanks. Had he been alone? She supposed that tomorrow she should try to raise the Soviet whale-watching station on her shortwave radio and let them know that he was all right.

Settling them both deeper into the water, she continued the languid stroking of his arms and chest, hips and thighs, his skin slipping like smooth, wet silk under her hands. The Russians' contention that they were whale watchers was laughable, and the idea that they thought anyone actually believed it was even more ludicrous. She had one hut with one antenna and a portable satellite dish the size of a typewriter. The Soviet site bristled with antennae; their satellite dishes were bigger than the Jacuzzi, and more radar equipment no doubt filled all eight of their huts. The only way they would ever watch a whale was if they thought it was a disguised American submarine sent to spy on them.

The water was cooling. Erin stretched an arm over her head to flip the drain lever and let the tub empty a bit before turning on the hot water again. She switched on the jets to increase the stimulation against his body and quicken his sluggish circulation. His body suddenly began to tremble as it regained the ability to shiver. Moaning, he thrashed his arms, sloshing water over the edge of the tub. "Sh, sh," Erin soothed, as she tried to keep out of the way of his flailing arms and still keep both their heads above water. "It's all right. You're safe now." She was glad the shivering reflex had returned, because it meant his body had warmed considerably, but his moans meant that he was also feeling the return of sensation in his limbs. Erin had experienced a touch of that agony once when she'd carelessly left her mittens behind one frigid day, thinking a few minutes outside without them couldn't matter. The pain in her hands when the feeling finally returned had been like a dozen angry ants under the skin, trying to sting and bite their way out. For him, it must be like thousands.

He continued to struggle, in his mind against the pain, in reality against her. Even in his weakened state, he was frighteningly strong, and it took all Erin's strength just to keep both of them from drowning. His groans were harrowing as she continued her quiet murmurs of comfort and reassurance. She didn't realize that the wet warmth on her cheeks was tears, not water from the pool. She could end his suffering immediately with a shot of morphine from her medical kit, but it would depress his respiration, making pneumonia almost a certainty. Silently, she asked him to forgive her.

Just when Erin thought that she could endure his misery no longer and would risk the morphine, his shudders and moans abruptly ceased. With a quiet sigh, he turned and relaxed against her, his cheek resting on her breast, his arms around her waist. His long legs tangled with hers and his body settled over hers. His skin had lost its icy chill; he felt as warm as she did now. Past exhaustion, Erin closed her eyes and drew a long, ragged breath. Thankfully, he had never become conscious, so he wouldn't remember his pain. Unfortunately, she would. She knew he'd been fighting her only by instinct, but she couldn't help feeling that she'd deserved it.

Rubbing his hips against her, he murmured something. Erin's eyes popped open, widening in consternation as she tried to shift out from under him. She bit her lip to stifle a startled giggle. There was nothing wrong with the rest of his instincts, either. He might be unconscious, but his body knew exactly where it was, naked and wrapped around a woman who might as well be naked for all the good her wet underwear was doing. She pushed hard against his chest to break his hold, but all he did was clasp her closer, his mouth nuzzling, searching across a soft, cushiony mound. His breath was warm through the cool, damp silk and, to her dismay, Erin felt her nipples hardening, straining. She shoved against him harder and only succeeded in pushing her own head under the water. She came up, sputtering and laughing helplessly. She knew she was more in danger of drowning than losing her virtue, yet even in his insensible state, this was no clumsy pawing. His hands slid over her back and hips, kneading gently. His body knowingly stroked against hers, and his mouth, she thought dazedly... His mouth!

It had found what it was seeking, his tongue finessing the hard point, his lips shaping her softness, his breath hot against her flushed skin, creating an even hotter coil of heat winding down inside her.

With a feeling curiously close to regret, she shoved him away as hard as she could. He frowned and mumbled something, but let go. Grabbing his arm, she towed him to the steps, then slumped on the bottom one. How was she going to get him out?

"Wake up." She spoke in a normal tone of voice, shaking him gently. "Time to wake up now. Come on. Wake up. We have to get out now." Erin sensed that he had passed from unconsciousness into a drugged-like sleep. If only she knew his name! She couldn't speak Russian, but maybe the sound of his name would rouse him enough so that he could walk. She repeated her command more loudly, shaking him a little harder. He murmured something in a foreign language, and then, to Erin's astonishment, he stood up. His eyes half open, he stumbled up the steps like a sleepwalker. She moved quickly to get her shoulder under his, wrapping one arm around his waist to help him navigate. The water streamed from both of them as they climbed out of the pool. Erin grabbed a bath sheet with her free hand. She didn't want to stop to dry him right now, but she didn't want him going to bed soaking wet, either.

Her hip nudging his, she guided him into her bedroom next to the bathroom. The long-haired cat followed, picking his way prissily to avoid the wet puddles they were dripping on the floor. Erin steadied the man at the side of her queen-size bed with one hand while she snapped on the bedside lamp and jerked the covers down with the other. He stood docilely, his eyes heavy-lidded and unfocused, as she rubbed him down quickly with the rough towel, resolutely ignoring the very male body under her hands. A gentle push, and he sat on the edge of the bed while she towel-dried his hair. The cat jumped on the other side and sat at the end of the bed, watching her and this intruder into their solitary domain with a faint air of puzzlement.

"Lie down now," she whispered softly, and he obeyed. His eyes shut, and he was deeply asleep again before his head hit the pillow. Erin decided against getting out her hair dryer. She swung his legs up onto the bed and, leaning over him, examined his cheek and both feet. The small patches of skin that she'd feared were frostbitten now had the same healthy tan as the rest of him. He was tanned all over, she noted absently. His breathing was quiet and even. Despite his ordeal, he hadn't gone into shock, and she was sure there was little worry of pneumonia now.

Still, she didn't move to cover him. She felt no embarrassing sense of voyeurism now, only an intense curiosity about this man who was lying in her bed naked. Even as exposed and vulnerable as he was, she sensed that he was about as defenseless as a sleeping wolf.

His light hair, rumpled and falling over his broad forehead, gave him a boyish look, but there were lines around his eyes and nose and mouth—not deep, but enough to show he was well past youth, late thirties, maybe early forties. His straight, slightly bushy eyebrows were the same pale color as his hair and lashes, and for a few brief moments, she'd again seen those startling ice-blue eyes. Under the soft glow of the bedside lamp, his thick lashes cast shadows on the high cheekbones that framed his straight blade of a nose. His mouth was thin and firmly set, his jaw square, his chin deeply cleft. Even in sleep, there was an alertness about him. His face had enough asymmetry and bluntness to keep him from being considered handsome in the classic sense, but he wouldn't walk into a room unnoticed, not if there were any women present.

Or men, either. She'd thought of a wolf earlier and realized now that it was an apt comparison. He had the look of a predator, but not the lankiness of a coyote, or the heavily muscled power of an adult male lion or tiger. His body, though obviously very strong, was lean, graceful and well-proportioned. Like a wolf, he was built for speed as well as strength and endurance. Weaker men would instinctively give way, while strong ones would offer wary respect.

He had little body hair. There was a light dusting of pale gold on his arms and legs, but his deep chest and abdomen were smooth—except for the thick, dark gold thatch down low on his flat belly. With an unconscious sigh, she pulled the covers over him, tucking them around him carefully.

After picking up the damp towel from the nightstand, she turned off the lamp. She tiptoed to the dresser on the opposite wall and eased open a drawer to take out an oversize flannel shirt and panties. At the door to the bedroom, she turned for a final look and, seeing the red sheen of the cat's eyes in the dark, she whispered, "Come on, Oscar. Let him sleep."

As soon as the cat brushed by her ankles she pulled the door nearly closed, then peeled off her damp long underwear and gave her body a cursory swipe with the towel. Slipping on the flannel shirt, she glanced down to see that it barely reached the middle of her thighs. "I'm going to have to stop running around half-dressed," she muttered as she did up the buttons. She spared a wistful thought for the thick fleece robe she'd left hanging in her closet back at the institute. She should have brought it, but then, she hadn't planned on having a house-guest.

After towel-drying her own hair, Erin mopped up the trail of puddles they'd tracked across the floor. Whoever he was, he wasn't a Russian. She might not speak the language, but she'd heard enough of it on her radio to know the sound, and whatever he had been speaking, it hadn't been Russian. It had sounded similar to German, only more guttural. Dutch, maybe.

After she'd finished with the mopping, Erin pulled the rag rug back into place and gathered up his clothes, her underwear and the towel, and tossed them on top of a compact washing machine in the kitchen corner of the main room. A sudden thought had her taking his clothes back out of the pile. She turned the pants pockets inside out, but they were empty. If he'd had a wallet or anything else that might have told her his identity, it had been lost in the ocean. She searched his clothing for a label that might at least give her a clue to his nationality and the language he spoke. A minute later she threw the clothes back onto the washer once more. All she'd learned was that he had international taste in clothing. The label in his sweater was in Greek, his pants came from Australia, and his briefs were all-American Jockey shorts.

After draping her snowsuit and mittens over a drying rack by the air lock, she set back the thermostat a few degrees, then stood in the middle of the room uncertainly. She was almost paralyzed with exhaustion; she ought to make up a bed on the sofa, but a peculiar restlessness kept her from going to bed just yet. Perhaps she would stay up a little longer, just to make sure he was really doing as well as he seemed.

Without consciously deciding to do it, Erin climbed up the ladder built in one corner of the room. The ladder and the odd, turretlike addition it led to had been built by the same man who'd engineered the Quonset hut's heating system from the thermal vent. Erin had guessed that once he no longer had to worry about energy conservation, he'd decided to indulge a whim and build an observation tower. For Erin, it had been a godsend, saving her from long hours outside in the frequently miserable weather. From the glass windows in the turret, she could observe the small bay in front of the hut in comfort.

She could clearly see the beach and the pod of beluga whales feeding in the cove. It was very late, after midnight, but true darkness didn't exist this far north in the summertime. Night was a long twilight as the sun dipped only briefly below the horizon. As she gazed out the window, she laughed quietly to herself. Now she knew why she'd thought of the wolf. It had been about the same time of night at the beginning of last summer, while she'd been keeping watch on a small pod of whales like the ones out there now, that she'd glanced up to the tall hill across the bay. She'd been astounded to see a wolf sitting there, silhouetted against the pale gray sky. She'd been so excited that she had run down and woken Daniel to make him look, so she could be sure she wasn't seeing things. All summer, she'd observed the wolf along with the whales. A magnificent animal, he was coal black except for the silver tips on his ears and tail. Since this was far beyond the normal western range of wolves in the Aleutian Islands, she had finally decided that he must have been trapped on a floe during the spring breakup of the ice packing the Bering Sea and ridden down on the current. He'd spent the summer decimating the island mouse population, but when she'd returned this year, he'd been gone. She had imagined him hopping another passing ice floe early in the spring to catch a ride farther east.

Now the cat sprang up on the high wooden stool beside her and rubbed luxuriously against her hand. Absently, she scratched behind his ears. The summer before, the sea had brought her a wolf. Now, it seemed, it had brought her another one. "Who do you suppose he is, Oscar?" she whispered softly.

A sudden whistle from below, jarringly loud in the silent darkness, made Erin jump. She ran down the iron rungs of the ladder as squeals, clicks and birdlike chirps filled the hut with an eerie symphony of sound. Simultaneously a computer printer clacked into life. With a twist of a knob on the speaker beside the computer module, Erin muted the sounds being broadcast through it. Sitting at a computer terminal, she read the lines that appeared on the screen, her fingers automatically typing responses to fill in the lulls.

Man lives?
Man lives.
Is your own kind. Is not good you alone.
Where you find him?
In sea. He came from great noisy bird. He pleases you?
He pleases me.

Chapter 2

Have you had any unexpected company drop in lately?"

Erin glanced away from the gleaming white Coast Guard cutter tied up at her dock to the young lieutenant standing beside her. "No," she lied with a bland smile. "No company since you came by last week."

She saw him looking at the bright red ATV parked at the door of the Quonset hut. Damn it! she cursed silently. She hadn't put the four-wheeler away. Would he notice it and ask her why she had it out? His glance slid over the machine without comment, and Erin decided paranoia must be a symptom of a guilty conscience. John Falk's gaze came back to her, and she gave him a brilliant smile. "Should I be expecting some?"

His appealingly homely face creased in a wide grin. "Even out here, in the middle of nowhere, you should expect company, Dr. Mathias. Erin," he corrected himself at her chiding look. "Every man at our station, for starters."

Erin laughed in appreciation of his gallantry, and only she knew the laughter was forced. It died a sudden death as he changed the subject.

"We got a request early this morning to look for some guy who was headed out this way." From the lieutenant's disgruntled tone, Erin knew that the request had been an order. "He gassed up his seaplane late yesterday afternoon at Adak, then disappeared from the radar scope about an hour later. Nobody's picked up a radio message or a signal from an emergency locator beacon, but somebody wants him found. An air search has started, too." He looked at her with studied casualness. "The gas jockey said he specifically asked about you and the island."

Suddenly Erin wondered if the lieutenant's questions were as innocent as they seemed. She shook her head with genuine puzzlement. "I'm not expecting anyone."

Falk shrugged. "He probably just set down near one of the uninhabited islands to ride out the storm." He sighed as he looked at the fog bank rolling in on the western horizon and, with obvious reluctance, took a step toward the cutter. "Well, I've got fifty square miles of ocean to search, but—" he gave her a hopeful smile "—I'll be back soon."

Erin waved as the cutter executed a smart turn in the small cove and headed for the open sea. Don't hurry back, she commanded silently, and began to trudge up the short hill to the Quonset hut. Why had she lied? When John Falk had mentioned that he was out looking for a missing plane and its pilot, why hadn't she spoken up? At least now she knew who the strange naked man sleeping in her bed was! She smiled unconsciously as she imagined the look that would have crossed the young lieutenant's face at *that* announcement. Her smile faded as she dragged open the warped metal door of the shed where she stored the ATV. She, who valued honesty above all else, who was so uncomfortable with lies that she could never tell one without blushing and stammering, had just lied with the best of them. Erin was starting to climb on the four-wheeler to drive it into the shed when she remembered the man sleeping in her bed. The buzz-saw racket of the engine would wake him up. She shoved the gear lever into neutral, then had to throw all her weight against the handlebars to start the unwieldy machine rolling into the shed.

After closing the door, she leaned against it to catch her breath. Staring out over the small half-moon bay below, she watched the waves pounding the high-tide line on the beach. The wind was bitter, the sky heavy with leaden clouds—just another balmy summer day in the Aleutians, she thought dryly. A weak sunbeam struggled through the sullen clouds, and Erin closed her eyes on a tired sigh, imagining warmth on her cold cheeks. Lying was exhausting. In addition, she'd gotten very little sleep last night. Eventually she had made up a bed on the sofa, but she had gotten up several times to check on her visitor, and spent most of the rest of the night lying awake, staring into the dark, listening in case he needed her.

She didn't think she had kept his presence on her island a secret because she was bored... or lonely. She had so much she wanted to do, and the summer season was so short that she resented even the need for sleep; and, although she was the only human living on the island, she was hardly alone. Had she lied because she wanted to protect him? It seemed almost ludicrous that he would need her protection, yet that awful scar was mute evidence that he wasn't invulnerable. Someone had once done him grave harm. Perhaps the sight of him, so big and strong, so alive and utterly male, yet lying helpless, dependent on her for his survival, had aroused some latent protective instincts that she hadn't even known she had.

Or maybe it's your overactive imagination, Erin, she told herself cynically. Just who do you think you have to protect him from? Russian "whale watchers" aside, the Aleutians were hardly a hotbed of cloak and dagger activity. More like a cold bed, she decided, shivering against the glacial breeze cutting through her flannel shirt. She had dashed out without taking time to grab a coat when she had seen the Coast Guard cutter coming, anxious to meet it at the dock before anyone could come up to the hut.

Outside of the thirty-man Coast Guard station on Attu, which was the westernmost of the U.S.-owned Aleutians, the "top-secret" Air Force base on Shemya Island next door, which was about as secret as the Soviet whale-watching post, and the Navy base on Adak two hundred miles to the east, the only people in the area were researchers like herself, a couple of game wardens and a few villages of native Aleuts trying to eke a living out of fishing. Hardly the characters in a spy thriller. If she'd had any sense at all, she would have piped up immediately and said yes, she had the man they were searching for and would they please take him off her hands. Somebody was already looking for him, worried about him. Probably his wife and a half dozen kiddies, she thought with less guilt and more irritation than was rational.

Erin shook her head at that thought. Somehow he didn't look like a man with a wife and children. And John had said he'd been heading for her island.... When you lived a thousand miles out in the middle of the Pacific Ocean, no one dropped by for a casual visit. On a map the Aleutian Islands looked like stepping stones dropped by a giant so he could walk from Siberia to Alaska without getting his feet wet. The islands were the crests of a chain of volcanoes—forty-seven of which were still classified as active—stretching twelve hundred miles across the ocean. Around them, the warm waters of the Pacific mingled with those of the cold Bering Sea, spawning what the natives perversely delighted in claiming as the worst weather on earth. Her island could hardly be considered a tourist attraction.

Even if it had been a tropical paradise, she wouldn't have had visitors. Her work wasn't secret, but neither she nor the group that sponsored her research encouraged them. Technically, the island was a closed research site, and anyone wishing to visit had to request her permission. No one had. But perhaps the stranger wouldn't have seen the necessity for that. Eyes still closed, Erin rubbed at the headache trying to form over her left eyebrow. There had been an attempt last year to break into the computer where her work was stored....

She opened her eyes and moved away from the shed. Lying made you paranoid, too, she decided while striding briskly around the corner. At the outer door to the hut, she paused to watch the small pod of white whales swimming across the bay. All her questions would be answered when he woke up—if he spoke English, she reminded herself as she opened the door.

She couldn't allow him to become a distraction; she'd already wasted too much precious time thinking about him.

Inside the air lock, she switched on the naked bulb dangling from the ceiling, checked on the black diving suit hanging near the inner door, then knelt in front of the air tanks lined up against the wall. She connected one to a nearby compressor, concentrating on the gauge as air began to hiss into the empty tank. The truth that she had so successfully ignored until now finally made itself heard. She had lied because she simply didn't want to let him go.

The heavy fog clouding his consciousness lifted slowly. First sound crept in around the edges, a low, steady rumble like a small motor running. Feeling returned. The motor seemed to be sitting on his chest, vibrating heat deep inside him. He remembered being cold...so cold.... Now he was cocooned in soft warmth. He fought the return of awareness, reluctant to give up the comfort and safety of the fog. His head tossing restlessly, his cheek scrubbed a cool, smooth pillowcase, and he breathed in the scent of it.

His eyes blinked open, and he was instantly fully awake—and staring into a pair of unblinking yellow eyes. The eyes and warm rumbling vibration on his chest slowly resolved into a very large and purring black, brown and cream-colored cat. Black markings across the cat's broad face made it look as if it were wearing a mask. The cat won the staring contest. With a bored yawn of victory, it rose from his chest and padded to the edge of the bed. With a heavy thud it landed on the floor, then disappeared.

Out of a habit that the years and experience had made second nature, his body remained motionless while his mind raced, assessing the information his senses were giving him. He was flat on his back in a large, very comfortable bed in a room he had never seen before. Besides the bed, there was a plain pine dresser, an unmatched nightstand in a dark finish with a cheap metal gooseneck lamp sitting on it, and a metal wardrobe. The windowless walls were finished with a rough paneling and were bare of any decoration.

The only door was half open, but he couldn't see anything of the rest of the building. Nor could he hear anything—no human or mechanical sounds, no natural sounds like the wind or the sea, nothing. Was he underground? The dim light could have an artificial source.

He took a personal inventory. He was naked beneath the quilt and sheet covering him. Beginning with his toes, he worked his muscles, testing each one. He felt no pain and no numbness, but his body responded sluggishly. Had he been drugged? No, he decided immediately. He knew the after-effects of drugs only too well, he thought sardonically, unconsciously touching the scar on his belly. Even if his body was reacting with an uncharacteristic slowness, his mind was sharp and clear.

How long had he been out? Running a hand over his lower face, he felt the stubble on his jaw. He had shaved the morning he'd left Anchorage, and his beard didn't feel more than two days old, so he couldn't have been out more than twenty-four hours. His last clear memory was of standing on one of the pontoons of his seaplane while it bounced like a ping-pong ball from one huge wave to another. He'd been trying to determine the cause of the sudden loss of oil pressure that had forced him down. He remembered hearing an express-train roar and looking up to see a wave as tall as a two-story building bearing down on him. The wave had crashed over the plane, tearing the wing strut he'd been clinging to out of his hands and burying him under tons of water.

He'd struggled toward the light and, as soon as he'd surfaced, he'd begun swimming, fighting endless waves that had pushed him back two feet for every foot of progress he'd made. His arms and legs had gone numb from the cold, yet something in him had refused to give up, and his arms had continued to stroke, his legs to kick, long after he knew the effort was futile. At some point he had blacked out. Then there was a confusion of images and sensations. He remembered a sense of being lifted and carried on top of the waves. Then there had been bitter, soul-chilling cold, pain as something sharp had cut him, and a bizarre hallucination involving a polar bear and a golden-haired angel.

He didn't try to force the memories or to make sense of them. They would become clear soon enough if he left them alone. His chest itched, and he rubbed it. The hem of the sheet brushed his nose, and he caught a tantalizingly familiar scent— light, sweet, unmistakably feminine—yet he couldn't remember ever having smelled it before. The scent was on the pillow, too, and—he sniffed his arm—him.

Throwing back the covers, he swung his feet to the floor. When he stood up, he felt a dizziness that cleared as soon as he shook his head. He took the few steps to the end of the bed with slow caution. His body felt as if all the moving parts had rusted. At the foot of the bed he found his clothes, neatly folded. Someone had washed and dried them for him. The socks weren't his, he thought, holding one up. It was a man's sock, but a couple of sizes too small. He remembered kicking off his boots; apparently he'd lost his socks, too.

He dressed rapidly, then positioned himself to see through the door without opening it any farther. The half of the other room that he could see was empty. With the flat of his hand, he slowly pushed the door open wider. The room was large and empty; even the cat had vanished. Noticing a closed door a few feet away, he opened it with the same cautiousness and saw a large, redwood-paneled bathroom, complete with Jacuzzi. The bathroom was empty, too.

He stood in the doorway, studying the main room before entering it again. Automatically he evaluated the advantages and disadvantages of the room, the potential dangers, the possible avenues of escape. There was one other door, a small window that didn't appear to open and a ladder that disappeared through a hole in the ceiling.

The walls and roof were one continuous curve, and he was certain that the building was a Quonset hut, most likely a relic left over from World War Two, when the Aleutian Islands had been fortified against a Japanese invasion. The main room apparently functioned as a kitchen, laundry, living room and office. The furniture would have lowered the class of a junk shop, except for the bank of electronic equipment on the opposite wall. The plank floor was mostly bare, but his feet, clad only in the thin socks, weren't cold, he noted absently. The room was warm, almost stiflingly so.

He skirted the perimeter of the room instead of walking across it, keeping out of the direct sight of anyone who might happen to be looking in from outside. Standing out of sight to one side, he gazed out the small window. The edge of a heavy steel shutter obstructed part of the view, but the landscape was what he expected. An arctic moor rolled away from the hut and up to a sharp pinnacle of bare gray rock. Long coarse grass, beaten down by the prevailing winds, covered the slope like a thick shag carpet. There were no trees—trees didn't grow naturally on the outer Aleutians—but there were bright-colored splashes of wildflowers growing in the emerald grass. A pair of arctic terns wheeled over the moor, their scolding, high-pitched cries muffled by the triple-paned window. He saw no other sign of life, no sign of the person who had saved his skin.

Turning away from the scenery, he examined the array of sophisticated electronic equipment. A shortwave radio sat on top of one of the two plain, metal, government-issue type desks. Next to the radio was what looked like a small hi-fi speaker. There was a knob on the front, and he turned it. The loud whistling and catlike mewing that suddenly filled the silence startled him. He listened to the incomprehensible sounds for a minute or two before turning the speaker off.

Between the desks was a compact mainframe computer. The soft whir of the drive seemed to indicate that the computer was receiving and recording information. A cable connected the speaker to the mainframe, and another tied the mainframe into a terminal sitting on the second desk. A half empty mug of coffee sat on top of the terminal. He touched the side of the mug. Cold. The back of his neck prickled, as if something was crawling through the short hair. The coffee mug, the running computer and the eerie, deserted feel of the hut reminded him of the tales of ghost ships found with dinner on the table, wine poured, candles lit and everyone aboard vanished without a trace.

He shook off the feeling and examined what looked like a combination radio receiver and cassette recorder. Beside it was some kind of modem, although telephone-transmission lines were hardly available here, and its radio-transmitter appearance wasn't usual. A printer was hooked up to the terminal and, leaning over, he rolled up the paper to read the few lines printed on it. It appeared to be the transcript of a conversation, and he seemed to be the topic.

There was a shorthand quality to it that indicated that at least one of the speakers was not completely fluent in the language of the other, but it wasn't the clumsy pidgin English of a tourist trying to make herself understood with two years of high-school French and a guidebook. He chuckled at the last sentence. He pleased her, did he?

A frown formed as he read the few lines again. Why had he automatically assumed the second speaker was a woman? An undertone to the conversation that he didn't have to hear to understand, he decided, and that scent.

A movement behind him caught the edge of his vision, but the natural reflexes that would have had most people whirling around before they could stop themselves had been rerouted in him by ruthless training and years of even more ruthless experience. In a seemingly casual move, he sidestepped to the right, putting himself behind the dubious protection of a padded metal desk chair. Then he turned around.

He relaxed; it was only the cat. The animal had silently reappeared and now sat halfway down the ladder, staring across the room at him. It stood up, arching its back and stretching out its front paws, then began to climb the iron rungs. Pausing, it looked back over its shoulder with an impatient twitch of its tail, as if to ask why he wasn't coming.

He followed the cat up the ladder. After the close, cavelike atmosphere below, the tower was almost too open, and he felt a moment's irrational unease at being so exposed. Three hundred and sixty degrees of glass gave him an unlimited view. Most of it was more of what he'd seen from the window downstairs—gray sky and rolling, empty green moor. He turned slowly in the middle of the floor, then stopped and drew closer to the window. The low knoll where the Quonset hut sat sloped down to a small natural harbor. A wooden dock ran out from the rocky beach, long enough to accommodate a good-sized ship, but the only "ship" moored there now was an inflatable Zodiac raft that bobbed against the tire fenders.

From the wind and the sky, he was sure the sea was still running high, but the water in the sheltered cove was relatively calm. It was the same tarnished silver color as the low clouds scudding across the sky. Easing a hip onto a wooden stool placed before the window, he watched a procession of white whales crossing the bay with slow stateliness. The cat jumped up onto a narrow ledge that ran around the bottom of the windows and reached out a paw to bat at his hand where it lay on his thigh.

Idly he scratched the cat under its chin as he followed the whales' progress. There were eight adults between twelve and fifteen feet long and weighing, he knew, close to a ton and a half each. In their midst were two brownish calves and a black shape, the length of the smaller calf but much slimmer. He watched a minute longer, recalling the strange memory of something carrying him through the water. Suddenly certain of the identities of the speakers in the conversation he'd read on the printer, however unbelievable his assumption might be, he stood up. The cat gave him a perturbed look but jumped from the ledge to follow him back down the ladder.

Twenty minutes later he slid open the last drawer of the dresser in the bedroom, ending a quick but very thorough search of the hut and its contents. There had been one toothbrush in the holder in the bathroom, one towel and washcloth hanging on the rack, one cereal bowl and spoon sitting in the kitchen sink. The clothing and personal items he'd found confirmed the suspicion that had been growing ever since he had awakened to that hauntingly elusive scent. A woman lived here. Alone. His hands moved through soft fabric to the hard wood at the bottom of the drawer. He straightened the clothes to their original positions so their owner would not know he had been in her drawers. He smiled to himself at the unconscious pun as he neatly refolded two garments that looked like bits of champagne-colored lace and nylon in his large hands. Absently he noted the size on one of the labels: 34C. She would fill his hand nicely. Unconsciously his long fingers caressed the silky fabric once before he slid the drawer shut.

Back in the kitchen, he drew a glass of water from the pitted chrome faucet at the chipped sink. His mouth and throat felt as if he'd eaten a box of salt, dry. He drank down the ice-cold water in a steady swallow, grimacing at the taste. It had a strong metallic flavor that took some getting used to, but he filled and emptied the glass twice more.

He set it down in the sink beside the solitary bowl and spoon. The movement reminded him of the cold sliver of steel resting at the small of his back inside his pants. Reaching around, he pulled a knife from the waistband of his slacks and stared at it thoughtfully for a moment. The knife was the type used for filleting fish, the blade sharp, thin and very flexible. It would probably snap before it could do any real damage, but it was the most formidable weapon he'd found in the hut, and old habits died hard. He'd had the knife tucked away before he'd even thought about it.

Despite the fact that she was alone, living on a remote island, isolated from help, the woman kept no protection, not even a .22 target pistol. His faint smile was grim as he bounced the knife lightly on his palm. A very foolish woman. As he pulled open a drawer, he heard a noise from behind the door he had already determined led to the outside. He pushed the drawer shut firmly with the knife inside, then turned toward the door. He wouldn't be needing the knife because, as fantastic as it seemed, he was exactly where he wanted to be.

Wearily, Erin set the air tanks down against the wall. Even with her insulated suit, an hour was all her body could tolerate of the frigid water. Unlike a wetsuit, which allowed a thin layer of water to seep between the skin and the rubber, this suit was watertight, made in one piece to cover her from head to toe. Her eyes and nose were covered by an oversized mask that formed another watertight seal, leaving only her mouth and chin exposed.

She still wore the suit, having removed only her flippers to make walking up from the beach easier. The thick material acted like a rubber sweat suit, trapping and reflecting the body heat generated by the exertion of walking. After the cold chill of the water, the sweaty, sticky warmth of the suit felt luxuriously comfortable. Shoving the hood back, she opened the inner door of the air lock.

"Oh!" Erin's hand went instinctively to her breast. "You're up! I wasn't expecting..." Her voice trailed off as she stared at the big blond man standing a few feet away. When no response was forthcoming, she took a step toward him, instinctively reaching for his arm to guide him back to bed. "You shouldn't be out of bed. Here, I'll help you...." Her hand dropped, and she didn't finish her offer as the expression on his face registered at last. He was frowning, as if slightly dazed or confused, and she knew her hope that he spoke English had been a vain one.

With a sense of fatalism, Erin racked her brain for any remnants of the semester of conversational German she'd taken in college. The language he'd spoken last night wasn't German, but it had sounded so similar that he might understand. *"Sprechen sie deutsch?"* she asked with what she knew was a terrible accent.

He had thought she was a hallucination. Then he had found the white fur parka hanging in the wardrobe, and he had told himself that she was a delusion. Even when he had found the long golden strands tangled in the hairbrush in the bathroom, he had still told himself that the yellow-haired angel who had rescued him couldn't be real. The real Dr. Erin Mathias would be sexless, with stringy hair and thick glasses, the stereotypical genius. Yet instead her hair was a glorious spill of bright sunshine, long and thick and straight. Christian looked down into the sea-green eyes of his delusion. And she didn't wear glasses.

"Ja," he answered slowly. *"Ich spreche deutsch."* Erin heard a deep voice that was slightly raspy, not at all unpleasant, and his accent was perfect. He paused a moment, still staring at her, then spoke again. "I also speak English."

His shift to English was so unexpected that it was a long moment before she could respond. When she finally did, some of her tension dissipated in a nervous laugh. "Thank goodness, because I just exhausted my knowledge of German." She offered her hand, startled again, this time by the intense surge of pleasure she felt because they would be able to communicate after all. "I'm Erin Mathias."

Her hand was cool and dry, her grip firm, but he was surprised by how small and fragile her hand felt in his. In fact, her size in general surprised him. He had seen her clothes and imagined the size of the body that wore them, but the real woman was smaller, slighter, than he had expected. The black diving suit she wore fit like another skin, leaving little need for imagination now. She had the broad shoulders of a swimmer and long, beautifully muscled legs, but she had a thin, almost delicate build.

There was an expectancy in her eyes that went with the questioning lilt in her voice. After making her own introduction, she was plainly waiting for his. Briefly he considered lying, but he had made himself a promise four years ago that he was finished with lies. "My name is Christian Dekker."

He watched carefully, but there wasn't even the slightest flicker of recognition in her eyes. If her late husband had ever mentioned his name, she had forgotten it. "I'm pleased to meet you, Christian Dekker," she said, shaking his hand.

Her tense, wary expression finally relaxed into a smile. She had a thin, narrow face, and cheekbones that would have gotten her an instant contract with any modeling agency. Arching delicately over large, clear eyes, her eyebrows, like her lashes, were unexpectedly dark. Her mouth was a little wide and had a sweet curve. And her smile took his breath away.

He laughed dryly. "Not half as pleased as I am." His hand tightened unconsciously around hers. "Thank you, Erin."

"You're welcome," she said with a soft smile. You're welcome. The words implied more than just the obligatory response to an expression of gratitude. They implied that she was welcoming him to her home and, abruptly, she wondered if that were true. Even when he was naked and unconscious, the strength and incredible vitality of his body had been obvious, but that still hadn't prepared her for the reality of him awake, moving, talking, touching her. The sheer physical size and power of him stunned her and, illogically, dressed in the black pants and sweater, he seemed even more male than he had naked. Carefully she withdrew her hand from his.

For the first time, she considered that she might have done something very foolish—and dangerous—in lying to John Falk. Christian Dekker's masculinity was a tangible presence in the room. She could see it in his big solid body standing before her, hear it in his deep voice that seemed to echo in the quiet corners of the room, even smell it in the still warm air—a faint trace of a musky tang that reminded her of the clean, sharp smell of the sea. And she could feel it—an overwhelming sexual force threatening the chaste little sanctuary where she lived like a pious nun, devoting her life to her work. For a moment she felt something very close to panic.

"What happened?" she finally thought to ask. If she'd had more experience with telling lies, she would have thought of it sooner, Erin thought disgustedly. He would certainly wonder about her if she wasn't curious as to how he had come to wash up on her beach.

"My seaplane had engine trouble. I managed to set it down. Then I climbed out on one of the pontoons to take a look and got washed overboard."

Erin looked at him in surprise. "Where do you think your plane is now?"

He grimaced wryly. "Probably at the bottom of the ocean. As high as the waves were, it wouldn't have taken them long to swamp and sink it."

Erin nodded in commiseration. "You couldn't have been very far from here. If only your plane had made it just a little farther, you wouldn't have lost it."

Christian shook his head. "I took a fix on my position just before I went down. I was about five miles west of Rat Island." He saw her go pale.

"Rat Island is miles from here. You must have been in the water for hours before I found you on the beach!" Even in an insulated diving suit, she could hardly tolerate much more than an hour in the frigid water, and he had only been wearing a thin sweater and pants.

Christian felt a perverse thrill of pleasure. He couldn't remember the last time anyone had worried about him. He shrugged matter-of-factly. "I knew the current would carry me to land eventually." He hadn't been nearly as certain, he remembered, that he'd be alive when he got there.

For an instant something of that uncertainty—and the acceptance of it—showed in his eyes. Suddenly, despite her thick diving suit and the overheated room, Erin felt ice cold. What kind of life had he led that he had faced his own death so calmly? Yet, paradoxically, the fact that he hadn't died was proof of his incredible will to survive. "Why don't you sit down and rest? I'll just change, then make us some lunch. I'm always hungry after I dive, and you must be starved. It has to be twenty-four hours at least since you last ate." Erin heard herself babbling and shut her mouth with a snap. Stepping around him, she started for the bathroom, where she'd left her clothes.

A light touch on her shoulder stopped her. Erin told herself that she imagined the tingling warmth she felt through the heavy material covering her shoulder. Looking up, she saw that his hard face had softened with a peculiarly gentle smile. "I've been 'resting' for almost twenty-four hours. If you'll tell me where things are, I can start lunch. It's the least I can do to pay you back for saving my life."

Erin regarded him soberly for a moment before nodding abruptly. "All right . . . thank you. I was just going to fix soup and sandwiches. The tins of soup and sandwich spread are in the cupboard over the stove. Pots and pans are in the cupboard next to it. The bread's in the plastic box on the counter."

The bathroom door closed, but Christian didn't immediately go into the kitchen area. Instead he picked up the object she'd had in her hand when she'd come in, and which she'd set down on top of the mainframe. It was a headset similar to the kind favored by joggers. It had the radio built into the earphones, with the addition of a microphone in a slender wand that would fit in front of her mouth. A sound from behind the closed bathroom door reminded him that he was supposed to be working on lunch, and he put the headset back where he'd found it. That piece of the puzzle could wait until later.

Ignoring the microwave on the countertop, he started a pan of tomato soup heating on an old-fashioned electric stove. The cat leaped up on one of the three chairs at the chrome and yellow Formica dinette table and looked expectant. With a chuckle, he opened another cupboard for a saucer, then splashed a little milk into it. Asking her where the lunch fixings were had been strictly for show, he thought as he watched the cat daintily lap up the milk. He probably knew the contents of her cupboards better than she did.

Their first meal together went better than Erin had hoped, with none of the awkwardness that she'd been expecting. When she'd come out of the bathroom, she'd found the table set, soup steaming in bowls, a stack of sandwiches on a plate in the middle and—bless him—a pot of tea. She looked at him wonderingly. How could he have known that she always craved tea, strong and scaldingly hot, after a dive? The heat of the tea spreading through her drove the chill from her body, and the mild stimulation of the caffeine got her moving again. Erin added two spoonfuls of sugar to her mug and took a grateful sip. It was just a happy coincidence, she decided, that he had made the tea.

The first few minutes passed in silence as they concentrated on satisfying their appetites. Erin refilled her mug, then held the teapot toward him in silent question. He shoved his mug across the narrow table, and she poured it full. After setting down the pot between them, she pushed aside her empty bowl and relaxed, her elbows on the table, her hands cradling the warm mug in her hands. "Thank you for making the tea. Do you like tea instead of coffee, Christian?" Erin was surprised to hear herself using his first name so easily but, under the circumstances, she reminded herself wryly, it was a little late for formality.

He shook his head as he swallowed the last of the sandwiches. He'd made the tea without thinking, following another old habit. "I like coffee, but I always wanted tea after a dive."

Erin noted his use of the past tense. "You used to dive?" Now that one ravenous hunger was appeased, she had another one to satisfy. She had the same problem, though, as a starving man confronted with a feast—she had so many questions that she didn't know where to begin.

"A bit," he said with a faint smile. Staring at her blandly over the rim, he took a long sip from his mug. She'd pulled that glorious hair back into a ponytail that made her cheekbones look even more dramatic. He smiled into his mug. She had a cowlick in her bangs, just off-center, a childish little imperfection that was completely charming. He knew that Erin Mathias was thirty-two, but right now, with the cowlick, the ponytail and her fresh-scrubbed face, she barely looked nineteen. He acknowledged that it was unrepentantly chauvinistic of him, but he was having a hard time believing that she had three university degrees and a genius-level IQ.

She had changed into the jeans and flannel shirt he'd seen hanging on the back of the bathroom door. The tight stretch fabric of the thick diving suit she'd been wearing had flattened the curves of her breasts and hips, but the soft flannel and even softer denim didn't hide the fact that she was very much a woman. The only photograph in the folder of information that Eisley had given him was a grainy blowup of her standing on the deck of some boat, wearing a wet suit, her hair a damp tangle. The quality of the photo had been so poor that he had hardly been able to tell she was a woman, much less what she looked like.

"What do you do now?" Erin asked, for the moment abandoning the subject of his past. Why had he been coming to see her? She couldn't very well ask him straight out, because then he would ask how she knew, and that would involve explanations that she didn't care to make.

"I own an apple farm north of Seattle, on one of the San Juan Islands. I also run a small air-charter service on the side.

I've gotten a few calls about flying to the Aleutians, so I thought I should come up and look things over before I take any charters.'' With a guileless smile, he sat back in his chair, assuming a casual relaxed attitude. ''When I stopped off at Adak to refuel, I asked the guy pumping gas about the islands to the west. He told me there were some archaeological digs, a couple of military bases, a wildlife refuge and your research station.'' It was an old but effective trick, to volunteer more information than had been asked for. It allayed suspicions and, despite her friendly tone, Erin Mathias was suspicious. It might be only the sensible wariness of a woman who was alone and vulnerable. Then again, something might already have happened to make her more guarded. Maybe Eisley's concern wasn't so farfetched after all. He emptied his mug, trying to wash away the bitter taste in his mouth. He hadn't broken a four-year old promise to himself, he thought cynically. He just hadn't told her all the truth...because the truth might make her even more suspicious.

Erin finished her tea and set down the empty mug. Everything about him said that he was a man with nothing to hide. His explanation was plausible. Naturally he would be curious about the area he was going to fly over, and her island would of course have been mentioned. The conversation between him and the gas jockey had no doubt reached John Falk third- or fourth-hand and been garbled in the process. His body language indicated that he was completely comfortable and at ease. His smile was open and honest; his eyes had no trouble meeting hers. So why was she so certain that he was hiding something? Because, she answered her own question, simple apple farmers didn't generally have people shooting them in the back, trying to kill them. And an apple farmer wouldn't have the eyes of a very old man, one who had seen and done things in his long life that he would like to forget—and couldn't. ''What did you do before you took up apple farming?'' she asked with a friendly smile.

A small grin quirked his mouth as he thought about the ancient orchard he'd shaped and pruned and the young trees he'd set out that had yet to produce a crop. Next year, maybe. "I'm retired from the Navy," he said briefly.

Picking up the teapot, he silently offered Erin the tea, just as she had offered it to him minutes before. She shook her head, indicating that he should finish the tea, and watched while he poured the last of it into his mug. Had a bullet in the back been the reason for retirement? She hadn't missed the fact that he hadn't mentioned whose navy, or what he'd been doing in it, either. His English was as American as his Jockey shorts, but she knew it wasn't his native language. He didn't have a discernible accent, but several consonants were a shade too guttural, and there was something slightly offbeat in the cadence of his speech. She met his easy smile with one of her own. "A friendly navy, I hope?"

His grin was wry. "Most of the time, I imagine. I was in the U.S. Navy." The relaxed attitude he'd assumed when she'd begun her subtle interrogation was no longer a sham, and he pulled himself back to alertness. It wouldn't be wise to get too relaxed, he told himself as he stretched out his legs under the narrow table.

His foot brushed hers. Even though she was wearing thick wool socks, her usual footwear inside, and he had on the socks she had given him, Erin felt the touch like the shock of bare skin on bare skin. Her foot jerked in reflex, and she carefully shifted it away from his.

"Thanks for the socks." He, too, had felt the contact, as well as her reaction.

She looked at him almost shyly. "I'm sorry they were too small."

His shoulder lifted philosophically. "The fit's close enough." If the socks had been her husband's, he more than filled them. The thought gave him a peculiar satisfaction.

He was smiling that oddly sweet smile again, and a small silence stretched between them. Erin had a dozen questions she wanted answers to, but suddenly she couldn't think of a graceful way to ask even one of them. The cat provided a welcome distraction. Leaping up onto the third chair, it popped its head over the edge of the table to see if there were any leftovers.

Erin clapped her hands. "Oscar! Get down!"

"Oscar?"

She heard the amusement in his murmur. "He looks just like a toy cat I had once. I gave all my stuffed animals names when I was a little girl," she answered before thinking, then realized how ridiculous that must sound to him. The man was going to think she was an idiot.

He suppressed a grin. She was embarrassed at having to admit she'd done something so silly as to name a cat after a toy she'd had as a kid, but he found it curiously endearing. "Where did you find him?"

"One night last fall I heard some noise out behind the institute, and when I went to investigate, I found him banging around inside one of the garbage bins. I guess he'd jumped in looking for dinner and then was too weak to climb back out. He was awfully thin and bedraggled." She laughed softly. "He wasn't too weak to try and bite me when I rescued him, though."

As she finished speaking she glanced toward the third chair. Erin closed her eyes briefly in mortification. Not only was Christian Dekker going to think she was an idiot, but he was also going to think she let the cat eat off the table when nobody else was around. Instead of obeying her command to get down, Oscar was easing his long body up over the edge of the table, sneaking toward Christian's soup bowl. "Oscar! No! Get down this instant, you bad cat."

Ears flattened, the cat glared at her, then, growling a feline expletive, backed down and stalked off. Erin laughed weakly. "He still has the same nasty disposition and manners he had when he was living in a trash can."

Christian nodded in solemn agreement, then changed the subject. "What's the institute?"

"The SOS Institute," she answered promptly. "SOS stands for Save Our Seas. It's the nonprofit environmental group that sponsors my work. Their headquarters and the research institute they support are on the west coast of Vancouver Island."

Christian listened to facts he already knew. A genteel organization, SOS didn't sail fragile rubber rafts across the bows of giant factory ships in an attempt to stop the slaughter of whales. Instead it sent out newsletters full of politely restrained outrage at the human population's careless treatment of the earth's greatest resource, the sea, coupled with almost apologetic requests for funds. Nor was its founder an environmental guerrilla. Phillip Damion was an urbane multimillionaire who had made his fortune in oil. Christian asked another question he already knew the answer to. "Do you live as well as work at the institute?"

She nodded. "Yes, in an apartment at the back."

"It must be pretty confining, living and working in the same place," he commented, giving her an ingenuous smile. The report Eisley had given him had been full of facts, but it hadn't told him why, almost immediately after her husband had died, she'd sold their home at a loss and moved into a tiny, one-room apartment at the institute. At the time he'd read the report, he hadn't cared why, but now, for reasons he didn't even understand, it was suddenly of tantamount importance that he know why.

"My husband died last fall," she said after a minute. "We had a house, but it was too big for one person to take care of, so I sold it." Too big, and too empty, too silent, too lonely. "Anyway," she continued briskly, "it's more practical for me to live at the institute. I don't have to waste time driving back and forth to work."

He drank the last of his tea, studying her over the edge of the mug. The shadows that had darkened her eyes when she'd mentioned her husband's death told him the answer to another question Eisley's file hadn't. She hadn't sold the house and gone to live at the institute because it was "practical," but because living in their house without him had been too painful. "I'm sorry," he said quietly.

"Thank you," she said simply.

"What happened?" he asked with equal quietness.

"An aneurysm. He died instantly."

Christian nodded his understanding. Eisley had told him that, unbeknownst to Erin, a second autopsy had been ordered to confirm that Mathias's death had indeed been from natural causes. Deliberately, he set down his mug harder than necessary, using the sharp sound to cut the subtle tension that the somber subject had created. "So why aren't you at the institute now, instead of out here in the middle of the middle of nowhere?"

"I'm studying the language of beluga whales, and learning to speak it."

She said it as if she were talking about taking Spanish lessons by correspondence, so he matched her casual tone. "Are you fluent yet?"

"Not yet, but—" Erin grinned at him "—I am beginning to get some of their jokes."

He laughed delightedly. "What kind of jokes do whales tell?"

She grimaced with mock dismay. "Mostly ones about me. They think I swim about as well as a rock."

"Why are you studying belugas? Why not another species?" Why had she chosen to study a whale she could find only in such an isolated area?

"I have studied some of the others, especially the pilot whales around Vancouver Island, but I decided to concentrate on the belugas because they're the most vocal. Actually," she confided, laughing, "they're nonstop talkers. Terrible gossips, too. I figured I'd have a better chance learning their language than any of the others because I'd have more of it to listen to."

Her laughter was a current of warmth flowing through him. "How do you pick up their conversations?"

"I have three underwater microphones placed out in the bay. The whales know where they are and go to one when they want to talk to me. That was how I knew you were on the beach. One of them called me to tell me they found you in the water and brought you to the island." Erin watched him closely to gauge his reaction. Would he find the truth, that he had been rescued by whales, too fantastic to believe?

Christian schooled his expression to show surprise. "I've heard stories of dolphins rescuing drowning swimmers, of course, but I never expected to have the proof firsthand." He grinned wryly. "Please give them my heartfelt thanks the next time you talk to them."

Erin nodded toward the array of electronic equipment across the room. "Technically, the computer does the talking, and the listening, too. Some of the sounds in their speech are beyond the range of human hearing," she explained, then smiled ruefully. "Even if I could hear them, I couldn't reproduce them, or most of the ones I can hear."

As if on cue, a long whistle came through the speaker she had switched on before sitting down at the table. Erin stood up quickly and went to the computer terminal and sat down. She kept her eyes on the screen, and her fingers hovered over the keyboard, ready to type her response, as the chirps, whistles and squeals coming from the speaker took on written form.

"I guess appreciation of an attractive woman is the same in any language," Christian muttered under his breath, biting back a laugh as he rose to follow her. The call coming through the speaker had been a classic wolf whistle.

Erin. Not come back to sea. Demons come.

You be safe?

We go out to sea. Demons not find us.

"You really can talk to them," Christian murmured, intent on the words forming on the screen.

He was bent over her, one hand braced on the desktop, as he read over her shoulder. Almost against her will, Erin's eyes were drawn from the screen to the strong arm stretched close beside her. She felt the warmth of him at her back and smelled the scent that already, on some deep animalistic level, she recognized as his. His heat and scent seemed to surround her, trapping her, and for an instant she knew again that inexplicable thrill of panic.

The whale's voice took on a strident tone, almost as if it were becoming impatient. Erin jerked her eyes back to the screen and saw the same line repeated three times on the screen, with her name added the last time. Hurriedly, she typed her response.

Erin, say stay out of sea.

I stay out. When you come back?

When demons leave. Stay safe with man.

Involuntarily Erin looked away from the screen and up to the man she was supposed to stay safe with. His eyes caught hers, as if he had been waiting for her to look at him. With their heads so close together, she could see each individual lash of the thick, white-gold fringe guarding his eyes. And guard was the right word, she thought as she stared at him. The expression in his blue-ice eyes was unreadable; whatever he was thinking was hidden. With more effort than it should have taken, she pulled her gaze free and looked back at the screen.

I stay safe. Be careful.

The speaker fell silent, and the printer stopped. Sensing the slight tensing of her body, Christian stepped away a split second before Erin pushed back her chair and stood up.

Her glance slid over the shortwave radio and, from the corner of her eye, she saw him looking at it, too. Although she'd certainly been in no hurry to bring it up, she was surprised that he hadn't asked about the possibility of notifying someone that he was safe. "I tried to call the Coast Guard station on Attu to tell them you were here, in case they were looking for you, but the storm has caused too much interference." She managed to sound regretful while not quite meeting the bright blue eyes that were watching her so steadily. "You won't be able to get a message out until the weather clears, and then I'm afraid you'll have to call someone to come get you. All I have is a Zodiac raft, and it can't handle a trip over the open sea to Attu."

That much wasn't a lie, at least. After the Coast Guard cutter had left, she truly had tried to get through to the station, knowing full well that the atmospheric disturbances caused by the storm made the gesture futile, but the attempt had pacified her guilty conscience for having lied to John Falk. And the approaching fog bank had assuaged the additional guilt she'd felt, knowing that men were out searching for a lost pilot who had already been found. The search would be called off, if it hadn't been already, and, as soon as the weather calmed, she would call Attu to tell them he was here. She should be able to come up with some convincing story to cover the lie she'd told John Falk, Erin thought sourly; she'd been getting in so much practice lately that she ought to be pretty good at lying by now.

Careful to hide his satisfaction, Christian looked back to her. "There's no one I need to get a message to."

Erin felt a rush of relief—from guilt, she told herself. Surely, if he had a wife, he would be anxious to let her know he was all right. Still, someone was looking for him, someone with enough authority to command an immediate, full-scale search.

"You don't have any way off the island, then?" he asked casually.

"No. A bush pilot flew me in, and he drops off mail and fresh groceries every two weeks. In an emergency, I could call him or the Coast Guard station to come get me, providing the radio's working, of course." He acknowledged the information with a nod, and Erin turned toward the kitchen.

Christian watched her busily clearing the table of their lunch dishes. How many people, he wondered, would appreciate, or even understand, the extraordinariness of what she had accomplished? Science fiction had become reality. Erin Mathias had established communication with another life form—not one from outer space, but from her own planet. And it wasn't the "language" of a trainer's hand signals telling an animal which trick to perform next, or the meaningless mimicry of a few human words. Erin spoke to the whales in their language, not hers.

"What you have achieved is incredible," he said quietly, joining her in the kitchen.

Erin turned from the sink to face him. "What it is, is the result of eleven years of research," she corrected.

Her tone might have been matter-of-fact, but he'd seen surprise, then appreciation, at his compliment in her eyes. "No big breakthrough, no blinding flash of revelation?" he teased her gently.

She shook her head, laughing. "More like a dim light bulb. Last fall I was listening to beluga tapes so much I was hearing them in my sleep, and finally I realized the basic structural pattern of their language."

Christian wondered at the timing of her discovery. Had she buried herself in her work after she'd buried her husband? "Were you speaking with one whale just now, or several?"

"Just one." She ran hot water into the sink and squirted in dishwashing liquid. "They each have their own individual signal," she explained as she shut off the faucet. "They speak over long distances and use the signal to identify themselves, the same way we give our names when we use a phone." Gingerly she tested the temperature of the soapy water, drawing her hand back quickly when it scalded her fingertips. "I've given each one of them a human name, though, one I can pronounce," she admitted with a sheepish grin. "That—" she glanced toward the speaker "—was Abner."

"And in their language, your name is—"

Dumbfounded, Erin stared at him as he did a perfect imitation of the wolfish whistle that was indeed the name the whales had given her. "H-how did you know that?"

"That was the signal the whale called you with. He used it again while you were talking, and 'Erin' appeared on the screen twice." The look on her face was, if anything, even more disbelieving, and he shrugged lightly. "I have a facility for languages." He drew out the dinette chair closest to her in a subtle invitation to sit, to leave the dirty dishes and come back to the table—and him.

"Obviously," Erin murmured as she sank down onto the chair. And what else do you have a facility for, Christian Dekker? she added silently as he sat down across from her. Besides languages, flying, diving and, of course, apple farming. And growing apples, she suspected, was the least of his "facilities."

"What are the demons he was talking about?" he asked.

"Killer whales," she said briefly.

Christian raised an eyebrow. "They're afraid of their own kind?"

Erin gave him a mild look. "We humans are afraid of some of our own kind, too. Killer whales aren't the playful clowns you see in the marine shows. Technically they aren't whales at all, they're dolphins, but—" her hand dismissed the point "—the differences between the two are minor. The real difference is their behavior. Killer whales are cannibals. Other cetaceans, like smaller dolphins and porpoises, are among their favorite prey, and they've been observed killing seemingly for the fun of it. They hunt in packs, and they'll attack a much larger whale if they know it's old, or weakened by illness or injury. They are very intelligent, very efficient killers. In fact, many cetologists think that killer whales may well be the most intelligent of all the whales."

Clearly the belugas were more than laboratory specimens to her. Although she spoke as if delivering a dry lecture, her fingers were systematically twisting themselves into knots. The thought that they might come to harm was causing her genuine anguish, and the strength of his desire to reach across the table, to take her hands in his and reassure her, astonished him. "If the belugas think the killer whales are demons, then they must believe in devils, evil spirits?"

Erin's hands stilled as she looked at him, puzzled by his inexplicably harsh tone. "No. The belugas consider killer whales an aberration, a disorder in the natural order of their world. They don't understand evil, but they understand that it exists. The closest I could come in English to their concept of it was the word demon, but I think it's an accurate translation. The Inuit gave killer whales the name orca. It means demon in their language."

The speaker, which had been silent for the past few minutes, began transmitting again. The cacophony of clicks, chirps and whistles was similar to what he'd heard before, but Christian knew immediately that he was listening to a different language, and to several animals, not one. The beluga's voice had had a softer, almost liquid quality, while the sound of these was harsh and ugly. The comparison reminded him of the contrast between Spanish and Russian in human speech. At the sounds, Erin's mouth had thinned to a narrow hard line. "Orcas?" he asked.

Her terse nod confirmed it. The printer began typing an occasional word, and he glanced at it, then back to her.

Erin answered his silent question. "All modern cetacean languages seem to have evolved from one ancient language— the way Spanish, French, Italian, Portuguese and Romanian evolved from Latin—and they still share a number of com-

mon words. The computer's programmed only with the beluga language, but it can translate words it recognizes from any
language." Rising, she went back to the computer terminal.

When he was beside her, Erin pointed to the scattering of
words on the screen. "See? The words for 'where' and 'search'
are the same."

"Are they trying to talk to you?" He breathed in the subtle
sweet scent of her hair.

"No, they just happen to be close to one of the microphones."

A translation of the shrill, staccato sounds wasn't necessary, Christian thought, to know that the killer whales were
annoyed that their quarry had escaped. The voices gradually
faded as the orcas moved beyond the range of the microphone. Erin whirled away suddenly, and he realized she was
heading for the ladder and the observation tower. Cursing the
lingering weakness in his muscles, which refused to match her
speed up the steps, he went after her.

Silent, he stood with her in front of the window, watching the
nine black-and-white torpedolike shapes cruising across the
cove below. In spite of what he now knew about their true na-
tures, Christian found himself admiring the sleek elegance of
the killer whales as they sped through the white-capped waves
with seemingly effortless ease. Compared to them, the belugas
he had seen earlier were clumsy and slow, and he knew that if
the orcas had caught them in the small bay, the white whales
wouldn't have stood a chance.

The pack disappeared through the heavy curtain of fog
drawing across the bay. Christian glanced down at the woman
beside him. Her fingers were busy tying themselves in knots
again as she pressed against the window, straining to see
through the gray cloud. Without thinking about it this time, he
reached down and gently unknotted her fingers. Keeping one
of her hands in his, he drew her away from the window until
they reached the first rung of the ladder. He waited several
seconds before she looked up at him. "They're safe, Erin," he
told her gently.

After another second, Erin nodded slowly. As irrational as it might be, his calm assurance that the belugas were safe did reassure her. Her hand was still in his, keeping her close to him. His body radiated heat, like a welcome crackling fire on a cold, stormy night, and, in the moment before she pulled away, she felt the even more irrational urge to draw nearer, to warm herself at that fire.

The young seaman tried to dash between the slow fat raindrops falling on the open parade ground between the communications center and a small building reserved for visiting VIPs. Since she'd been assigned to the Whidbey Island Air Station a few months before, she'd negotiated the asphalted field mined with puddles more times than she cared to remember. With its proximity to the huge Navy yard at Bremerton and the port of Seattle, Whidbey Island saw more than its share of traveling VIPs, and all of them seemed to have an endless trail of messages following them around.

The seaman glanced down at the room number written on the outside of the paper in her hand as she tugged open the heavy glass door. Scuttlebutt had it that this one was Naval Intelligence. The radio operator who had dispatched her had said it was as likely that McBride, the name on the message, was his real one as it was that there would be a cloudless blue sky and sunshine tomorrow. Fake names, travel to exotic places—Whidbey Island aside—sounded so romantic and exciting. Maybe she should put in a transfer request to Intelligence. It would sure beat playing carrier pigeon under a perpetual cold shower, she thought wistfully as she climbed the stairs to the second floor.

Her knock was answered by the best-looking man she'd seen in quite a while, maybe in her whole life. He was the classic picture of "tall, dark and handsome." Yes, indeed, a transfer was looking better and better. Momentarily dazzled, her tongue tied up. "M-message for you, s-sir," she finally managed.

"Thank you—" his eyes flicked to the stripes on her sleeve as he reached for the paper "—seaman."

His voice was wonderful, too, she thought absently as his dark head bent to scan the brief message, deep and smoothed by a touch of the South, but she was no longer bedazzled. Never had she seen eyes like his. The color of sleet and just as cold, they were empty, as if there were no soul behind them.

He handed the message back. "Request that they resume the search as soon as visibility improves. They should check the island again before looking elsewhere," he ordered tonelessly.

A minute later she paused inside the glass door, looking out at the gray rain that didn't seem so cold after the eyes of the man upstairs. Maybe she would turn in an application to the sonar school in warm, sunny Pensacola instead.

Chapter 3

Shoving aside his plate, Christian glanced at the woman on the other side of the table and then away. For a man who had sworn he was done with lies, he had a remarkably elastic definition of the truth, he thought derisively. He knew he should have told her immediately who he was and why he was here. He knew, too, that with each passing minute, the inevitable explanation would only be more awkward, his dishonesty more indefensible, but damn it, he couldn't tell her anything. Not when he didn't know if what he'd found in the engine of his plane had simply been bad luck or sabotage. And if it had been sabotage—which of them was the target? He'd made more enemies than friends in his years in "the Navy," as he'd so euphemistically put it for Erin, and then made a few more since. If she hadn't been in danger before, his presence might well be putting her life at risk now. And the real hell of it was that by the time he knew whether his suspicion was right or not, it might be too late.

Unobtrusively, Erin studied the face of the man across the table from her. She told herself that it was because she was trying to see below the surface to the real man underneath, to find the answers to some of her questions about him, but the truth was that she simply enjoyed looking at him. His hair was so light blond that it was almost silver. Cropped close, it lay flat, fitting the curves of his skull like a sleek pelt. Her eyes lingered on his profile, clean and unrepentantly masculine, on the hard mouth that could smile so sweetly.... His eyes shifted suddenly and locked on hers. She saw cool assessment and sharp intelligence, and again Erin was reminded of a wolf.

"Not hungry tonight?" Christian asked when Erin stuck her fork into the congealed brown mass on her plate. The label on the can had identified it as beef stew, but with his first taste, he'd resolved to try out the fishing rod he'd found at the earliest opportunity.

Giving up, Erin pushed her plate aside. "I guess I just haven't acquired a taste for canned glue yet." She sighed. "This stuff is proof that there is no truth in advertising."

He laughed at the horrible face she pulled at her dinner. He'd laughed more in the past few hours, Christian thought wonderingly, than he had in the past six months. "From the number of cans in the cupboard, you may develop a taste for it yet."

Erin shook her head with total conviction. "Never, although, at the time, bringing canned food did seem like a good idea." Reaching for the loaf of bread and the butter on the table between them, she slanted him a guileless look. "Somehow, going to all the trouble of cooking a meal from scratch when you're the only one there to enjoy it seems like a waste of time, doesn't it?"

She was trying to find out if he lived alone. He had to admire her skill. All throughout the meal he had parried her feints. Against a player less skilled than himself, she would have found out everything she wanted to know. Although he knew the risk of relaxing his guard, Christian answered honestly, not because he wanted to let her score, but because he was tired of playing the game. "It does," he agreed as he pulled the butter plate and bread toward him, "until you get tired of canned glue. That's when I learned how to cook."

Erin knew it was only a small point, but it felt like a major victory. Watching his straight white teeth bite through a folded slice of whole-wheat bread, she considered her next question. Maybe she'd get lucky again.

A movement near the third chair caught their attention, and they both looked over to see Oscar's black bandit mask inching up over the edge of the table to see what he could steal. He sniffed in the direction of her half-eaten plate of stew. Erin was opening her mouth to scold him when the cat recoiled in an attitude of repulsion. Throwing them both a look of disgust, he jumped down and walked off, tail and nose high in the air to convey his opinion of their taste.

Their eyes met across the table, and they both burst out laughing. There was something she had been lonely for, Erin realized suddenly—the sound of laughter. More than any other human emotion, humor, the appreciation of life's little sillinesses, was meant to be shared, and she'd had no one to laugh with for a long time.

Their laughter faded to soft echoes. "What have you been working on all afternoon?" Christian asked with a lazy smile. For hours she'd been absorbed in her work, and he, admittedly, had been absorbed in her.

"Just an article for a scientific journal." Erin twisted the plastic tie around the neck of the bread wrapper, then snapped the lid on the butter tub. Standing, she picked up the butter and milk to put them away.

He stood and began stacking their dishes. "On your work with the whales?"

Her back to him, she juggled the butter tub so she could open the door of the refrigerator. "Uh-huh."

"I'd like to read it."

Erin shut the door and came back to the table. "You probably wouldn't find it very interesting," she said, trying to discourage what she was sure was only an attempt to be polite, though he did do it better than most. Her work was the kind that tended to make most people's eyes glaze after the first paragraph. Pointing toward a metal bookshelf behind the couch crammed with paperbacks, she suggested, "If you want something to read, there's nearly a whole library over there. I think everyone who ever stayed here left at least one book behind." She reached for the loaf of bread. "Just help—"

He took the loaf out of her hand. "Leave that." He softened the order with a smile when he saw another protest coming. "I'll clean up while you print me out a copy of your article."

Christian set aside the sheaf of computer paper and switched off the floor lamp beside the couch. Slouching down comfortably on his spine, he put his feet up on the wooden cable spool that served as a coffee table. He glanced at the papers on the couch beside him. The striking advances she'd made in understanding the language of whales were the subject of the monograph. It might be destined for a dry scholarly journal, but it was as readable and entertaining as anything he'd ever seen in one of the popular pseudo-science slicks. He hadn't been entertained, however. With each new paragraph, he'd become more and more convinced that Eisley's concern was justified.

He looked across the room at the golden head bent over the computer terminal. The lamp on her desk was the only illumination in the hut, a pool of light that made her hair seem as bright as the sun and the dusky shadows in the rest of the big room even darker. She played the keys of the terminal like a piano, and the bizarrely beautiful music of whale song began to fill the air.

The melancholy sounds formed the perfect counterpoint for his brooding thoughts. He was all the things he'd told her—retired, the owner of an air-charter business, a farmer—but he had failed to mention his other business, the one that had paid for the plane and the farm, the business that had brought him to her.

When he had retired four years ago, he'd had few marketable skills that would be accepted in polite society. With his pension and the money he'd been stashing away for years, though, there hadn't been any pressing need for him to look for work. The first thing he had done was buy a car, because he didn't own one. He hadn't owned much of anything back then—no car, no house, not much more than the clothes on his back. After an aimless drive up the West Coast, he'd found himself one afternoon on Orcas Island in the San Juans, between Washington and Vancouver Island. With an hour to kill before the ferry returned, he'd picked up a local newspaper.

The ferry had left without him. Instead he'd spent the next two days with a real-estate agent whose name he'd gotten from one of the ads in the paper. Late the second afternoon the agent had taken him by boat to the seventh and last possibility on his list, an entire island that was for sale. As they approached, he'd seen rugged gray cliffs and giant evergreens, and the agent had told him that this was Mary's Island. Roughly circular, the island was small, only about a hundred acres, and included a house in the first stages of falling down and an apple orchard gone wild.

The owner's heirs had accepted his cash offer without haggling, and less than a week later, he'd closed the sagging front door of his house and set down his lone suitcase on the warped floor. He had an empty bank account and no idea how he was going to come up with the money it was going to take just to make the place livable, but he was home.

Unexpectedly, it was Eisley who had come up with the money. How Eisley had found him so quickly Christian never knew—no one knew how Eisley did a lot of things—but he'd looked up a week later from the rotted floorboards he was ripping up in the kitchen to see a tall dark man walking in the back door. Over a cold beer Eisley had told him that he had a job for him, if he wanted it.

A Persian Gulf emir was marrying his favorite daughter to the oldest son of another emir. The dowry included a sizable ocean of oil reserves, and the U.S. government was very anxious that the marriage take place, since the bride's prospective father-in-law was friendly to the West. However, others were not so pleased about the upcoming nuptials and the resulting increased U.S. influence in the area. There had already been an attempted kidnapping of the bride by rebel terrorists, as well as a bungled assassination attempt. Understandably, the U.S. government couldn't give the emir's daughter official protection, but a private citizen could, and the father of the bride would show his gratitude in a very practical way.

Three weeks later the bride and groom were honeymooning in Monaco, and Christian was flying home with the emir's check for a hundred thousand dollars in his pocket. Soon there had been other clients, other jobs, from rescuing an oilman's missionary son from a Central American prison to retrieving the stolen plans for a revolutionary new microchip. Eisley had sent a few of them his way, but most had come by word-of-mouth within that rarefied circle who considered his fee cheap at twice the price—a minimum of one hundred thousand dollars, escalating with the degree of difficulty and danger. There had been no shortage of those desiring his services, but even at the beginning, he had turned down nearly all of them. Most he'd rejected because what they'd wanted was simply wrong, and a few because the job was too easy and he had sensed that he was just to be their latest status symbol. For the past six months he'd turned down every job. Rebuilding his house, tending his trees and watching them grow had given him a satisfaction that his former life never could have. Finally he had found a measure of peace and—if not true happiness—at least contentment.

Through half-closed eyes, he watched her hand come up to tuck back a wisp of hair that had escaped from her ponytail. Her hair would be soft and smell of that elusive scent. Yes, he mused, watching the strand of hair float free again, he had turned them all down... until a dead man had asked him to protect his wife.

The request had come in a letter, and Eisley had been the postman. He had received it from an attorney in Vancouver, British Columbia, who had been commissioned to send it by Daniel Mathias shortly before his death. Christian remembered every word of the letter and the conversation that had followed.

His thoughts drifted back three days to an afternoon when Eisley was again enjoying a cold beer while Christian read the letter he'd brought. After finishing, he'd set the letter—as well as the cashier's check that had been enclosed with it—on the kitchen table between them. "This is legitimate?" He knew Eisley had already read the letter, because the envelope, although addressed to him, had been opened.

"The attorney is a kid just out of law school. Mathias probably picked him for that reason, knew he'd be hungry enough for the money not to ask too many questions." At Christian's raised eyebrow, Eisley explained. "Jansek, the attorney, said Mathias walked into his office one day, laid down a manila envelope and five one-hundred-dollar bills. In return, Jansek was supposed to watch the obituaries until he saw Mathias's death notice, then find out if and when Mathias's wife was going back up to the Aleutians to study whales. If she did, he was to forward the envelope on to me. A cover letter to me and that—" he indicated the letter and check Christian had set aside "—were inside. I showed Jansek Mathias's picture, and he said it looked like the same man. Both letters were typed, but the signatures checked out."

Christian nodded. Eisley had vetted the letter and the attorney; he would have expected nothing less. He glanced down at the check again. The amount was three times his usual fee. Where had Mathias gotten that kind of money?

"The money came from an account that his wife apparently knew nothing about," Eisley said, as if he'd read the direction of Christian's thoughts from the direction of his glance. "Mathias had patented several of his devices. Apparently he didn't tell her about the specialist he'd been seeing for the past four years, either. She didn't know he had an inoperable aneurysm until he died."

"Why didn't he have the lawyer contact me directly? Why did he go through you?" Christian wondered aloud.

Eisley shrugged. "I knew him better than you. Maybe he thought his request would have more credibility if it came through me."

Christian looked at Eisley without speaking. He didn't believe that any more than Eisley did. The letter had been sent through Eisley because Mathias knew Eisley would alert Damage Control. Apparently Mathias had believed he would need their help to protect his wife. Created at the start of the Cold War, Damage Control was a very select, very secret branch of Naval Intelligence. Someone with a perverse sense of humor had borrowed the name from the teams assigned to handle the results of torpedo attacks; however, it was never the job of this Damage Control to hold back water flooding through a hole in the side of a ship. Instead they tried to contain another kind of disaster, the even messier kind that the State Department liked to call "unfortunate incidents."

"How does Jansek know that Mathias's wife has gone back to the Aleutians?"

Eisley opened a file folder he'd brought with him and took out the newspaper clipping on top. "Dr. Mathias is somewhat of a local celebrity in the Vancouver area," he said, sliding the clipping over the tabletop.

Christian skimmed a full-column article explaining that Dr. Erin Mathias, linguistics expert and the leading authority on the language of whales, was planning to spend the summer on a remote Aleutian island, studying beluga whales. It briefly reprised her research and mentioned her recent widowhood. Christian glanced at the date in the top margin of the clipping, then to the man across the table. "According to this, she's already been on the island for a month. In the letter, Mathias said he wanted me with her before she left."

Eisley answered the implied question in a neutral tone. "I didn't pick up my mail until two days ago."

Christian translated Eisley's answer. He'd been on a mission, and it hadn't gone smoothly. He tapped the letter with a long forefinger. "He said there was an attempt last year to breach the security on the computer where her research is stored. It would make more sense to try that route again, with better talent, than to kidnap her." His tone clearly conveyed his doubt that there was any need for his services.

Eisley took a long pull on the beer sitting in front of him. "Mathias was almost as good with computer security systems as he was with bugs. Almost as good as the Librarian, in fact. I imagine he recoded her research information, making it impossible for anyone else to access it. The only way to get it now would be from her."

Christian set down his own beer, shaking his head. "I still don't buy it. Why would anybody want to kidnap a woman just because she talks to whales?"

For an answer, Eisley pushed the file folder forward. "Nelson had the Librarian work this up for you. I advised him after I read Mathias's letters and ran a check on the lawyer. He said to tell you that if you needed more information or backup, you would have it. Unofficially, of course."

"Of course," Christian agreed with a dry smile. Eisley hadn't shown a sign of conscience at admitting he had read a letter intended for someone else. Christian hadn't expected any; he had often doubted that Eisley had a conscience. He picked up the file folder, flipping open the cover. He remembered Nelson well, sitting in his windowless gray office in Washington like a plump spider in the middle of his web of agents, pulling their strings. He wasn't surprised that Nelson was still in charge of Damage Control. Nelson had seen three presidents come and go, and would very probably outlast at least one or two more.

Christian pulled out the first page of the Librarian's report. He hardly remembered the Librarian at all, although he'd met with the man numerous times. Thin...thick glasses...stooped shoulders...and a face so completely forgettable that he couldn't bring it into focus in his memory. Christian couldn't recall ever having heard the Librarian's real name. Damage Control hadn't gone in for code names, nor had anyone been known by a nickname. Nicknames implied affection, and affection, or any feeling at all was considered a major liability in their work. "Librarian" wasn't a nickname; everyone called him that because his identity existed only as a function of his job, a job he was very good at. Supposedly there wasn't a computer system in the world that was safe from the Librarian's myopic eyes. Compared to picking the electronic brains of the KGB, gathering information on Erin Mathias would have been child's play for him.

"After you read that," Eisley's smooth drawl intruded as he began to scan the page, "I'll tell you what I know about her."

* * *

Eisley could have told him a hell of a lot more than he had, Christian thought sardonically now as he watched her strain to reach a drawer in the other desk. The motion pulled her shirt tight across her chest, silhouetting the high, full breasts under the flannel against the strong light of the desk lamp. Unconsciously, he rubbed his suddenly itchy palm on his thigh. She got the papers she wanted, and he found himself staring at her back again.

The Librarian's report had held a few surprises. The first was that Daniel Mathias had gotten married. They had served in Damage Control together and, although he hadn't known Mathias well—one didn't make close friends in their business—he had worked with him. The resident wizard in electronic surveillance, particularly listening devices, Mathias and he had spent long hours together, eavesdropping. They'd laughed about the public's misconception that the life of a secret agent was glamorous and exciting while they'd been cramped in a sewer tunnel, drinking cold coffee, making bets on the size of the next rat and trying not to fall asleep from the incredible boredom. Light-headed from lack of sleep and too much caffeine, they had agreed that the British Secret Service must pay a hell of a lot better than the U.S. Navy for James Bond to be able to afford all those fancy clothes, cars and women, and decided that maybe they should apply. And they had talked, as men will to pass the time. Christian had gotten an impression of a man with no life outside Damage Control, certainly no woman. And that was why he'd been surprised to find out that Mathias had married scant weeks after retiring from the service.

They had both retired at about the same time. Unconsciously, his hand covered the scar under his sweater. The reason for his own retirement was officially listed as medical, but, had he chosen to, he could have returned to active duty. Lying in a hospital bed, he had begun wondering if he hadn't become one of the very people he was supposed to be protecting his country against. The darker side of life had seduced other men, and he came to the realization that if he continued to live in the shadows, he would never find his way back into the sunlight again. Why Mathias had retired, he didn't know.

Whatever his reason, Mathias had then married Dr. Erin Jane Clarkson who, contrary to the current trend, had taken her husband's name on her wedding day. Even with the resources at the Librarian's disposal, the file Eisley had given him on her had been slim. Her private life remained exactly that—private. Even her research was not particularly well-publicized. There had been no television specials on her astonishing successes, only occasional newspaper articles and progress reports in the SOS newsletter. He did learn that her childhood had been spent on an Alberta wheat farm with a widowed mother, a grandfather and a bachelor uncle, and that by the time most students were lucky to be completing their bachelor's degrees, she had earned a Ph.D. in linguistics. The subject of her doctoral dissertation had been the language of whales. SOS had sponsored her research even then.

In the years that followed, she'd had the rare privilege of sailing on the *Calypso*, twice, and spent two months on one of the Falkland Islands, alone and under very primitive conditions, while England and Argentina settled their ownership dispute. Then she had married.

By all accounts, the marriage had been happy and productive, professionally, at least. There had been no children. Christian was sure that Mathias's skill with microphones and transmitters had added invaluable refinements to Erin's ability to communicate with the whales, yet the haunted look in her eyes at the mention of her husband told him that the marriage had not been another "practicality." And certainly a man wouldn't pay three hundred thousand dollars to hire a bodyguard for a woman he had no feeling for.

In his letter, Mathias had accurately predicted the breakthrough that Erin had made not long after his death. He had been certain that it would be this breakthrough that would put Erin's life in danger. Unfortunately, he'd given no hint as to from where or whom he thought the threat would come, only that it would come when she was alone and defenseless on the isolated island. That Mathias had expected him to have a particularly difficult and dangerous time protecting her was evidenced by the size of his check.

Christian wasn't quite sure why he'd agreed to Mathias's request. He didn't need the money. Maybe it was to honor the last request of a man he had respected. And maybe it was because he was curious to know why Nelson thought a woman who talked to whales might become an "unfortunate incident." Now, after seeing her talk to them firsthand and reading her paper, he knew.

The word altruism wasn't in Nelson's vocabulary. He wasn't offering unofficial help out of loyalty to an old employee. The Navy's marine-mammal program was classified, but there had been few secrets in Damage Control. The "Flipper Force," as most referred to the program, recruited and trained dolphins, seals and whales to detect mines, rescue divers and perform various other military missions. If they had Erin Mathias, the Navy could keep surveillance on unfriendly ships without risk of detection. Valuable underwater mineral deposits that were too expensive or difficult to mine with human hands could be developed, oceanic research carried out. The possibilities were almost endless—and some of them were not so innocuous. If she had been a U.S. citizen, Erin and her work could have been declared a risk to national security, classified and put under government "protection." But Erin had retained her Canadian citizenship after her marriage, and the Canadian government frowned on U.S. "protection" of its citizens. According to the Librarian's report, the Navy had offered her their research facilities and unlimited funds in an attempt to lure her into their control, but she had turned the offer down flat. No wonder Nelson was eager to provide him with help. Like a jealous lover, they must have decided that if they couldn't have her, neither would anyone else.

He hadn't agreed to accept the check. He was due a little time off, he'd reasoned, and he actually had had a charter inquiring about a possible flight to the Aleutians. He had decided to check out the area and Dr. Erin Mathias at the same time, talk to her, satisfy himself that absolutely nothing suspicious was going on, then report back to Eisley that her late husband's fears had been unfounded. That was what he had planned to do: to see her, give her a straightforward explanation of his visit, then be on his way home.

Only it hadn't worked out quite that way, he thought, watching through hooded eyes while Erin raised her arms above her head with an unconscious voluptuousness in a long, languid stretch. Her back arched, her hands closing into fists while she slowly lowered her arms. It was more than possible that something was going on, and he didn't need to remind himself that he had been less than straightforward with her. Her head rolled in a lazy circle as she tried to loosen muscles that had grown stiff from sitting still for too long. The thought that someone might be trying to harm her suddenly filled him with a cold, remorseless fury.

Erin glanced out the window over the desk. The heavy fog had blocked out the bright twilight of the arctic summer night, giving the illusion of true darkness. Too bad the hut didn't have a fireplace, she thought wistfully. With the fog wrapped around the island like a cold wet blanket, it was the perfect night for a fire. They could drag the sofa over in front of it, curl up and... How ridiculous! Determinedly, Erin punched a command key on the terminal. Of what possible use would a fireplace be when the Quonset hut already had more heat than she knew what to do with? And besides, a small wishful voice slipped in, where would they get wood?

"That sounds like someone singing to a baby."

He hadn't made a sound crossing the creaky floor. Erin raised her eyes from the keyboard and met his reflected in the dark mirror of the window. "That's exactly what it is, a mother singing to her calf." She laughed softly. "The whale version of 'Rock-a-bye, Baby,' I guess." She looked back down at the images on the split computer screen. A transcript of the whale speech appeared on the right half, seismograph-like scratchings on the left. Glancing back up to their twin reflections in the window, she saw his eyes automatically tracking the graphic depiction of the pitch, tone and loudness of the soothing sounds from the speaker. Pressing a key, she froze the images on the screen. "That's the voice print of what you're hearing," she said, pointing to a pattern of small even zigzags slanting upward. "Interestingly enough, this same crooning pattern appears in voice prints of birds, humans, bears, whales, almost every animal that has a voice." Her fingers hit the keys again, and the images on the screen and the sound fast-forwarded. "Actually, there are quite a few of these voice patterns that cut across species lines."

The speed slowed to normal. He couldn't understand the words, of course, but the voice he heard now was an unmistakably belligerent growl. Stretching an arm across the back of her chair, he crouched down beside her to get a better view of the screen. "That one sounds just a little annoyed."

Erin leaned forward slightly to break the contact of her back and his long warm arm. It felt just a little too right there. "More than a little," she agreed with a small laugh. "That's Abner again, warning off a lone killer whale that came into the bay last week." She stopped the graph once more. "See how the zigzags are in a straight line now, how they widen, then narrow, widen and narrow? That's the growl pattern. Now listen to this one," she commanded, fast-forwarding again until she found the section she wanted.

"Surprise?" he murmured, hearing the same inflection in the whale's voice that he'd heard in Erin's a few minutes before when he had correctly identified the first pattern.

"Right. This is the pattern for it." Leaning, she traced her finger along what looked like a row of small mountain peaks on the screen.

He leaned forward, too, to get a better look, a move that brought their heads close together. Her ponytail grazed his cheek, teasing him with the softness and the scent of her hair. "How many of these common voice patterns are there?" he murmured. How would it be to fill his lungs with that clean sweet scent, to feel her hair sliding between his fingers? Like silk, he knew, like the finest, softest silk...wherever it touched him.

The warm puffs of his words stirred a loose strand of hair by her ear, creating a disturbingly delicious tickle that took its time shivering its way down her spine. She shifted away. "Oh, a dozen, at least. I can show you more," she began eagerly, only to bring herself up short after a quick glance at him.

She sat back, folding her hands in her lap. His eyes were glazed, not with boredom, but with fatigue, and there were bruises of exhaustion under them, reminding her that he'd barely escaped death less than twenty-four hours ago. She castigated herself with the stinging whip of guilt. How could she have been so selfish? Was she so starved for a little human conversation? He needed more rest, and here she was, keeping him up, blathering on about something that probably interested him about as much as fruit flies. "Well, perhaps another time. It's getting late, and you must want to get to bed."

She studied her hands. Yet he had seemed genuinely interested. They'd joked and talked with the ease of old friends—or lovers. But Christian Dekker wasn't an old friend, she reminded herself as she scooted back her chair and stood up quickly. He was a virtual stranger, with too many questions about him still unanswered.

In the bedroom she gathered up the quilt and pillow she would need for another night on the couch. "You can use the bathroom first," she offered, coming back into the main room. "I have a little work to finish up before I go to bed," He was standing in her path, and when she halted and looked up at him questioningly, he took a step closer. Erin found herself hugging the quilt and pillow, as if their puny softness could protect her, though she wasn't quite sure from what.

He reached out his large hand, and his fingers tucked an errant wisp of hair behind her ear. "I take it we're not sharing the bed," he said lightly.

"No," she said with something that felt curiously akin to regret. "We're not."

His long fingers lingered for several heartbeats; then she felt the callused tips feathering down her cheek as his hand dropped away. He smiled, the gentle smile that softened the harsh line of his mouth. Turning to look at the sofa, he said, "I'll take the couch. You shouldn't have to give up your bed."

"I don't mind," she said quickly. "The lumps are comfortable, and besides—" her small laugh was strained "—you're about six inches longer than the couch." She kept her gaze fixed on his face, denying her eyes the chance to look up and down his body, to prove his size to themselves again.

He smothered a deep yawn, then gave her a bleary grin. "Unfortunately, you're right, and I'm too tired to argue with you, anyway." His hand brushed her shoulder as he turned away, another light caress that felt as potent as a hard kiss. "Good night, Erin," he said softly.

"Good night," Erin echoed after him while he crossed the floor to the bathroom. Still clutching the blanket and pillow to her breast, she watched the door close and wondered if she would sleep any better this night than she had the night before.

Chapter 4

Erin peered over the arm of the sofa. She shouldn't have worried about sleeping; she should have worried about waking up, she decided. Christian Dekker was standing in front of the stove, stirring something in a small frying pan. As she looked on, he bent down and gave Oscar, sitting at his feet, a piece of bacon. He had cooked breakfast not thirty feet away from her, and she hadn't woken up until he was almost through. The thought was disquieting. She hadn't even known him forty-eight hours ago, yet now it seemed so natural for him to be here that the sounds of him moving around hadn't even disturbed her.

"Do you want breakfast in bed, or do you want to eat at the table?"

Erin didn't know how he had known she was awake, because he didn't turn around until after he spoke. Sitting up, she pushed her hair out of her eyes. "At the table." Her voice was froggy from sleep, and she cleared her throat. "It will just take me a few minutes to get dressed." She threw aside the quilt, then paused. Despite the oversize flannel shirt and long-underwear bottoms she was wearing for pajamas, which more than adequately covered her, she felt reluctant to parade across the hut in front of him.

Her voice had a sexy huskiness from just waking up, he thought, and her green eyes still had a soft, drowsy look. With her tousled hair and rosily flushed cheeks, she didn't look like a genius. She looked like a woman who'd spent the night in a man's bed and wasted little of it sleeping. "If you take the time to get dressed now, your breakfast will get cold," he pointed out.

As if that settled the matter, he began dishing up scrambled eggs onto the two plates sitting on the kitchen table. Erin inhaled another whiff of bacon and fresh coffee, and hunger won out over modesty.

A few minutes later Christian poured them both a second mug of coffee, then carried his with him to the couch. Erin hesitated a moment; then, picking up hers, she followed. He hid a smile against the rim of the mug at the sight of the big red shirt and blue long johns she was wearing. She sat at the other end of the couch, cross-legged, her bare feet tucked under her. "I checked the radio a little while ago. I'm afraid there's still nothing coming in but static," he said with just the right tone of apologetic regret to give sincerity to his lie. He took a sip of his coffee, then changed the subject. "What are you going to do today?"

Erin glanced from the shortwave radio to the hut's sole window, which was still heavily misted with fog. Never had she been so grateful for bad weather. "There are a couple of things I need to catch up on," she answered vaguely.

"What things?"

She looked back to him. "One of the areas I'm researching is how quickly newborn whales acquire language." At his look of interest, she elaborated. "Cetaceans are the only species besides man that have to teach their language to their young. That's because, like us, they have a very complex, highly evolved language. I've been studying the language development of Elizabeth, a calf born just after I arrived this year, and comparing it to William's, a calf born last summer. Daniel rigged up a collar with a transmitter in it for William to wear so

I could make tapes of his 'baby talk.' " She pointed across the room to the receiver-cassette recorder whose function he had wondered about. "Elizabeth's wearing a collar now, too, but I haven't had a chance to compare their tapes yet, to see if the way they learn their language is similar to the way a human child acquires language."

"Too bad you and your husband—" Christian found that the word seemed to stick in his throat "—didn't have any children. Then you could have had a human subject as part of your experiment."

Erin set down the mug of coffee, which had suddenly lost its taste, on the table in front of the couch and stood up. "Yes, too bad," she agreed in a cool tone. "Thank you for fixing breakfast," she added with exquisite politeness before turning away.

"Erin." His quiet voice stopped her halfway toward the bedroom. She looked back to see that he was standing now, too.

Christian waited until she was facing him. "I'm sorry, Erin. That was a thoughtless thing to say."

With a small nod and a smaller smile, she accepted his apology.

He stared at the closed bedroom door. He hadn't needed to see the flash of pain in her eyes before they'd blanked over to know that what he'd said had been thoughtless...and cruel. He knew as well as he knew his own name that a baby could never be just the subject of an experiment to Erin. He also knew just as surely that she had wanted a baby with Mathias and had grieved for that loss, as well, when he died. That thought lit another fire in his gut from the fiercely hot jealousy that had prompted his nasty remark in the first place. The emotion was as inexplicable as it was unfamiliar, but Christian found that he couldn't bear to think of Erin having another man's baby, or another man, period. And that was inexplicable, too.

Erin pressed a command key, then watched in disbelief as the computer screen went blank, wiping out the vocabulary analysis she had been working on for the past hour. Closing her eyes on the cursor winking rudely at her from the empty screen, she swore eloquently under her breath. The whole day had been like this, one stupid mistake after another, because she couldn't seem to keep her mind on her work.

Opening her eyes, she grimly set about reconstructing what she had just destroyed by pushing the wrong button. She'd been at the computer all day. Christian had puttered around and done the few housekeeping chores. He'd fixed the water pump that previously had only worked when it wanted to, then made lunch, because, involved as she was in her work, she had forgotten it. After lunch, he'd asked if there were any fishing equipment around, and she'd shown him to one of the tall metal lockers in the entrance tunnel. The contents of the locker were a garage-sale jumble of odds and ends that past residents of the hut had left behind, and almost immediately he'd found the saltwater fishing rod and heavy-duty reel. Maybe they would have fresh fish for dinner, he'd announced.

She glanced over at the kitchen table, where the source of her distraction had spent the afternoon taking apart and patiently cleaning and oiling the fishing reel. He picked up one of the pieces that were spread out over a newspaper covering the tabletop. Oscar, sprawled at the edge of the paper, batted lazily at his fingers as they fit the tiny gear expertly in place. He paused before picking up another piece to scratch the top of Oscar's head, and the cat closed his eyes, rubbing his furry head against Christian's fingers with a voluptuous pleasure. Unbidden images of other things those long clever fingers would be expert at, other pleasures they might give, flashed into her mind, and she jerked her eyes back to the computer screen.

Erin scowled at the screen while she deleted an entire paragraph because she'd typed it with her fingers on the wrong keys. Quiet, undemanding, helpful, able to entertain himself—Christian Dekker would be the perfect houseguest, she decided, if she just weren't so... aware of him. It was an awareness that bordered on witless fascination, she admitted dryly, as she tried to remember what the paragraph had been about.

Christian set down the reassembled fishing reel, then looked across the room. He grinned at the sight of Erin's toes, clad in hot pink socks, curled over a rung of her chair. She'd come out of the bedroom after breakfast dressed in the socks, green corduroy jeans well broken in to the curve of her slim hips and those impossibly long legs, and a baseball-style gray jersey with long raspberry sleeves. She'd left her hair loose to fall across her shoulders and halfway down her back, the only sunshine on this dismal day. By necessity, her clothing had to be sturdy and serviceable, pants and shirts, but they weren't masculine. The colors were bright pastels, the fabrics, even the denim and corduroy of her jeans, soft. Her long underwear was silk, and he thought of the other soft, delicate things he had found in the dresser. Erin Mathias was a very sensual woman.

She was also, he realized suddenly, one of the most completely feminine women he'd ever known. It wasn't just the obvious things, like the sweet curves of her body, her clear soprano voice, her scent and her hair. It was a basic, intrinsic sense of womanliness that determined the way she moved, the words she chose, the textures and colors of the clothes she wore, the gentleness of her hands when she petted the cat—the same gentleness, he knew, with which she'd touched his body when she had cared for him.

Oscar abandoned the table and padded across the bare floor to his mistress. Christian watched as he climbed up onto her lap and kneaded a place for himself. She gave him an absentminded pat as he draped his long body over her corduroy-clad thighs. The cat's fur wouldn't be as soft as the lace and silk she wore underneath, he thought, or the even softer skin under that.

Abruptly, Erin shut off the terminal and stood up. Oscar landed on his feet with an indignant yowl, then shook himself and ambled off to take the next in his endless series of naps. Turning her head, Erin saw Christian watching her with that stillness that seemed so at odds with the size and obvious strength of his body. One didn't expect a body like that to be still, she thought; one expected immediate, explosive action. Folding her arms across her chest, she looked away and realized she was pacing. Erin laughed humorlessly to herself. He was supposed to be the wolf, but she was the one prowling the living room like a caged animal.

Forcing herself to stop, she stood with her back to him and stared at the shreds of fog drifting past the window. She told herself that her lack of concentration, the restlessness she was feeling, were simply cabin fever.

Christian saw her rub the back of her neck as if she were trying to work out the kinks left from sitting over a computer all day. "I'm going out for a walk," she said suddenly, without turning around.

"I'll go with you," he said, ignoring the sudden stiffening of her back. He had a few kinks to work out, too.

The catchall locker yielded up an old army flight jacket two sizes too small and a pair of Wellingtons that, miraculously, fit perfectly. After fastening her parka and tying on her own boots, Erin looked him over critically. The black pants tucked into the tops of the Wellingtons emphasized the length and power of his legs. The jacket looked as if it had survived several crashes, barely, and his wrists were left dangling out of the sleeves. It should have looked ridiculous, but it didn't. "I think I saw a pair of gloves in the locker," she said, pulling a red silk balaclava over her head.

He rummaged around in the locker for a few seconds, then silently held up a pair of gloves for her inspection. In spite of herself, Erin giggled. The wool gloves looked as if they had been attacked by a pack of rabid moths. "Maybe there's another pair?" she said hopefully.

He took another look, then shook his head. "That's what they make pockets for," he said equably. After pulling on a black wool watch cap he had found in the locker, he opened the outer air lock and silently indicated that she should precede him.

The wind swirled a last few wraiths of fog around them, but Erin saw another long, low gray line waiting on the horizon. Thick dark clouds boiled overhead as the storm ponderously moved on. It would be another day, at least, before anyone was looking for Christian again, she thought, leading the climb up the low grass-covered hill behind the hut. A fierce wind buffeted the hilltop, but she paused, turning her face into it, reveling in its power. The wild weather spawned a wildness in her that released the tensions that had been accumulating over the past two days. Filling her lungs with the chill clean air and the strong sharp smell of the sea, Erin angled a look up at the man beside her. The wind ruffled the narrow band of white-gold hair beneath his cap against the black wool, and whipped back the open edges of the flight jacket. His hands stuffed in his pockets, he stood with his legs slightly spread and braced like he was challenging the wind. He tilted his head back, as if he were sniffing the scents it carried. Erin was studying the strong line of his exposed throat when his head turned suddenly, and he grinned at her.

The balaclava covered everything but her eyes and the golden fringe of her bangs, but Christian saw her lips curving under the thin silk. Framed by the narrow opening in the hood, her eyes sparkled with silent laughter. Her eyes were exactly as he remembered them from the night she had found him on the beach, clear, sea-green pools with flakes of gold glinting in their depths.

Knowing he couldn't hear her over the howl of the wind, Erin tilted her head questioningly toward the beach below and saw him nod in reply. The back side of the grassy hill was a steep cliff of bare rock, which wind and water had faceted into sharp planes and angles. Erin started down, a quick glance over her shoulder assuring her that he was right behind her and handling the treacherous climb with ease.

Near the bottom, one of her boots skidded on a patch of rotten rock, and, almost before she realized she was falling, Erin was lifted off her feet. Instinctively she clutched at his shoulders as Christian turned her, securing her body against his with his arms clamped across her hips and back. The powerful muscles of his thighs bunched and flowed against hers as he continued the descent, and, despite the layers of clothes separating them, Erin could feel a body that was even harder and stronger than she had imagined.

As soon as they reached level ground, he set her down and released her. Erin took a quick step backward, staggering a little. He wasn't even breathing hard, she noted, while her breath seemed to be lost somewhere in the middle of her chest. "Thanks," she gasped when she finally found it.

"You're welcome." His smile warmed the blue ice of his eyes, and, when he held out his hand, it seemed only natural that she should put her hand in his. He tucked both their hands into the pocket of his jacket as they began walking up the beach. Her parka offered more than adequate protection from the raw wind, but the warmth seeping up her arm from her hand clasped in his gradually suffused her body with a different kind of heat.

Long, rolling waves broke heavily on the gravel beach, dashing a cold salt mist over them. They walked a mile or more, picking their way over thick, greasy-looking strings of kelp that the waves had torn loose and strung along the shore. The strip of gray gravel narrowed as the cliff crowded closer until the beach finally dead-ended against a wall of solid rock.

An ancient stream had carved rough steps down the face of the rock. By unspoken agreement they chose to climb the wall instead of retracing their paths. It seemed he wasn't ready to return to the claustrophobic closeness of the Quonset hut, either, Erin thought as she watched the man climbing ahead of her. The natural stairway was glass slick in places, broken in others, yet he never slipped, never made a clumsy move. It seemed almost impossible that a body as big as his could move with such agility and grace.

The last step was nearly five feet high. He levered himself up in one smooth, powerful motion, then reached down to grab her hand and hoisted her up with the same seemingly effortless ease. Kneeling beside him, Erin pulled the hood off her head and shook her hair free. "I didn't know this was here," she murmured in surprise. They were in a shallow cave that had been eroded out of the softer rock beneath the overhanging cliff. The roof was too low for either of them to stand up, and if Christian stretched his arms out, she was sure his fingertips would brush the sides, but it provided a shelter from the raw weather, muzzling the howling wind to a low whine.

Erin sat on the smooth floor and wrapped her arms loosely around her knees. Christian remained close beside her, one knee resting on the ground. The cave offered an endless view of the sea and sky. Both were the same dirty gray color today, and, out of habit, Erin scanned the water for any sign of the whales. Her gaze sharpened and focused on something several miles offshore. She studied the bobbing object for several seconds, trying to make out what it was, but it was too far away. Erin glanced up to see if Christian might be watching it, too, but he was looking in the direction of the beach on the other side of the rock wall they had climbed. When she looked out to sea, the object had disappeared. Although she watched for several minutes, it never reappeared, and finally Erin dismissed it as a trick of the dusky light.

"That's where I found you," she said, seeing that he was still looking at the beach below.

"I was wondering if that was where it was," he answered in a soft, reflective tone.

Erin looked at him curiously. "Do you remember it?"

He slanted her a dry look. "All I remember is freezing to death, literally." *And you,* he added silently. He remembered nothing of the beach. He had been dying, his awareness almost gone...yet his memory of her was perfect. How could that be? he wondered as he studied her upturned face. Perhaps because he had wanted to take the vision of her with him into eternity.

A gust of wind eddied through the cave, whipping Erin's long hair into her face. While she was fighting for control of her hair, Erin felt Christian shift behind her. Then she felt his hands in her hair, gathering it in his fists and holding it until the tiny whirlwind spent its furious energy.

His hands opened, freeing her hair, and Erin started to turn her head around to thank him. Before she could speak, she felt his long fingers tunneling through her hair as if combing it into some semblance of order after the wind's messy play. He had moved so that she was now sitting between his legs, his chest at her back. She sat very still as his palms smoothed over her head and his thumbs paused above her ears. The short, blunt nails raked lightly against her scalp while his thumbs worked up to the crown of her head, parting her hair. She felt his fingers sectioning it, then a gentle tugging, and she realized he was braiding it.

Her hair was softer than he had imagined. When he had been trying to work out the tangles, the long strands sliding between his fingers had felt like threads of the finest, softest silk, and he'd barely controlled the impulse to bury his face in it. Now the sweet scent of it floated up to him as his fingers divided and braided, and he had to resist the urge again.

Erin unfastened and opened her parka as it suddenly became much too warm in the snug cave. A shiver worked its way under her scalp, then down her back, but it wasn't from the sudden rush of cool air on her heated chest. She felt as if she were a child again, being petted and lavished with attention; yet his long, strong fingers moving through her hair, the gentle tugging, produced the most erotic, unchildlike sensations she had ever experienced. Erin caught herself arching her neck, trying to rub her head against his hand, much as Oscar did when he petted him. "You're very good at that," she said, her voice slightly husky. Whose hair had he practiced on? she wondered. A wife's? A lover's? He was old enough to have had several of each, and with that thought came a painful prick of...jealousy?

"Every sailor learns how to braid rope in boot camp," he murmured. That's what her hair was, he thought, silky ropes so fine that they were almost invisible, twining themselves around his fingers and wrists, binding the two of them together. He had never allowed himself to become involved with a woman who was part of a job. It was a personal rule he'd never broken, not in his time with Damage Control or in the years since. It was the only rule he hadn't broken, he reminded himself with a trace of bitterness. His hands stilled in the act of gathering the last strands at the nape of her neck. Maybe the reason he hadn't broken it was because he'd never really been tempted before, he realized abruptly. She had caught him off guard. He had been prepared for someone asexual, someone who was more computer than human. Instead he'd found an arrestingly attractive, totally feminine woman full of wit and humor. Despite her formidable intelligence, she was unassuming and completely natural, with an honesty and directness that were disarming. He looked down at his hands, which were still wrapped in her hair. He felt drawn to her as he had been to no other woman, as if there truly were ropes binding them together. And he wasn't struggling very hard against them, Christian admitted ruefully.

He finished the braid, tying the end with a bit of fishing line he found in a pocket of the flight jacket. "There. All finished." He gave her shoulder a brisk pat. Christian heard her murmur thank you and expected her to pull away. Instead she seemed content to stay where she was between his knees, her back brushing his chest, her head almost on his shoulder. He touched her shoulder again, ruffling the coarse white polar-bear fur covering it. "Where did you get the parka?" he asked.

The parka and the pants that went with it were an authentic Inuit snowsuit made in the traditional style. Although the fur suits were superior to anything commercially available, few Inuit bothered to make them anymore, preferring to buy their clothes like everyone else, and even fewer non-Inuit were lucky enough to own one. His hand drifted down her arm, and her hand just naturally seemed to come back into his. He closed his fingers around hers gently, resting their joined hands on his thigh.

"Daniel and I spent two summers living in an Inuit village on the Alaskan coast, studying belugas, before we came here." Her voice was soft, almost drowsy sounding. "I stopped to see them on my way here this year, and the women of the village gave me the parka and matching pants." She turned her head to smile at him over her shoulder. "They made them for me as a gesture of friendship, sort of an informal adoption into their tribe, because I have no husband or sons to provide for me. I was wearing the parka and pants when I found you. I put them on you, to keep you warm until I could get you back to the hut. I expect they saved your life."

His hand tightened involuntarily around hers. "If you gave me your parka and pants, what did you wear?"

"My long johns and boots," Erin answered, puzzled by the sudden fierceness in his eyes.

His mouth thinned to a hard, narrow line. "You were out in that storm wearing only your underwear?" he asked in an ominously soft tone. He hadn't considered that she might have endangered her own life to save his.

"There wasn't time to go back for more clothes," she explained patiently, as if he were a slow three-year-old. "You were dying."

He stared into her wide, clear eyes and felt as if he could see down to her soul. He was humbled before such selflessness, and he didn't know how to respond. "Oh, Erin," he said helplessly, his voice harshened by the emotion that was threatening to swamp him. Locking his free arm across the front of her shoulders, he drew her against him. "You shouldn't have risked your life for mine," he whispered into her hair.

"I had no choice," she answered softly; then he heard her quiet sigh and felt a pressure against his arm. He relaxed it immediately, and she sat up. Suddenly Christian remembered something she had said earlier. "How did the Inuit know Daniel had died?" he asked, his tone indicating only mild interest in her answer.

"I imagine Sam told them. He probably saw Daniel's obituary in the newspaper." Erin knew she should pull away from him and remove her hand from his, but, like the little cave, his body was a haven of warmth and comfort that she was loath to give up.

"Sam?"

"Sam Akiachak. He's the headman of the village. He used to have a law practice in Vancouver. In fact, SOS was one of his clients. Then, about three years ago, he moved back to the village, but I know he still gets the Vancouver papers, because he passes them on to me. He's the bush pilot who brings me supplies," Erin added as an afterthought.

Christian kept his voice easy. "Why did he give up his law practice in Vancouver?"

"He felt he should try to do more for his people." Erin laughed sadly. "The village has a twenty-foot satellite dish and every house has a television set, but no indoor plumbing. Sam works for free as the tribe's lawyer and business manager. They got a generous sum of money under the Alaska Native Claims Settlement Act, but they didn't invest it wisely, and now most of the money is gone. Sam is trying to conserve what's left and raise more to finance improvements in the village, and also a small fishing fleet and a cannery to provide income for the tribe.''

"Why didn't you go back there this year to study the whales so you wouldn't have to be alone?"

"That's what I'd planned to do," Erin admitted. "But then, about a month before I was supposed to leave, Phillip Damion, the founder of SOS, told me he'd gotten permission for me to come back here." She gave him a wry grin over her shoulder. "You might not believe it, but it's easier to get a room in Buckingham Palace than to get reservations for this place. Different research groups have it booked up years in advance. I don't know what strings Phillip pulled, what favors he called in, but they must have been major. After that, I couldn't tell him no."

"You couldn't find someone to come with you?"

Erin shook her head. "No. None of the other researchers I know is studying belugas." She looked down, seeing their linked hands lying on his thigh. His hand was square, and, like the rest of him, large and very powerful looking. The skin was darkly tanned, the palm callused from hard work, with those odd thicker calluses along the outer edge. His fingers were long and blunt, dusted with white-gold hair. Her hand looked absurdly small in comparison, weak and pale, barely half the size of his. One good squeeze and he could easily break it, crush the fragile bones. His fingers tightened slightly, speaking in eloquent silence of the great strength he could use against her—but which she knew instinctively he wouldn't.

Erin raised her eyes slowly to meet his. "Why is it," she said quietly, "that I feel so safe with you?"

Christian didn't give her an answer. He knew she wasn't really asking for one, and he didn't have one to give her, anyway. All he had was a vague suspicion taking shape at the back of his mind that told him that she wasn't safe at all. If only he could have had just ten more damned seconds with his plane!

None of the frustration he felt showed on his face as he watched his hand smooth the funny little cowlick in her bangs. "We better be heading back," he said with a smile.

Moments later, Christian landed with an agile leap on the first step, then reached up for Erin. She locked her hands over his shoulders as he got a firm grip on her waist. Just as he was about to swing her down, he felt her body stiffen, and she pushed against his shoulders in a silent demand for him to wait. Glancing up, he followed the direction of her gaze out to sea.

Erin narrowed her eyes, trying to bring into focus the object she'd been subconsciously watching for ever since it had bobbed out of view nearly half an hour ago. It had reappeared at last, closer to shore. "Christian?" she asked uncertainly. "Is that your plane?"

Chapter 5

Is there anything out there to keep it from washing ashore?''

"I'm afraid so." Erin paused to catch her breath after their mad scramble down the cliff. She looked at him standing at the edge of the rocky beach, the surf boiling around his black boots, his big body straining forward, as if he could bring the plane ashore by the strength of his will alone. "About a hundred yards offshore there's a reef. If the sea weren't so rough, you'd see it."

He spared her a glance. "There's no opening?"

"A small one, too small for a plane to get through."

"And if the plane hits the reef, it will break up," he muttered. Christian stared at his plane, thinking hard. Lighter parts, like the pontoons and body panels, would probably wash ashore, but the heavier ones would sink, and the engine was the heaviest of all. He estimated the distance the plane had traveled since Erin spotted it, then rapidly calculated the time it would take to reach the reef and the time it would take him to bring her Zodiac raft around. He turned to her suddenly. "Do you have any heavy rope or chain?"

Erin knew immediately why he was asking. "I—I think so, but you can't be thinking of going out and getting it! The sea's too rough, and the fog is coming back in," she argued forcefully.

"I'm damned well going to try," he said grimly, already heading for the other side of the island.

From his tone and the set of his jaw, Erin understood the futility of further argument. She followed him at a near run, unconsciously retracing the same route she'd taken two days before. The trip had seemed to take hours then; now it took only a few minutes to reach the Quonset hut.

Erin raced up the ladder and turned on every light in the observation tower. On her way out of the hut, she stopped long enough to get the life jackets and her rain poncho, which were stored in one of the tunnel lockers. It wasn't raining, but the spray thrown up by the boat would drench them in seconds. Whichever one of them rode in front could wear the poncho and, she hoped, shield the other.

She paused in the act of closing the locker door. Whichever one of them? Without realizing it, she had made the decision to go with him. Although she had exaggerated the danger in hopes of discouraging him, trying to handle the raft in rough seas and attach a towline to the plane at the same time really was too dangerous for one person alone. She could understand his reluctance to watch his livelihood smash up on the rocks, and if he was determined to try to save his plane, she would help him. Erin slammed the locker door shut and, scooping up the life jackets and poncho, ran down the tunnel to the outer door. After saving his life, she wasn't about to lose him now.

Erin glanced at the tower as she ran down to the dock. With the light streaming out of the windows, it looked as bright as a lighthouse beacon. It had better be, she thought grimly. If the fog caught them out at sea, the light would be all they had to show them the way back.

Christian was already in the boat, checking the level of gas in the outboard engine's tank when she arrived. Erin saw a long coil of heavy rope, which she knew he'd found in the shed, lying on the bottom of the boat. He screwed the gas cap back on, and Erin silently handed him a life jacket. He buckled it on, then picked up a square of canvas tarp she knew had also come from the shed. He grasped the middle of the tarp in his big hands and, with a quick jerk, ripped a foot-long tear in the heavy canvas. Dropping the tarp over his head, he settled it in place with an impatient twitch of his broad shoulders.

As Christian bent to untie the stern rope, he caught sight of Erin pulling on her own poncho. He straightened slowly, the rope still in his hand. "Where do you think you're going?"

"With you." Erin stepped into the boat.

He tossed the rope down. "Like hell."

"It's my boat," Erin observed mildly. "And besides, you can't manage it and the plane both. There are also other reefs out there, and you don't know where they are. I do," she added with maddening reasonableness. She cast off the bow rope, shoved them away from the dock, then settled herself on the front seat.

Christian stared at her for a long moment without speaking. She met his stare with a calm implacability that told him the only way he was going to get her off her boat was to throw her off. The real hell of it was that she was right. Erin knew as well as he did that he had a poor chance of recovering the seaplane without her help. She probably thought he was worried about losing thousands of dollars' worth of plane, Christian thought, laughing humorlessly to himself. He didn't give a damn about the plane—insurance would cover it—but her willingness to help touched him in ways he didn't have time to think about now.

He studied the sea beyond the mouth of the bay, feeling a rare sense of indecision. The wind had died to almost nothing. The plane was off the lee side of the island, where the water was calmer, and he was confident of his ability to handle the small rubber boat. They would probably get wet and cold, but there should be no real danger. Still, he knew he wouldn't even be considering the risks of taking her if getting another look at that engine weren't so damned important. She might be in

greater danger if the plane sank before he could confirm his
suspicions.

Bending suddenly, Christian took out his frustration on the
outboard's starter rope. The engine started on the first jerk and
settled into a smooth idle as he dropped onto the wooden plank
that served as a seat. "All right!" he shouted over the noise of
the engine. "But you do exactly as I say."

She gave him a demure smile, and he read the words "of
course" on her lips before she swung her legs over the seat so
she could face forward. Staring at her straight back, he chuckled in reluctant appreciation of how neatly she had outmaneu-
vered him. His face sobered as he twisted the engine throttle
open wide and they roared away from the dock.

The pointed bow of the Zodiac butted through the waves,
throwing back a heavy spray. Huddled under her poncho in the
prow, Erin maintained a lookout. A wild wave bounced the
small raft up like a rubber ball, and for a moment she was eye-
to-eye with a sea gull that was cruising low over the water. The
gull squawked in alarm and veered away, and Erin laughed.
Despite the rough ride, she felt no fear. She wasn't even particularly worried. In fact, she was enjoying it. She felt that same
sense of freedom and exhilaration she'd felt on a windswept
hilltop a few hours before.

The raft smacked through a wave, and Erin blinked the salt
spray out of her eyes. If it had been anyone else, she thought
wonderingly, she would have tactfully insisted that she handle
the boat, because she knew she had experience with the small
craft that few others could equal. Yet she hadn't even thought
of suggesting it. Automatically she had assumed that he knew
what he was doing, and he did, controlling the small boat in the
rough water at least as expertly as she would have.

She had to blink again, and when she opened her eyes, she
saw his plane about seventy-five yards ahead of them and a little to the left. "There!" Erin shouted, turning to glance back
at Christian to be sure he heard her. She saw him follow the
direction of her pointing arm, then nod, and then she felt the
boat turn.

Christian circled the green and white plane slowly, looking for damage. One of the struts that connected the floats to the body had buckled, giving the plane a drunken list, but it was riding the waves easily. The tail rudder was flapping in time to the rising and falling of the waves, indicating that it was loose, and the door was open and sprung, as if a huge wave had tried to rip it off its hinges. He cut the throttle back to a notch above idle, giving the outboard just enough gas to hold their position in front of the plane's nose. It was a little short of a miracle that the plane had survived—and with such relatively minor damage, he thought. His glance passed over the woman sitting quietly in the bow and paused. But then, his own survival was something of a miracle, too.

Christian raised his voice above the clatter of the outboard motor. "We're going to have to go in from the side to tie on the tow line. Going in under the nose would be easier and faster, but the sea's running too high, and we'd take a pounding."

As if to demonstrate his point, a large wave slapped the belly of the plane, and Erin realized that if they had been under the nose, they would have been slammed up against the unyielding metal body and sharp propeller blade. Christian picked up the coil of rope and started toward her. Keeping low, just as he did, to avoid rocking the boat any more, Erin moved to change places with him. They met in the middle, and, as she started to step over the seat, he stopped her with a hand on her arm. She looked up to see that the lines around his mouth were harsher than usual.

"I can still put you ashore, Erin, and pick you up later," he said quietly. "You don't have—"

She stopped him with a quick smile. "I didn't come along just for the ride, Christian."

His hand lifted to tuck damp wisps of her hair under the hood of her poncho while his eyes searched her sober face. At last the harsh lines around his mouth softened a little as he gave her another of those heartbreakingly gentle smiles. "Okay, love." The soft endearment was so right for the moment that neither of them took notice of it.

A few seconds later they were both in their places, Christian's tone crisp with command now. "Take the boat in under the wing and keep it as close to the float as you can. I'll reach across and tie the rope on the front strut. Then back out, and we'll do the other side."

Seated in the stern, Erin nodded. Her hand tightened on the throttle, and the boat eased forward. The rubber skin of the Zodiac and the metal pontoon bumped gently, and she cut back on the gas. She looked at Christian, who was standing in the bow, one foot on the edge of the raft, ready to tie the rope. Silhouetted against the gray sky, his makeshift poncho swirling around him like a long cape, he looked larger than life. Like some eighteenth-century swashbuckler, she thought whimsically, poised to leap aboard an enemy ship, cutlass in hand, and do fierce battle to claim it as his own.

The raft pitched into a trough, rolling wickedly, and Erin hastened guiltily to adjust the steering arm to compensate. What he was trying to do was almost as dangerous as fighting a pack of pirates, and he didn't need her mooning around, Erin berated herself. He stepped up onto the float and grabbed the metal strut, keeping the boat and the plane together with just the strength of that one long arm, despite the ferocity of the angry sea trying to tear them apart. Erin held her breath. Now she was worried. If she misjudged the size of a wave, or another wild wave hit the plane, or his foot slipped on the wet pontoon, or any of a dozen other things happened, he could be jerked out of the raft. And even with the boat, she might not be able to rescue him before the swift current dashed him up against the sharp, tearing teeth of the reef.

Words weren't necessary as Erin sensed what he needed from her. She held the Zodiac steady in the rough water, giving gas to the engine in small spurts timed to the fall of the craft as each new wave slid out from under it. Christian whipped the end of the rope around the strut and tied it on almost too fast for her eyes to follow. Erin backed out from under the wing as quickly as she dared, keeping an anxious eye on the white line of breakers that marked the reef. They were close enough to hear the muted roar of the tons of water trying to bury the rock, and she knew it was going to be a close race between them and the reef to see who would have the plane.

Erin watched Christian play out the rope, then loop it back up as she nosed in under the other wing. Except for one heart-stopping moment when a wave broke over the pontoon he was standing on and she was terrified he would be washed away, the rope-tying maneuver went as easily as the first time. Christian dropped back into the boat and flashed her a wide grin as he held up his thumb and forefinger in a circle to indicate success.

Erin forced an answering grin and backed away from the plane once again. None of the disasters she had envisioned had happened. They had worked together to accomplish the difficult and risky task as if it were routine, something they did every night before dinner. She swallowed, sending her heart back to its proper place, and abruptly realized that every muscle in her body was shaking. Now that he had both feet safely back on the wooden floor of the raft, she could admit how frightened she had been.

Drawing a deep breath—the first, she was sure, since they'd left the dock—Erin shoved the steering arm of the outboard hard to the left. The prop churned the gray-green water into a white froth as the boat swung one hundred eighty degrees on the axis of the engine shaft. The stern was now facing the seaplane, and Erin watched Christian come down the twelve-foot length of the Zodiac toward her. His body adjusting automatically to the pitch and roll of the boat, he moved with the same surefooted grace he had on solid ground.

She scooted to one side on the seat to give him room to work while she kept her hand on the throttle to maintain the distance between them and his plane. Christian looped the rope around the cleats set on either side of the wood transom where the outboard was mounted. He closed his hand over hers on the throttle and twisted gently.

The raft moved forward slowly, straight away from the plane. It bucked when the slack in the rope was used up, and Erin could hear the engine straining as it took on the additional weight of the plane. She kept her eyes fixed on the pitted chrome cleats, silently willing their rusted screws to hold in the salt-bleached wood. She knew he was watching them, too. They groaned ominously, but they held.

Christian twisted his hand on hers again, and they stopped dead in the water. The momentum of the plane carried it forward, the taut rope began to slacken, and Christian quickly threw a couple of additional loops around the cleats to keep it from slipping any more. Erin got up to return to her place in the bow. A long arm was wrapped around her waist, and suddenly she found herself sitting down on the seat, hard. Startled, she turned to stare at the man now sitting beside her.

"You'll stay drier back here," was all he said before turning his attention to getting them under way. Gradually he increased their speed, keeping a close eye on the buckled strut until he was apparently satisfied that it would bear the strain of the rope.

He glanced down at her with a smile. "That was quite a job you did handling the boat."

Erin laughed shakily. "One thing whale watching teaches you is how to handle a rubber raft in six-foot seas."

In response his arm snuggled her closer. To try to sit up straight while she was wearing the bulky life jacket and he was holding her so close was too awkward, so Erin didn't even try. She leaned against him, her head finding its natural place on his shoulder. The rough canvas under her cheek was damp, and it smelled of motor oil and mildew, but, oddly, she didn't mind. The growling drone of the engine, the warmth of his body, the strength of his arm around her, had a soothing, soporific effect that helped her forget that the boat seat was as hard as a rock and her bottom was cold and wet. She lay in the circle of his arm for what could have been hours or a few seconds, rousing only when a cold, damp finger of fog brushed her cheek.

Erin pushed against his chest, and his arm loosened enough to let her sit up comfortably. The lack of wind was a mixed blessing. It made the job of towing the plane easier, but the still air allowed the fog to settle faster. From the sweeping turn the Zodiac was making, she knew they were rounding the spit of land that marked the entrance to the small bay below the hut. He really had an uncanny sense of direction, Erin thought absently, as she searched the gray mist for the lights of the observation tower. She spotted a golden glow in the grayness and knew he had seen it, too, by the slight relaxing of his body.

"We're almost home," he murmured.

Erin had the sudden realization that the rusting hut with its shabby furniture did seem like home to her, certainly more like home than that sterile apartment back at the institute.

Minutes later the raft bumped against the end of the wooden dock. Again acting in wordless coordination, Erin jumped out, holding the bow rope, while Christian loosened the tow rope. As soon as he stepped onto the dock, she walked the raft down to its usual mooring place to leave him room to tie up his plane. After securing the raft, she glanced back to see him climbing into his plane.

At first glance, at least, it seemed relatively undamaged. From what she'd seen of his handiness, he'd probably be able to make whatever repairs were necessary himself. Then he'd be leaving. The sudden sharp misery she felt almost made her cry out. It was the same situation as when one found an injured animal and nursed it back to health, she tried to tell herself. It was normal to feel possessive, not to want to let it go again, to let it return to where it belonged. She had no right to keep him.

He'd discarded the tarp and his life jacket in the raft. Mechanically, Erin took off her own jacket and poncho, then gathered everything up and started to carry it up to the hut.

"Erin!" His shout commanded her to stop. Pausing halfway up the beach, she turned around and laughed to see him loping toward her, a boyishly pleased grin on his face. For a moment she felt a bittersweet pang at this glimpse of a younger, happier Christian, before whatever it was that had put the harsh lines in his face and given him the eyes of an old man had happened.

Erin staggered slightly from the impact of his body as he hooked his arm around her shoulders and pulled her against his side in a rough, one-armed bear hug. "We make a pretty good

team, don't we, sweetheart?'' His deep raspy voice was rich
with satisfaction.

Erin looked up to find him grinning down at her. "Yes, we
do." She laughed. Caught up in his exuberance, she reached up
and kissed him.

It was just a spontaneous, friendly kiss, but it changed the
moment her lips touched his. His mouth crushed hers lazily, as
if they had all night and were lying in the comfortable bed inside, instead of standing outside in the cold, damp fog. It
wasn't an aggressive kiss, not at all threatening or frightening;
it was warm, wet, a little rough . . . and incredibly arousing.

His lips were firm, his teeth hard and sharp as they nipped
into her soft bottom lip, his tongue slow and gentle as it bathed
away the tiny hurt. The tip traced the curve of her upper lip,
then teased at the corners of her mouth. Erin acquiesced to his
artful demand for entry. Her lips parted on a sigh, and his
tongue began a languid journey of discovery.

Gradually Erin had become aware that she was leaning full
length against him. He still had one arm around her shoulders, the other one tight across her back. She wondered dimly
what had happened to the things she'd been carrying, not realizing they were lying around their feet where she'd dropped
them so she could wrap her arms around his waist. He changed
the angle of the kiss, and she forgot about them.

She stretched up along his body, her hands sliding under his
jacket, pressing herself closer so she could kiss him back. Her
lips twisted against his, and her tongue ventured forth, hesitantly at first, then more surely as her hands locked behind his
neck.

The tip of her tongue touched his, and Christian felt the light
contact in the soles of his feet. He withdrew his tongue, coax-
ing hers to follow, and it did, gliding along his before exploring his teeth, the roof of his mouth, the insides of his cheeks
with slow, delicate licks. He widened his stance, drawing her
deeper into the kiss and his body. Their jackets were open, and
through her jersey and his thin sweater, he could feel her nipples, hard and raised, rubbing against his chest.

His hand dropped down and settled unerringly on her breast. The hard little nub stabbed through the soft jersey into his palm as he rotated his hand slowly. He felt her sigh of pleasure as much as he heard it, a warm gust on the cool skin of his cheek as her body suddenly seemed to go boneless, melting into his. His hand moved on, plucking at the buttons of the placket closing her shirt, and it was his turn to sigh as his fingers slid inside the opening, under lace-edged silk. Her skin was so hot after the chill air that his hand felt scorched. His fingers spread and flexed as he took the soft weight of her breast, and he sighed again. She did fill his hand.

His thumb rasped slowly over the tight tip, and Erin moaned deep in the back of her throat. She only vaguely heard the sound and didn't register at all that it was her own voice. The exquisitely arousing friction between the rough callus of his thumb and the satin smoothness of her nipple created a heat that spread through her body, gathering at the junction of her thighs where, paradoxically, it turned into a deep ache. Her nails bit into his neck as she held his head for her hungry kiss, her body squirming, rubbing, trying to relieve the ache. His mouth bit back, softly, while one rock-hard thigh pushed between hers, and his hand slid down to cup her bottom. He pulled her up high and hard against him. Her hips did a slow bump and grind against his, and she moaned again. It relieved the ache, and made it worse.

Only slowly did Christian realize that the jeans covering her hips were clammy and that the tremors shivering through her body into his were coming from cold as much as passion. He worked his hand up into her braided hair and began to ease her away. Her mouth released his very reluctantly, and her arms fell away from his neck. Her body stopped straining, and she lay quietly against him. Pressing her head against his shoulder, he tilted back his own and drew a deep, ragged breath of the cold fog, trying to clear his brain of ideas he had no business thinking. Ideas of setting her on that big bed inside, slowly stripping off her practical jeans and shirt and the impractical lace and silk underneath, filling his hand again with her softness, of

his hands and mouth finding other places even softer, feeling
her hair brush across his . . .

The insistent throbbing that had eased in his groin grew demanding again. Perhaps he'd better not think at all. He
chuckled ruefully to himself. Never, even when he was a kid,
had he lost control so fast or had such a hard time finding it
again. Her chest rose and fell in an unsteady sigh, and the
chuckle became a groan as her nipples stabbed into him. They
were still hard. He wished he'd thought to pull their jackets
closed. Lowering his head, he rested his cheek on the top of her
silky head. He knew she had kissed him on impulse, but the
moment his mouth touched hers, her impulse had become the
hottest, sweetest, most explosive kiss he'd ever experienced.

Closing his eyes, he rubbed his cheek in her hair. Her mouth
might have been made for his, so perfectly did they fit. And she
had responded totally, with such an unguarded honesty that he
suspected one of his preconceived notions about her might not
be so wrong after all. She couldn't be a virgin—Mathias might
have been a loner, but the man certainly had been no monk—
yet there had been something innocent, almost virginal, in her
ardent response, as if she'd never experienced passion before.

She raised her head suddenly, and he wondered if he looked
as stunned as she did. Her breath still hurried jerkily through
her parted lips, and confusion hazed the lingering glitter of excitement in her eyes. His fingers had loosened her braid, and he
smoothed back the loose hair; then his hands dropped to the
buttons of her shirt and he did them up with matter-of-fact
briskness. Bending, he picked up the life jackets and ponchos
scattered around their feet. "It's getting chilly out here. We'd
better go in," he said, his deep voice raspier than usual.

Erin wondered at the fierce, almost feral smile she'd surprised on his face just now. She stared up at him with a faint
frown, trying to remember what he'd said. "Yes," she said finally. "It's . . . getting cold."

They walked up the hill in silence. He was walking beside her,
not touching her, yet she was still intensely aware of him. She
could still taste him, Erin thought dazedly, and her blood
seemed to have been replaced with something hot and fizzy. In

the tunnel, she reached automatically for the life jackets so she could store them away. Her hand inadvertently brushed his thigh, and the cold, sodden fabric her fingers encountered shocked her out of her half daze. "You're soaked!" she cried, looking at him in dismay. She grabbed the life jackets, her poncho and the tarp out of his hands, ordering, "Go in and change. You've got to get out of those wet clothes before you get a chill." She jammed everything in the locker, then had trouble closing the door. Impatiently she slammed it shut with both hands, then turned around to find him still standing there. "Christian!" she began sharply. "You've—"

"I didn't arrive with a suitcase full of clothes," he reminded her. He could also remind her that she was just as wet as he was.

"I know," Erin muttered, feeling stupid that she had forgotten.

He reached past her to open the locker door and free the life jacket she had caught in it before closing it again; then, with a light touch on her elbow, he started her toward the inner door. "It's just my pants that are wet, anyway. They'll dry soon enough."

Erin held back. "Wait! You must have had a suitcase and some clothes in your plane. I can run down and get them." Without waiting for his reply, she turned for the outer door.

He wrapped his fingers around her arm to stop her. "I did have a duffel bag," he admitted, "but it's gone. It was near the door, and it must have fallen out at some point." He didn't mind losing his clothes, but he did mind losing the nine-millimeter pistol that had been with them, almost as much as the modified M-16 that had been in a case next to the duffel bag. Christian felt a tremor run through the arm under his hand, and he realized that she was still shivering. He tugged on her arm, not gently. "Come on. You need dry clothes more than I do."

"There are some old clothes I use for rags in the kitchen," Erin said, remembering once they were inside the Quonset hut. "Clean ones," she added hastily, straining against his grip to detour him into the kitchen.

"I'll look while you change," he said, propelling her in a straight line toward the bedroom. A corner of his mouth lifted in an exasperated grin. "I've never met a woman more determined to get me out of my pants." His grin broadened as he saw her mouth tighten primly. Her lips were rosy and a little swollen from his, and he was sorely tempted to kiss that tight, prissy line until they were soft and wanton again.

Minutes later he was standing under a hot shower. The bathroom boasted a minuscule shower stall as well as the Jacuzzi. He would have liked for her to have taken a long, warming soak in the Jacuzzi, or at least a shower, he thought as he lathered his chest, but she'd been back in the kitchen in less than five minutes, dressed in dry jeans and a sweater the same sea-green color as her eyes. He'd considered suggesting it, but he was fast learning something else about Erin Mathias that Eisley hadn't bothered to tell him. Her seemingly demure, retiring nature was simply a front for a stubborn streak a yard wide. And it was the worst kind of stubbornness. He laughed ruefully while the hot water rinsed long streams of lather down his body—the kind that smiled sweetly and then did whatever the hell it pleased.

Erin glanced away from the pot she was stirring and toward the bathroom door when she heard the shower shut off. She almost wished he wouldn't come out. Ever since she had pulled him out of the sea's grasp, she had been feeling a pull herself, to him. He was feeling it, too, she knew. That almost palpable tension between them that she'd been trying so hard to ignore was sexual—simple, basic lust, a biological itch understandably aggravated by their situation. A man and a woman, stranded alone on an island . . . all they needed were palm trees and a grass hut to have the classic fantasy. But this was no fantasy, and, like mature, sophisticated adults, they'd scratched the itch with a few kisses and a passionate clinch to relieve it.

But it wasn't relieved, Erin thought a little desperately while she turned down the heat under the pan. Opening a drawer, she took out silverware to set the table. Instead, it was worse than ever. Something that she hadn't even suspected was trapped inside her had suddenly begun scratching and clawing to get out, and she'd realized that, despite her degrees and her supposed genius, there was one vitally important area in which she was abysmally ignorant—her own sexuality. She had been helpless to control the sensations rioting through her because she'd never felt them before, and she didn't have the experience to know how to control them. She closed her eyes briefly. And he had to know it. She had been so lost that she hadn't even noticed the fog, the cold or her wet clothes. Christian was the one who had called a halt to the kiss.

Erin folded paper napkins into haphazard rectangles. She didn't feel mature or sophisticated; she felt as gauche and unsure as the most inexperienced teenager bumbling around in the back seat of her boyfriend's Chevy. Maybe because she never had bumbled around in a back seat, Erin decided as she laid forks on the napkins. She'd never even had a boyfriend. While other high-school-aged girls had been going steady, making out at the drive-in on Saturday nights, learning how to handle those itches and urges, she'd been in college, going steady with textbooks, spending her Saturday nights alone at the university library. Other girls had collected those pretty little enamel and gold pins with the Greek letters; she'd collected Latin initials after her name.

Erin added knives and spoons. Her first and only sexual experience before her marriage hadn't come until after she'd earned her Ph.D. She'd been curious to know what she'd been missing all those nights in the library. Not much, she'd discovered. Curiosity was a poor substitute for love.

She straightened the forks, knives and spoons into rigidly parallel lines. She had truly loved Daniel, but lying by his side in the dark, after he'd fallen asleep, she'd wondered—shouldn't there be more? An emotional and spiritual sense of becoming one, as well as the physical act? Finally she'd decided that she had expected too much.

Erin heard the bathroom door open. Now, thanks to a man she hardly knew, one she wasn't even sure she trusted, she understood that there might indeed be more.

Christian walked into the kitchen area, pulling a holey gray sweatshirt with the sleeves raggedly lopped off over his head.

The shirt and the navy sweatpants he was wearing had come from the ragbag. The pants had originally belonged to someone almost as tall as himself and about a hundred pounds heavier. The drawstring wrapped nearly twice around his waist, but he was glad of the loose fit, since the only pair of shorts he had were now in the washing machine chugging away in the corner. Erin had loaned him a pair of tube socks that were probably knee socks on her but were nothing of the sort on him.

"Something smells good," he said as his head came through the neck of the shirt and he got a good whiff of whatever was on the stove. He smiled at her standing beside the table with plates in her hands, watching him.

"It's canned spaghetti, but I doctored it up. Maybe it won't be too bad," Erin said absently. She'd noticed just before he'd pulled the shirt down that his nipples were erect from the shock of cooler air after the steamy warmth of the bathroom. They reminded her of the persistent ache in her breasts.

Christian saw that she was looking over his clothes. He glanced down at himself with a rueful laugh. "I have the makings of a good clown outfit, don't I?"

Erin's echoing laugh was a little strained. "Yes, you do." No, he didn't. The stark contrast of his black sweater and pants with his blondness had somehow accentuated his masculinity, making it overwhelming. Paradoxically, the raggedy, wrong-sized clothes didn't lessen it. He leaned back against the counter, crossing his arms loosely over his chest, then stretching out his legs and crossing them at the ankles. The raveling, uneven edges of the sleeveless shirt made his shoulders seem even wider, his arms even more powerful. The muscles in his biceps bulged, and the strong tendons in his forearms stood out in sharp relief as he tightened his arms over his broad chest. The smooth bronzed skin covering them glowed. Too short by several inches, the shirt left a gap between its bottom hem and the waistband of his pants. Even relaxed as he was against the counter, the flesh around his waist was tight, with no sign of even a fraction of an ounce of fat. The sweatpants rode low on his hips, accentuating their leanness. He shifted slightly, and the soft fleece pulled tight over one thigh, defining the heavy muscle. She glanced up to his face. He had towel-dried his hair, and it was still damp and a little rumpled. The light caught in the blond stubble on his uncompromising jaw. No, he didn't look funny in the funny clothes. He looked even bigger and rougher and better than he had before.

Erin swallowed to wet her dry mouth. "Do you want some garlic toast to go with the spaghetti?"

"Sure. What can I do to help?"

He pushed himself away from the counter, and Erin felt herself flinch. She knew now what the panicky little thrill was that she felt when he was close to her, when he touched her. It was an instinct that had probably been born when the first man and woman had walked upright. It was the primal female in her reacting to the primal male in him, recognizing his greater strength and dominant power, making her aware of her own softness and weakness, and how she could use them to tame him, to bind him to her.

Chapter 6

Christian put aside the novel he was having little luck getting into. He reached up idly to scratch Oscar's head, which was lying heavily on his shoulder. The cat was stretched along the back of the sofa, his head positioned as if he'd been reading over Christian's shoulder. Christian laughed softly to himself as he listened to Oscar's steady snore. The book had apparently put the cat to sleep.

He swung his feet off the cable spool and stood up. Yawning broadly, he stretched his arms slowly over his head, then swooped them down in a rush, trying to get his blood circulating again after a lazy hour on the couch. He noted the laxness in his muscles, the reluctance of his body to obey quickly. The aftereffects of his near-fatal swim were still with him, and he knew it would probably be several more days before his normal strength and speed returned.

For a moment he listened to the taped voice of a whale coming from the speaker, the only voice he'd heard since dinner. If it weren't for the soft clicking of the computer keys and the fact that he could see her, he wouldn't have know Erin was there. No, he would have known, he corrected himself wryly. Deaf, dumb and blind, he would have known. There was that unforgettable scent, and something else he felt but couldn't quite define, almost as if there were a subtle magnetic current flowing across the room.

She had spoken in monosyllables during dinner and immediately afterward retreated in silence to her computer. It didn't take any great intelligence to figure out that she was trying to ignore him, or why. She was disturbed by what had happened between them earlier, embarrassed, he suspected, by her response.

Silently he padded across the wooden floor in his stockinged feet. "What are you listening to?" Standing behind her, he touched her hair, so lightly that she couldn't feel it, but he felt a subtle increase in the current.

"Elizabeth's baby talk."

Christian smiled at her choice of words. The "baby" was as long as Erin was tall and weighed at least three times as much. "What's she saying?"

Erin's shoulders lifted a little. "I don't know. It's mostly gibberish. She's probably complaining that she's hungry."

"Or wet."

Erin glanced quickly over her shoulder. His face was perfectly deadpan, but his eyes were full of teasing mischief.

"You're probably right," she agreed with a solemn nod, then ruined the effect by giggling. His deep chuckle harmonized with her higher-pitched laughter.

"What were you listening to a little while ago?"

"Just a vocabulary tape, for practice. The computer doesn't translate baby talk very well, but sometimes I can pick out word bits." He was hunkered down beside her now, his arm across the back of her chair. As usual, Erin thought absently. Then, with a small shock, she realized what she was thinking. There was no "as usual" for them. He'd only done it once before, last night, when she was showing him the voice-print patterns, yet his position beside her, his arm almost around her, felt so comfortably familiar that it seemed they were together like this every night.

"Word bits?"

"That's what I call them. To really understand their language you have to break the words apart into bits." She saw that he was waiting for an explanation. "Most modern human languages use an alphabet of sounds—letters—that have no meaning of their own. We put those sounds together to make words. The whales have more of a dictionary of sounds. Each sound has its own specific meaning, and they put them together to make complete words. It's similar to what the ancient Egyptians did with their hieroglyphics. They used picture symbols that represented the basic aspects of their world, then combined them in an infinite number of ways to represent any idea they had, even the most abstract."

His eyebrows were drawn down in a frown as he stared intently at her, and Erin could almost see the workings of his mind as he assimilated what she was trying to explain to him. "Give me an example," he commanded.

Erin frowned back at him absently, thinking. "Okay. Let's take your plane for an example. The whale language is a pure language, meaning that it's not an amalgamation of several languages, the way English is. The whales don't borrow words from other languages the way we do and adapt them to describe something new. They can't, so every time they encounter something new, they have to make up a word for it out of these bits. Your plane is a 'great noisy bird that floats,' except that float is a rather rough translation. The word doesn't mean in their language exactly what it means in ours. In the ocean, the only things that float are either dead, like a bloated fish or a piece of wood, or inanimate objects, like a glass bottle or piece of plastic, so 'float' to them means without life."

Her fingers rapidly punched a series of keys, and Christian heard a raucous note that sounded exactly like the cry of a gull. "Bird" appeared on the computer screen. "An airplane is like a bird, so they used this sound. Planes are bigger, of course, so they added this." He heard a low-pitched squeak, and the screen recorded "great." "Planes are also loud." There was an appropriately loud squeal, and the word noisy. "The sound that means float is too low-pitched for us to hear it. It is also the word for death," she added in an aside. "A dead whale is called a 'whale that floats.' " She hit the keys again, and the sounds he'd just heard separately were put together. The word 'plane' formed in green letters on the screen.

Erin saw him nod in recognition as he listened to the words, but he was still frowning. "That's clear, but what about live birds that set down for a while on the water and float. Do the whales consider them dead, too?"

Shaking her head, Erin touched several more keys. "No." Christian heard a click and saw "buoy" on the screen. "Again, this was the closest I could come in a translation. The whales can sense the life in something, no matter how small. They know that a twenty-foot frond of kelp that has torn loose from the bottom is dead, while an almost microscopic bit of plankton is alive."

"They don't have words for specific species of birds?" Christian asked. As he had hoped, getting her to talk about her work had relaxed the constraint between them, but that wasn't the only reason for his continued questions. He was truly interested in her answers. He was beginning to understand why she had devoted nearly half her life to these giant creatures.

She shook her head again. "Birds to them are sort of like rocks are to us. A rock is just a rock. It's usually not important what kind it is, except to a geologist." She laughed a little. "And as far as I can tell, none of the whales is an ornithologist." He smiled at her little joke, and she smiled back automatically, an open expression of pleasure. "They have no word that just means water," she added. "The Inuit have over two dozen words to describe snow in all its forms and conditions, because it's so important in their environment. The ocean is even more important to the whales, because it *is* their environment. They're sensitive to the smallest change in it, every little nuance. I've counted over twenty-seven words so far that they use to describe it, and I know I haven't begun to collect all of them. I usually just use the word sea though, when I'm translating." Glancing sideways, she saw him listening closely as she brought up the various words for ocean, the words playing through the speaker.

At the end of the list he nodded in understanding. "I see what you mean, but you can tell the words relate to the same thing because they all have that same bit of sound, kind of like a low rumble."

Erin gave him an odd look that he didn't see. "*I* didn't hear that until the fifth time that I listened to the tape," she muttered under her breath. This was too good an opportunity to pass up. Never before had she known someone with this aptitude. She gave the computer a series of commands as she said, "Tell me what you hear now."

The screen gave him no help; she'd wiped it clean. Head cocked to one side, Christian listened intently to the new sounds playing out of the speaker. There was a long mewling note, almost like a whimper, which he remembered vaguely hearing the day before, a pause, then a descending whistle. Then the bits of sound were put together, with the mewling note slightly shortened. "The first one—" he gave an imitation of the mewling whimper and knew by the widening of her eyes that he had come very close to reproducing it exactly "—is the word for demon. I remember it from yesterday." His brow furrowing, he said slowly, "The second one sounds like the last part of their name for you."

Erin studied him with a wondering look. "How many languages do you speak, Christian?" she asked him in a seeming non sequitur.

He shrugged indifferently. "Probably five or six fluently, with a working knowledge of another half dozen or so. I don't know."

"Which ones?" she persisted.

He frowned at her. "Well, my native language is Dutch—"

"I knew it!" Erin interrupted, then explained at his puzzled look. "You mumbled in a foreign language while you were unconscious the night I found you. It sounded like German, but not exactly, so I thought it might be Dutch. That's why I spoke to you in German the first time. I don't know any Dutch, but I figured they were so similar that you'd understand me."

"I was meaning to ask you about that." He grinned at her. "Your accent is lousy, by the way."

She laughed. "I know." Her hand motioned for him to continue.

His arm stretched across her back as he relaxed onto his haunches. "Let's see. My Swedish grandfather lived with us when I was small, so I learned Swedish. The kids next door to us were French, so I picked that up, too. I was learning English and German in school. Then my folks emigrated to the U.S. when I was twelve, and we became citizens. I took Russian in high school, and later," he added without thinking, "I picked up Spanish, Arabic, Vietnamese, Lao, and a little Farsi and Cantonese."

Mostly the languages of the world's trouble spots, Erin thought. And the U.S. Navy had excellent language schools. With his aptitude—genius, really—he must have been their star pupil. Aloud, she said blandly, "That certainly is an interesting mix."

One broad shoulder lifted. "You travel around a lot in the Navy," he said, mentally cursing his slip. She'd pounced on it immediately, and, despite the look of polite disinterest on her face, he knew she was busily adding this new information to what he'd already told her and what she had guessed. If Mathias had told her anything about his former job, she could all too easily come up with the right—or wrong, from his viewpoint—answer. "What was that I was listening to?" he asked to distract her.

Erin knew why he had changed the subject. He'd just opened up several fascinating new topics for discussion—his "traveling," his family—but she knew he was far more skilled at avoiding a straight answer than she was at getting one. She would have to sneak her questions in, as she had the one about how many languages he spoke, although that one hadn't been planned, and hope she could catch him off guard again.

She replayed the tape. "The last word you hear is the whales' word for man. I imagine at first the whales thought men were some kind of bear, because early men wore furs, of course, and bears walk upright at times. Polar bears even occasionally kill beluga calves." A sad, almost bitter note crept into her voice. "The whales probably realized their mistake as soon as men learned how to make boats and began hunting them in packs, just like the orcas. The bit that sounds like part of my name means 'legs' or 'with legs.' So their name for us is—"

"Demon with legs," Christian finished for her. "But that's not what they call you."

"No, they don't," Erin agreed. "The first part of my name is their name for themselves, so I'm the 'whale with legs.' Not terribly romantic, but—" she laughed impishly "—the wolf-whistle sound of it is flattering."

Christian didn't laugh. "Your name is an indication that you've earned their trust," he said quietly, his arm tightening around her. "Given that they think the rest of us are demons, that's quite an achievement. You obviously mean a great deal to them."

"With that trust comes a responsibility, too," Erin said softly.

Unwittingly, she'd given him the opening he had been looking for. He had wanted to question her about the attempted theft of her work without arousing her suspicions that he knew anything about it. "I suppose someone could use your work in a way that might harm the whales?" Using the seemingly casual question as a subtle probe, he waited to see if she would mention the earlier incident. She stared at him without speaking, as if she were considering something.

Even though he was crouched and she was sitting in a chair, he was so tall that their eyes were still on the same level, Erin thought absently. She searched the clear blue depths of his eyes, and he met her probing gaze unflinchingly. She was all too aware that when she wanted answers to her questions, she seemed to end up answering his, instead. She had thought earlier that she wasn't even certain that she trusted him, but now she realized that, although it might defy logic, she did trust him. Despite his reticence about his past, she intuitively knew that there was nothing in it that she should fear. She sensed an uncompromising sense of honor and a strength that was far greater than that in his powerful body.

She relaxed within the protective curve of his arm. "Someone has already tried," she admitted with a sigh. "When we got back to Vancouver last fall, Daniel discovered that there had been an attempt to break into the institute's computer where my research is stored—the language tapes, translation programs, everything." From the stark look in her eyes, Christian knew that she realized only too well how her work could be used against the creatures she loved.

"Daniel tried to trace it back to whoever was responsible, but the break-in was apparently attempted through one of the terminals at the institute, so there were no tracks to follow. The institute was crawling with students last summer, any one of whom could have used a terminal."

"Why were so many students there?"

"Phillip Damion, the SOS founder, allows students from the universities in Vancouver to use our facilities for their research projects. Most of them would have been familiar with my work," she said matter-of-factly, without false modesty, "and one of them could have tried to get a look at it out of curiosity or in hopes of stealing some of it and passing it off as his own."

He slowly rubbed away a knot of tension his fingers had discovered at the back of her neck. "How did you protect it?"

She arched unconsciously against his hand. "With a password. Daniel was an expert in computer security, and he'd been after me to let him code my work to make it more difficult to access, but it seemed like a lot of bother to have to remember some complicated code." Erin grimaced. "It turned out he was right after all. He recoded everything, using three different access codes, one layered over the other. Anyone trying to get into the computer memory has to know both the codes and the right order. He said it would be virtually impossible to breach them."

All this only confirmed what Eisley had told him: the only way to gain access to her work now was through her. And once they had it, they wouldn't need her anymore. His hand clenched involuntarily on her shoulder, not relaxing until he felt her flinch, when he looked down to see his white knuckles. He resumed his slow massage. "Did anyone at the institute have any idea who might have tried to steal your work?"

She looked at him with a shrug. "No. Phillip was very upset, of course, when I told him what had happened. He was going to stop the graduate-student program immediately, but I convinced him that it couldn't happen again.'' Her wide soft mouth tightened, and her eyes took on a momentarily hard glitter. "I did have a suspicion or two, but—" she laughed mirthlessly "—they wouldn't have been so clumsy."

Christian didn't need to ask who. If the Navy had decided it wanted to "acquire" Erin's work after she'd turned them down, the assignment would have been given to Damage Control, and Nelson was never clumsy. "Does Damion know the codes?" he asked casually. If she hadn't told him, was it because Erin was suspicious of him or just being cautious?

She hesitated a beat before answering. "No. My mother is the only other person who knows them. I told her after Daniel died. I thought someone should know in case something happened to me, so all my research wouldn't be lost." She stopped abruptly, giving him a wondering look. "I hadn't told anyone that," she said quietly.

"I'm safe," he said lightly, ignoring the twist of guilt in his gut.

"Except in airplanes," she reminded him with a smile.

Her smile was soft and hazy looking, like her eyes. She's exhausted, Christian realized with another twist of guilt. "Why don't you call it a night?" he suggested softly.

Erin nodded, realizing suddenly how tired she was. She took a few seconds to shut down her equipment; then his arm slipped to her waist, and he brought them both to their feet.

She turned within the circle of his arm to face him, and Christian saw desire mixed with an anguished uncertainty in her wide eyes. With a quiet sigh, he folded her against him.

Erin felt the soft stubble covering his jaw rub against her temple. Linking her arms loosely around his waist, she scrubbed her cheek against the cotton fleece covering his shoulder and breathed in his warm, familiar scent. She closed her eyes to concentrate on the strong, steady rhythm of his heart, trying to remember when she had last felt so safe.

Before she was ready, he was pulling away, and Erin felt his lips brush her forehead, in a brief, curiously sexless caress. His raspy voice was barely above a whisper. "Sleep tight." Erin opened her eyes to see that oddly sweet, gentle smile on his face again.

Minutes later she was lying on the sofa, staring through the murky shadows at the closed bedroom door. She wished he would have called her sweetheart again, she thought sleepily.

Because lots of time for rest was rarely part of a mission, Christian had long ago mastered the trick of simply closing his eyes and falling asleep. But tonight the trick didn't work. He rolled over onto his back and looked in the direction of the door. With it shut the room was completely dark, but he knew exactly where it was. He'd like to tell himself that the ache in his gut persisted only because he hadn't had a woman in a long time. In truth, he couldn't remember the last time he'd had sex, and his celibacy might have worried him—if he'd thought about it. It was always easy to find a woman who wanted the same thing he did, mutual pleasure with no strings and no hard feelings when he said goodbye—physical intimacy and emotional anonymity. Lately he hadn't even looked for anyone. He needn't have worried in any case, he thought sardonically as he eased the sheet away to relieve the friction. His sex drive and all the necessary body parts were in full working order.

He didn't have to look for the woman, either. She was in the next room, sleeping alone. Only a few steps away, it was even fewer steps to imagine her without the long silk underwear and big flannel shirt she wore to bed. She'd be surprised to know that her modest choice of sleepwear was sexier than the sheerest lace. And it was the shortest step of all to imagine her naked, under him.

His hand curled unconsciously as if it were again fitting around her bare breast, taking the firm weight while the hard nipple burned a hole in his palm. He knew her by scent and by touch—knew the feel of her soft, satin smooth skin, knew the size of her breast, the slim tautness of her body—but he didn't know all her colors, her tastes, textures. Her nipples were surprisingly small and pebbly like wild raspberries. Would they taste as sweet on his tongue...or sweeter? He imagined her breasts milk-white, flushing to a delicate pink as he took his time finding out.

She would blush that same beautiful pink all over, like the color inside a perfect shell, before he was finished. He would undress her slowly, revealing her to himself an inch at a time, drawing out the anticipation. Some men preferred total softness in a woman's body, soft muscles as well as soft skin, but for him, that softness had always been a little like being smothered in a featherbed. He preferred firmness under the softness, muscles that had some strength. His own muscles rippled in helpless response as he imagined the feel of her wonderfully strong, graceful body beneath his, moving with him. He would explore that beautiful body, learn its secrets, until they were both ready to go out of their minds with pleasure.

It wasn't some anonymous woman he wanted; it was Erin Mathias. It was her arms he wanted curling around his neck like strong silky ropes, her long smooth legs locking around his hips, her sleek supple body sheathing his. It was her soft skin sliding over his that he wanted to feel, her nails raking down his back, her lush breasts filling his hands. He wanted her taste in his mouth, her sweet wild cries in his ears, every sense glutted with her as he buried himself so deep that she would feel empty when he wasn't inside her. He wanted her like no woman he'd ever known before, and he could have her. He could open the door, slip into her dreams, become a part of them and make her ready and begging for him before she was even fully awake.

But he wouldn't. The door would remain closed because beneath her strength he sensed her fragility. Trust. She trusted him, and trust had been lacking in his life for too long. It was such a fragile thing, so easily destroyed. He saw it in her artless eyes, felt it when she kissed him with such giving honesty and came into his arms as if she believed he could keep her safe from all the demons in the world. And he wanted to keep her safe.

He didn't want "emotional anonymity" anymore. Perhaps he wasn't entirely comfortable with her trust because he knew he didn't deserve it, but he craved it, hoarded it like a miser with his gold, steeped himself in the warm feeling it gave him that was almost as good as the feel of her in his arms. He could take her, teach her the unbelievable pleasure that her body was capable of, but he couldn't teach her to trust him again if he violated it now. Because that was what it would be if he took her now with his lie between them. He lay quietly in the darkness, absorbing the feminine essence of her that scented the still warm air of the bedroom. When the time came, he wanted a sharing, not a taking. He would give her pleasure and joy, and she would give him some of her innate goodness and honesty that he wanted, *needed* in himself.

Chapter 7

With a disgusted curse, Christian tossed a wrench back into the open toolbox sitting on the dock and slammed down the engine flap on his seaplane. He still didn't know who or why, but he did at least know how. Whoever had sabotaged his engine had known what he was doing. His unknown enemy hadn't used the usual bit of explosive with a timer; he'd used a fifty-cent clamp, and he hadn't even had to buy it.

The clamp held the vent line for the crankcase in place. The line had a small hole in it to allow the crankcase to breathe. If the clamp should somehow become loose, it would slide over the hole, creating a siphon effect that would suck all the oil out of the crankcase. The ultimate result would be a complete loss of oil pressure, then engine failure. On an engine the size of the Cessna's, the siphoning action would take about an hour and cause the oil gauge to fluctuate, making the pilot think there was something wrong with the gauge, not the pressure. That was exactly what he'd thought, until the engine had begun to sputter.

Christian could almost admire the man's ingenuity. The sabotage was diabolically simple. If, by some fluke, the wreckage of his plane had been found, there would have been nothing to prove it had been tampered with. An investigator would simply assume the clamp had worked itself loose. That was what he would have assumed, Christian thought as he stepped back from the plane, if he hadn't just overhauled the engine himself. He knew beyond a shadow of a doubt that the clamp had been tight; if it had moved, it had had help.

He stared hard at the green and white plane, not seeing it, but instead the public dock on Adak Island three days ago. Adak had been his last stop, and, since it had only taken an hour for the oil to be siphoned out, that was where the sabotage must have taken place. He remembered that there had been several fishing boats tied up, waiting for diesel fuel, and another seaplane, a Cessna 185 like his. It stuck out in his memory because the head of a sea hawk, in the traditional, highly stylized Inuit design, had been painted on either side of the nose. He closed his eyes, trying to bring faces into focus. He remembered the gas jockey well, a short, thin man with a red nose and sparse grizzled hair who'd introduced himself as Ski, and a few others vaguely. He didn't remember seeing the pilot of the other seaplane anywhere around it, or anyone else around his own plane.

The sabotage would have been almost absurdly easy to accomplish. He'd been at the dock for over an hour and away from the Cessna several times, to get coffee, to pay for his fuel and to check a map posted in the dock office against his. The Cessna had been left unguarded each time for five or ten minutes. Loosening the clamp would have taken no more than fifteen or twenty seconds, and no one would have given a second glance to a man tinkering around in his engine.

Christian took another wrench out of the toolbox to see what he could do about the sprung door hinge. It was fortunate that the toolbox had been bolted down, or it would have gone the way of his guns. Given a choice, he would rather have had the guns, he thought sourly, giving a bolt a vicious twist. Now that he knew the source of the engine failure, he could discount the possibility that the sabotage had been done by someone with an old score to settle. Nobody would have gone to all the time and trouble of trailing him to Adak when the clamp could have been loosened anytime back home with the same effect. Which meant that Erin was the real target, not him. He had simply been in the way, and someone had wanted him out of it.

The wrench slipped, and Christian skinned his knuckles, cursing again. He suspected the tampering had been unplanned, a spur-of-the-moment decision. He hadn't advertised his destination, but neither had he tried to keep it a secret. He'd filed the standard flight plan, and anybody keeping a check would have known where he was going almost as soon as he did, but it made no sense that someone had been specifically watching him, waiting for him to visit Erin Mathias. There was no connection between them, and he knew that neither Eisley nor Nelson would have mentioned Mathias's request to anyone.

He straightened up and tried shutting the door. It almost closed now, and he went to work on the other hinge. What made more sense was that someone was monitoring her visitors from Adak. The gas jockey was the logical suspect. Anyone visiting Erin would come either by seaplane or boat, and invariably they would stop first at Adak to refuel after the long crossing from the mainland before going on to her island. While pumping their fuel, it was only natural that the garrulous Ski would ask where they were heading.

Christian tried the door again. It latched, reluctantly, and he moved back along the fuselage to take a look at the loose tail rudder. He didn't believe Ski was the saboteur, however. Unless the man had a talent that could be earning him millions in Hollywood, he was just a gabby old coot who'd seen the bottom of a few too many bottles. More likely he was bird-dogging for someone else and had relayed the information that she was about to have company. That person would have to work on the dock or nearby, but all he would need were some quick thinking and a few seconds of opportunity to come up with a way to keep her company from arriving. Or maybe the old man wasn't involved at all. Maybe it was just a coincidence that the person who wanted to keep Erin isolated just happened to be on the dock that day, and eavesdropping.

That was what was wrong with this case, he thought as his hand delivered a hard slap to the rudder. It wobbled back and forth drunkenly, the control cable obviously broken. There were too damn many maybes and unknowns. All he had were nebulous suspicions ... and a cold emptiness in the pit of his stomach.

Neither of which was going to help when he told Erin who he really was and why he was here, he thought as he walked along the tail section. He'd decided last night to tell her, delaying until this morning because he had hoped to find something when he examined his plane that would convince her that she was indeed in danger. Something, he admitted to himself, that would help mitigate the fact that he hadn't told her immediately.

There was also the small matter of his pride, although he didn't like having to admit even to himself that that was part of the reason he hadn't told her sooner. He wouldn't blame Erin for being skeptical if the man whose life she'd just saved announced that he had come to protect her.

He was crouched down, checking the buckled strut, when he heard the heavy throb of a diesel engine. Christian straightened up to see a white Coast Guard cutter rounding the small rocky point that marked the entrance to the bay. The fog had moved out overnight, and now a weak sun was battling the omnipresent heavy gray clouds.

The ship announced itself with a raucous blast from its air horn, and a few minutes later Christian caught the bowline, snubbing it around a cleat at the end of the dock while one of the crew leaped ashore with the stern line. Behind him he heard the rapid thud of feet racing across the warped planks of the dock. While the crew positioned the gangway, he turned around to see Erin running toward him.

When he'd last seen her an hour ago, she'd been lying on her side on the sofa, asleep, her body loosely curled under a blanket. Oscar had been lying next to her, his body snuggled into the curve of hers. One of her arms had been lying outside the blanket, and the cat had been using it as a pillow, one of his paws draped possessively across it. For the first time in his life, Christian had been jealous of an animal.

She reached his side as a lanky, sandy-haired man wearing the uniform of a Coast Guard officer strode down the gangplank. From the looks of her, she'd just awakened, probably when the cutter's horn had blasted. Her hair was still sleep-tousled, and she'd taken time to throw on only the sweater and jeans she'd worn the night before. His mouth tightened as he saw her shoulders hunch unconsciously against a brisk breeze that felt a few degrees warmer than an icicle. Was she so anxious to see this guy that she couldn't even take the time to put on a jacket?

The young officer spoke first to Erin, a warm, slightly sappy smile creasing his good-natured homely face. "Hi, Erin. I got back sooner than I thought."

"John."

Christian wondered at her tight smile and the wary note in her voice. The Coast Guardsman turned to him, and Christian noted that his smile was noticeably cooler.

"You must be Dekker. I'm John Falk."

Christian took the hand the man offered, and they very briefly shook hands. "Lieutenant," he said, addressing him by the rank displayed on his thin shoulders. So Eisley was keeping tabs on him. This close to the Soviet border, they would have been routinely tracking him on radar, and when he disappeared from the scope and didn't respond to radio calls, Eisley must have had Nelson call out the bloodhounds. He laughed silently. He didn't flatter himself that he was the one Nelson was really worried about.

Erin was beginning to feel the strain of maintaining her smile. Would John Falk unknowingly give her away? When something had awakened her and she'd seen that the fog had lifted, she'd started immediately for the radio to call the Coast Guard station on Attu to advise them that they needn't bother to resume their search for the downed flier. Then another glance out the window had told her that she needn't bother. They'd already found him.

"Christian had engine trouble," she volunteered, praying that would satisfy the lieutenant's curiosity, and he wouldn't ask any embarrassing questions, like how long had Christian been there.

"Engine trouble?" John Falk looked over the green and white seaplane moored to the dock, and Erin saw him focus on the crumpled pontoon brace. "It looks like you had a pretty rough time," he said to Christian. "Will you be able to fly out? I can take you back to Attu, and you can radio for parts, if necessary."

"Thanks for the offer, but I think I can patch it together well enough to make it home," Christian said easily. He didn't bother to point out that, now that the weather had cleared, Erin's radio would be working just as well as the one on Attu. He felt as if he were reading a book with the first hundred pages missing; something was going on here that he didn't quite understand. He hadn't missed the Coast Guard lieutenant's surprised look at Erin's easy use of his first name, nor the tension emanating from the body beside his.

Erin had sensed a subtle undercurrent between the two men in their brief exchange. John Falk's face was sober and not particularly friendly looking, despite his offer. Christian was smiling, but his expression was—she winced mentally after her fanciful thoughts about him earlier, but the description was accurate—decidedly wolfish. Summoning her brightest smile, she said, "Well, John, now that you know he's safe and sound, I imagine you'll want to let everyone know they can call off the search." She looked significantly at the white cutter idling behind him. "As soon as possible."

"Yeah, I probably should," he agreed reluctantly. He gave the big, blond, rough-looking man standing beside Erin another brief, unsmiling look. "I'll relay the message that you're all right, Dekker." He would have liked to ask Dekker just who the hell he was that a full-scale military search could be ordered to find a civilian, but he'd gotten the impression from his commander that it might be wiser not to ask too many questions. He turned to Erin, and his expression softened. "I'll check in with you on my next patrol, Erin. If you need anything—" his eyes cut to the man at her side "—just call the station. We'll come running."

"I know, John. Thank you." Ignoring his last puzzled glance from her to the man at her side, Erin dismissed him with another bright smile. As he stepped onto the short gangway, she allowed herself to begin to relax.

In the middle of the gangplank he turned around.

John Falk had decided to risk one question. "We searched this area three days ago, Dekker, and didn't see any sign of you. Neither had Erin. Where were you?"

Erin waited in numbed silence for the answer that would dig her grave deeper.

"I put down by Rat Island during the storm and managed to get the plane here last night," she heard Christian reply in a casual tone.

Falk nodded. "We didn't have a chance to search over there before the fog closed in." He sent Erin a final warm smile. "Bye, Erin."

She raised a leaden arm in response. The crew scrambled to pull in the gangway and cast off, the cutter's powerful engine revved, and the ship began to pull slowly away from the dock. She stared after it until the cutter disappeared around the point at the mouth of the bay, the growling throb of its diesel engine fading to nothing.

Christian hadn't exactly lied; he had sorted through the truth and chose those parts that wouldn't embarrass her, but the speed and ease with which he'd done it disturbed her. Such skill suggested that he'd done this before, many times, and she couldn't help wondering if he'd kept her secret to protect her... or himself.

The wooden thump of the sections of the floating dock knocking together as the cutter's wake reached shore sounded loud in the sudden silence. She took a deep breath, then turned to face the man behind her.

He was standing at the edge of the dock, where he'd helped the cutter crew cast off. His hands were in the pockets of the open flight jacket, his long legs spread a little, braced against the rhythmic dip and rise of the dock, his body relaxed. He was watching her, as she'd known he would be, an unreadable expression on his face. "Why didn't you tell Lieutenant Falk I had lied to him?" she asked tonelessly.

Her devastating honesty made his own dishonesty seem that much more a sin. "Did you want me to?" he asked expressionlessly.

Her short laugh was harsh. "No." She glanced away. "I lied to you, too."

He moved to stand beside her, not quite touching her, and she heard his quiet question. "Why?"

Erin looked up at him and saw that his eyes were guarded. "You didn't speak English when you were unconscious, and I wasn't sure you would want anyone to know where you were."

She saw surprise flicker through his eyes, but his tone was even. "You were protecting me, then?"

Her laugh was less harsh this time. "Foolish, wasn't it?" There was something else in his eyes for a moment, something that passed too fast for her to identify. He didn't say anything, and she went on. "There was another reason, too, probably even more foolish." She looked away quickly as she felt the sudden inexplicable burn of tears. "I just didn't want you to go," she whispered.

There was a moment of silence; then he said lightly, "I'm not ready to go yet."

His arm came around her shoulders loosely, drawing her inside the warmth of his jacket. Erin looked up with a hesitant smile.

He tightened his arm around her shoulder and turned her in the direction of the beach. "Come on, let's go see if we can find some baling wire in that mess in the shed."

They were halfway up the hill when they both heard a familiar drone overhead. Erin looked up, shading her eyes from the weak sunlight. "That's Sam," she said in surprise. "I wonder why he's here now. He's not due until next week."

Christian's eyes narrowed on the white seaplane circling the bay. He could just make out the head of an Inuit raven painted on the nose. His eyes went cold and hard as he started back down the hill. "Let's go find out."

The small Cessna glided down to the water like a giant drag-onfly, then taxied to the dock. Christian steadied the craft with a hand on one of the pontoon struts while the pilot climbed out. He stepped down onto one of the floats, then jumped the short span to the dock.

While the man took a minute to tie up his plane, Christian took a good look at him. He judged him to be about thirty-five, and his appearance was typically Inuit. His build was short and stocky, and the medium-long hair under his blue baseball cap was black and straight. His black eyes behind his wire-frame glasses had the characteristic epicanthic fold, and the mus-tache under his flat nose was sparse. He had a soft-looking, moon face, which was split now in a wide grin.

"Erin!" After enveloping her in an exuberant bear hug, he turned to look at Christian with friendly curiosity. "Hi." He stuck out a pudgy hand with short, stubby fingers. "Sam Ak-iachak."

Christian shook it and found that the soft pudginess dis-guised a hard strength. "Christian Dekker." He had detected only a trace of the staccato accent with which many native Americans spoke English.

Sam frowned for a second, as if trying to place him; then his brow cleared. "You were on Adak a few days ago, weren't you? Buying gas on the dock?"

"Three days ago," Christian confirmed. He glanced at the white seaplane. "I remember your plane."

Sam laughed, revealing straight, blunt teeth. "Yeah, there aren't too many painted up like mine." His glance passed over Christian's plane, pausing on the bent strut. "I remember your plane, too, but not like that. What happened?"

"I had engine trouble, a problem with the oil pressure." He watched closely, but Akiachak didn't so much as flick an eye-lash.

"That can be trouble," Sam agreed; then his tone sharp-ened. "Say! You must be the guy everybody's looking for." He looked at Christian curiously. "I don't know who you are, buddy, but they've got the Navy, Coast Guard, everybody mobilized, trying to find you."

"My banker probably got nervous. I still owe money on the plane," Christian said dryly.

Erin didn't join in Sam's appreciative laughter. Christian's answer had been quick and glib, and she was certain it wasn't the truth. She was equally certain that he knew who had initiated the search for him, but, since he was clearly unconcerned about being found, she couldn't figure out why he was hiding the person's identity. "One of the Coast Guard ships was just here," she said, joining the conversation. "The storm knocked out my radio, so Christian couldn't let anyone know where he was. I imagine they're already calling the search off." Puzzled, she looked at Sam. "Why are you here, Sam? I wasn't expecting you until next week."

"I flew a couple of archaeologists over to Amchitka this morning, so I thought I'd bring you your mail while I was in the neighborhood." After reaching into a deep pocket of his quilted gray nylon vest, Sam pulled out several envelopes and handed them to Erin. He watched as she quickly scanned the return addresses. "Phillip called me, too, Erin," he admitted. "He asked me to check on you the next time I was in the area. I think he's worried about you being here all alone." His eyes flicked to the big blond man who stood close beside her.

Erin slipped the letters into a pocket of her jeans. "Thank you, Sam. You can tell Phillip I'm perfectly fine, and—" she smiled up at Christian "—I've even had some company for a few days."

Sam nodded, then turned around to look over the green and white Cessna. "Can you fly it out as is, or do you need some parts?" he asked over his shoulder. "I could fly you out to get them and bring you back. Probably wouldn't take more than a day or two."

"I can repair it with what's lying around here. I'm in no hurry," he added deliberately. Sam Akiachak didn't want him here with Erin any more than the Coast Guard lieutenant did. The question was, why? Was it the natural protectiveness of a man for a woman alone, or was he the one who had loosened a fifty-cent clamp? He'd had the opportunity, along with the fifty other people on the dock that day.

Akiachak walked across the dock to the damaged plane. "Let's take a look," he said, slapping the tail. "Maybe I can give you a hand."

In the next few minutes, Sam Akiachak proved that, as well as having had the opportunity, he had the knowledge to make murder look like an accident. The lawyer-turned-bush pilot could always find work as a mechanic if the charter business turned sour, Christian thought as he followed him out of the plane. He turned to help Erin down, holding her hand until she was safely on the dock.

Sam absently wiped some grease off his hands onto his baggy khakis as he stared at the seaplane. "I think you're right." He glanced at Christian. "You can probably fix everything at least well enough to get back home with what Erin's got around here. Some oil ought to take care of the engine, and splicing the cable for the tail rudder shouldn't take too much time. The worst part will be pulling up the floor. And the flaps are probably just jammed, like you said." He bent and ran his hand down the buckled strut. "I think I would brace this with some pipe or something, though, if I were you," he said, rising.

Erin spoke up. "There's some in the shed." She had tagged along on the inspection, not because she had any desire to learn airplane mechanics, but because she wanted an idea of how long the repairs might take. Two full days at the most, Sam and Christian had agreed. Maybe adding the pipe brace would stretch it to three.

Sam looked at the heavy chrome watch on his wrist, then sighed. "Well, I better get going. Those two bone diggers were so eager to leave this morning, they left half their stuff behind, and I've got to go back and get it."

"Have you got time for a cup of coffee, Sam?" Erin asked.

He shook his head regretfully. "Better not, Erin." He turned to Christian. "Good luck. If you find you need a part after all, call the dock office on Adak. They'll get a message to me. Erin knows the call letters."

"Thanks. You live on Adak, then?" he asked idly. Erin had said he lived on the Alaskan mainland.

Sam's smooth round cheeks creased with a grimace of disgust. "No. You couldn't give me that place. I live on the mainland, near Bethel, but I've been flying a couple of oil geologists around the past few weeks. They're staying on Adak, so I have to, too. But—" he shrugged philosophically "—the money's good."

"Speaking of money, have you heard anything yet on the grant for the village, Sam?" Erin asked him hopefully.

"We got turned down."

Erin laid a hand on his arm in commiseration. "Oh, Sam! I'm so sorry. I know how much you were counting on that money."

Patting her hand, Sam smiled. "Don't worry about it, Erin. I've found another source." He glanced at his watch again. "Well, now I've really got to go."

A few minutes later, Christian and Erin were walking slowly back up the hill to the Quonset hut. The breeze gusted, and he saw her shiver. Reaching out, he pulled her close with an arm around her shoulders. After a moment's hesitation, he felt her arm come around his waist. "How much money does Sam need?" he asked casually.

"Three hundred thousand dollars," Erin told him soberly. "That's how much the grant would have been worth. Even that wasn't going to be enough, but it was a good start." She leaned against his shoulder unconsciously. "I wonder what this other source is that he's found."

So do I, Christian echoed silently as he swung open the door to the air lock.

He closed the inner door behind them. "Erin, there's something—"

Her upraised hand stopped him. "Wait." Head down, she stood listening just inside the door.

Over the past three days Christian had become used to the background music of clicks, whistles and chirps as Erin played her language tapes. Whenever she wasn't playing the tapes, he knew that she switched the speaker over to the underwater microphones. Right now the speaker was emitting a monotonous rhythm of metallic clicks, like the sound of a gun being cocked over and over again. He looked at Erin in silent question.

She raised her head. "That's called a click train. The whales use it for echo location."

"Do you think the belugas are back?"

Erin shook her head. "I don't know. It could be the orcas again. I can't tell them apart."

Her fingers had begun worrying each other. Christian took her hand and tugged gently. "Let's go up to the tower and take a look."

From the tower they could see a small pod of white whales swimming slowly across the bay. Her eyes shining, she turned to him. "Look! They're back!"

Christian heard the tearful relief in her voice that was evidence of how worried she had been. Squeezing his hand happily, she listed the names she had given them, assuring herself that they were all there. "There are Elizabeth and her mother, Martha. William . . . Alice. . . ."

Christian followed the progress of the pod across the bay. The water was almost calm, a dull green color under the pale sunlight. The white whales were in the same loose formation he'd seen them in the first day. One adult whale swam alone in front. Behind the lead whale were two more adults, then the calves Elizabeth and William, flanked by their mothers. Behind them swam two more adults side by side. He remembered that the whales had had Erin in the protected center of the formation with the calves the day he had seen her swimming with them. "Which one is Abner?"

"The one swimming behind the pod."

He moved behind her to follow her pointing finger to the whale who had warned Erin to stay out of the water when the orcas had come. He swam very slowly, the distance between him and the others increasing steadily. "He looks old," Christian said quietly.

"He is. The usual life span of a beluga is about twenty-five years. Abner is at least thirty. This is probably his last summer." There was profound sadness in her voice.

Christian reached one arm over her shoulder to point to the far side of the bay. An ancient lava flow, evidence of the time when the island was an active volcano, had formed a natural dam halfway across a narrow inlet, creating a secluded pocket of water. "What is all that splashing over there? Are the whales playing?" He bent his arm across her chest, his hand loosely clasping her opposite shoulder.

"They're making love," she said softly.

Christian looked down. Her face was turned in a three-quarter profile toward the inlet, and he could see her lips curved in a soft smile. She hadn't said they were mating or having sex or any of the cruder terms that he knew instinctively she would never use. She had said they were making love. He brought his other arm up and across her breasts, his hand closing over her shoulder. Flexing his arms, he exerted a slow backward pressure, and she relaxed against his chest. "Do they make love only at certain times of the year?" He found that the words came easily to him, too.

"You mean a mating season? No. Whales are very sensual animals. They make love all year long, and often."

Their voices were naturally hushed, although neither of them, he knew, felt any embarrassment. The whales' bodies were only blurs at that distance, screened by the flashing veils of water. "Like us," he said in a soft rasp.

Erin laid her cheek on his hand, which was still resting on her shoulder. "Like us. Some scientists believe sexual expression is an indication of evolutionary development. The more frequent, and the more sensitive and complex their lovemaking, the more highly evolved a species is supposed to be." She rubbed her cheek over his hand. His thighs brushed the backs of hers as they shifted, widening his stance, and her hips settled into the saddle of his. "If that's true, whales may be the most highly evolved of all species. They're very affectionate, very caring and considerate of each other."

Christian lifted his hand to thread his fingers through her hair, guiding her head back to the hollow of his shoulder. He combed through the silky strands with exaggerated sloth so his thumb could trace the shell of her ear, her jaw, finally coming to rest in the small hollow at the base of her throat. Her pulse fluttered under his finger, fast and uneven. "No wham, bam, thank you, ma'am?"

His gentle laughter was a warm caress on her skin; then she felt the cool, moist touch of his tongue as the tip lightly traced the line of her throat. A shiver rippled through her, and she arched her head back to give him greater access. His tongue reached the hollow of her throat, displacing his thumb and he filled the small depression with a soft kiss. "No." The word came out as a quiet moan in a voice she didn't recognize. "They touch, tease . . . caress with their flippers as we do with our hands, to give each other pleasure. It's prolonged and mutual."

Her hands, which were still hanging idly by her sides, rose to his arms. Her fingers reached his elbows first; then she rubbed her suddenly itchy palms hard over the thin wool up to his shoulders and back down. The hand displaced by his mouth slid lower, under the loose neck of her sweater. His long fingers splayed over her bare skin because she hadn't taken time earlier to put on a bra, and the lowest one slid naturally into the hollow between her breasts to anchor his hand in place. His other hand skimmed down her chest and settled over her stomach, opened wide, then began to rub small lazy circles, as if trying to soothe a tummy ache. The ache only got worse.

His mouth had moved back up her throat, and now his tongue was investigating the hollow behind her ear. His whisper shivered the moist skin. "Sounds like they could give lessons in foreplay."

Erin nodded against his shoulder, closing her eyes. The hand that had been lying still on her chest had begun moving, rubbing in the same rhythm as the one lower down. The sensations produced by those twin frictions were almost too intense to bear. "They devote a great . . . deal of time to it. Nuzzling . . . nibbling . . . stroking . . ." The breathless catches in her husky voice counterpointed the rhythm of his hands. "It's . . . nice."

Christian's hands froze. Nice? *Nice?* In that one little word, she had told him all he ever needed or wanted to know about her relationship with Mathias. His hands began moving again, both of them dipping lower. *Nice.* By God, he'd show her nice.

His hands stilled again. He'd show her nothing, not with his deception still between them like an unscalable rock wall. Again her scent, the feel of her body, the mere warmth and closeness of her, had tempted him almost beyond his control. Helped along, he had to admit with a silent chuckle, by a discussion of the mating habits of whales, which had been the most erotic conversation he'd ever had.

An honesty as pure as Erin's deserved no less in return. He would finish what he'd started to tell her downstairs; he would tell her everything. His hands moved to her arms and set up another rhythm, long strokes from her shoulders to her wrists, this one meant not to arouse but to soothe both of them. She would be angry, and justifiably so, but once she got over it, they would work together, as they already seemed to do so well. They would discover who was trying to steal her work, and then he would teach her the difference between nice and having your body burned, your soul scorched... because that was how it would be.

Erin opened her eyes and gradually focused on the small inlet across the bay. The water was calm now, much calmer than her feverish body. It frightened her a little to realize how quickly she became lost in a sensual haze every time he touched her. His strong hands slid soothingly down her arms once more, this time over her hands as well, linking his fingers with hers. She felt his chest expand against her back as he took a deep breath.

"Erin—"

He was interrupted by a two-note whistle on the speaker below. One of the whales was calling her.

The call was made twice more, and there were already several lines on the computer screen by the time they got down below.

Erin. Erin. Erin. Where are you? Come out. Come play.

The printed words reflected the same childlike impatience he heard in the voice. "William?" he murmured, standing beside her.

"Yes." She laughed softly as she typed her response. "He's a typical little boy. He hates to wait for anything."

I come. Wait by great noisy bird.

I wait. Come soon.

Erin turned away from the computer to hurry into the bedroom to change. After a step, she turned back to Christian, who was still standing beside the desk. "When we came in, you were going to tell me something. What was it?"

He ran a finger down her cheek. "It can wait," he said, holding his impatience in check. "We can talk later."

It took her only a few minutes to change into the one-piece suit of thermal underwear she had to wear under the diving suit. When she got out to the air-lock tunnel, she found Christian already checking her air tanks.

He glanced over his shoulder. "I don't think you should use this tank." He tapped the left one in the harness. "The pressure gauge indicates a slow leak. I'll check it out later, see if it's just a faulty gauge or a bad connection."

"Okay." Erin watched him rapidly remove the questionable tank and replace it with one of the spares he'd obviously already satisfied himself was all right. As she had suspected, he'd done far more diving than the "bit" he'd said he had.

From a locker she took the heavy insulated rubber suit that made diving in cold water possible. Sitting down on the small bench beside the lockers, she stepped into it, then stood up and began pulling it over her body. Glancing up, she saw that he was watching her. The black underwear she wore had the close fit of a body stocking, leaving nothing to the imagination, but, oddly, she felt no embarrassment.

Because of the cool temperature of the air lock, the rubber was stiff, and Erin had to struggle to get the legs of the stubborn suit over her own. She heard him laugh and looked up, her face flushed with her exertions. "What's so funny?" she demanded.

"Seeing you wrestling with that suit reminds me of the time I used to have trying to put on panty hose. I don't know how you women can stand to wear them. They're the damnedest things to get on. I used to ruin two pair for every one I managed to put on."

Seeing her eloquently expressive eyebrow, he laughed again. "The SEAL teams wore them in southeast Asia. You'd be in muck for days on end, out in the jungle and swamps, and the nylon kept you from getting rubbed raw. There was the added benefit, too, that when you peeled them off, you also peeled off most of the leeches." He stared past her with a reminiscent smile. "It was quite a sight to see us get ready for a mission. Here would be a dozen or so of the roughest, toughest guys you ever saw, dressed in camouflage, faces all painted up green and black, struggling to get their hairy legs into a pair of panty hose and complaining about snags and runs."

"How did you get them?"

Erin's voice had an odd choked sound, and his eyes snapped back to her. She had collapsed on the bench, her suit only halfway on, and her face was bright red. Not from the struggle with the suit, he suspected, but from the struggle to keep from laughing. He grinned. "Somebody's wife or girlfriend would buy them and send them over. We didn't have guts enough to go into a store and buy them ourselves."

Erin felt her face burn a shade redder, and tears squeezed out of her eyes with the effort to contain her laughter as she conjured up the hysterical image of big tough men sidling up to the hosiery counter in a department store and whispering to the clerk that they wanted a dozen pairs of panty hose in the largest size she had. "What size did you wear?" she asked in a smothered voice.

"Big Mamas, size double X, extra long," he said, deadpan.

Erin choked. "Big Mamas?" she finally managed to squeak in incredulous disbelief.

His large, consummately masculine body struck a prissy pose, and when he confirmed it with a mincing simper, it was too much. Her laughter exploded uncontrollably.

A few minutes later, Erin fell on the bench sideways, holding her sides, moaning. Her body still shook at regular intervals with tremors of mirth. Finally she worked up the energy to sit up and wipe the tears out of her eyes. "Oh, Christian." She groaned as she struggled to her feet. "I don't think I've ever laughed so hard in my life." She pulled ineffectually at the suit, trying to get it up the rest of the way, but even her fingers were weak from laughing.

"It wasn't *that* funny," he said in an aggrieved tone as he came over to help her.

"Yes, it was," she insisted as he stuffed her rag-doll arms into the sleeves and jerked the zipper closed across the top of her chest. "I could just see you—" More laughter bubbled out of her when she caught sight of his disgruntled expression. She scrubbed her hand down her face and tried to look contrite. "I'm sorry," she said in a small voice.

"No, you're not." He gave her a black glower that broke up into a grin at the sight of her trying to look serious.

Her head dropped weakly to his shoulder. "You're right. I'm not," she moaned. He let her lean on him to catch her breath. It had been hysterically funny—except for the leeches. The mental image of their hideous bodies obscenely bloated with blood was like a sharp slap to remind her that while the thought of men wearing panty hose might be funny, the mission the men had been on hadn't been.

Erin sobered and, with a quiet sigh, pulled away from him. In the past five minutes she'd gotten a few more answers to her questions. The news that he'd been a SEAL didn't really surprise her. The acronym stood for Sea Air Land Team, the U.S. Navy's most elite commando force. Some said the SEALs were the toughest men alive. Without so much as a sniffle, Christian had survived an experience that would have killed other men, proving that he was still one of the toughest of the tough. She knew SEALs were experts in weaponry, explosives, sabotage—destruction. If he was reticent about that part of his life rather than eager to brag about it as a lesser man might be, it was only further testimony to what a truly extraordinary man he was.

She stepped back to the locker and took out the depth gauge she always wore strapped to her left hand. As she fastened it, Christian reached into the locker, then silently handed her the compass and diver's watch when she was done. While she buckled them on, he knelt and strapped the rubber sheath holding a large, wickedly sharp knife around her right calf.

Next he placed the buoyancy compensator around her neck. The vest was a horse-collarlike affair that was used for emergency ascents. Like a Mae West life jacket, it contained two carbon-dioxide cylinders that would inflate immediately if she pulled the lanyard on the front. "There's a ritual quality to dressing for a dive, isn't there?" she commented as he knelt again to pull the straps snugly between her legs.

He looked up at her, his face sober. "I always thought it must be a little like a matador getting ready for a bullfight."

"How many times did you face the bull?" she asked him quietly.

Rising, Christian met her direct gaze. "Three hundred times? Four hundred?" He smiled faintly. "I never kept track." Had his admission that he'd been a SEAL been unconsciously intentional, he wondered, intended to prepare the way for what he had to tell her? Or was he just becoming so comfortable with her that he no longer worried about watching what he said?

Erin picked up the thick rubberized gloves that went with her suit. "How many years were you a SEAL?"

"Twelve," he answered immediately. "I went into the Navy right out of high school, then the SEALs after basic training." If he was going to be honest with her, he might as well start now, Christian decided sardonically—then had to lie again at her next question.

"Did you ever know a man named Eisley? He's about your age. You and he would probably have been in the SEALs at the same time."

He reached for her weight belt. "No, I never met him." It was better not to admit knowing Eisley yet. If Erin knew Eisley was with Damage Control, she might, with her quick mind, guess that he had been, too. He wished he knew how much Mathias had told her. If he had told her about his years with Damage Control, it might make his own explanation easier.

Erin stared at him. "You know, it's funny," she said, as if to herself, "you don't look anything like him—he's dark, and you're so blond—but you remind me of him somehow." She looked at him a moment longer, then shook her head with a little laugh and reached into the locker for her mask and flippers. He would have been about thirty when he retired, she decided, and he looked to be around forty now. That awful scar wasn't ten years old. Erin looked at him from under her lashes as she fiddled with the flippers. Perhaps there were other parts of his life he was reticent to talk about, as well.

Christian hefted the weight belt to make sure it was neither too heavy nor too light. The belts were easily adjusted. All that had to be done was to add or subtract small blocks of lead from the pockets of the belt. His eyes had told him that Erin weighed about one hundred ten or one hundred fifteen pounds, but his hands had found a body that was almost solid supple muscle. Now he would guess she weighed about one hundred twenty-five pounds, and that meant she needed to carry about eighteen pounds of lead in her belt. He weighed the belt in his palm again. It felt about three pounds too light, despite the additional object, which looked like a large hand-held microphone dangling from it. "Your belt's too light."

Erin looked up from adjusting something on the headset he'd seen the first day. "It would be if I dove down very far, but mostly I stay on the surface. Any more weight tends to drag me down."

Christian accepted her explanation. Critically, he looked her over from the top of her bared head to her toes hidden in the feet of the black diving suit. Going back to her face, he frowned. "Don't you have something to put on your chin?" The face mask would leave her mouth and chin exposed to the frigid water, and she was risking damage to her delicate skin if she didn't insulate it with something.

Erin made a face. "Vaseline, but I don't like it. My hair always gets stuck in it."

"You won't have to worry about your hair if your face goes numb and you can't keep your regulator in your mouth," he growled as he started searching through the locker that held her diving gear. He found the small plastic jar he was looking for in a back corner.

"Hold still," he warned when she started squirming as he smeared the thick jelly liberally over the lower part of her face.

"You're getting it in my mouth, and it tastes terrible," she whined.

"Keep it shut, then," he suggested.

Erin glared at him, but followed his suggestion.

Finished, he snapped the lid back on the jar, then leaned down to give her mouth a sound smacking kiss. He licked his lips with an exaggerated motion. "You're right. It tastes terrible," he told her with a grin.

"I don't know how I ever managed without you," she said with acid sweetness. She *had* managed, Erin thought, but it hadn't been nearly as much fun.

Laughing, he tossed the jar into the locker, then picked up her air tanks and gestured her toward the door. He was beginning to wonder, he admitted, about managing with her.

"What do you use the headset for?" he asked once they were outside. He recognized Mathias's handiwork, but he'd never seen him use one underwater.

"I use it to talk with the whales while I'm diving. Daniel adapted it from one of his designs. In fact, that's how I met him." She picked her way through a patch of loose rock, mindful of the thick rubber covering her feet, which could still be punctured by a misstep. "I should have remembered my boots," she muttered to herself. She felt his hand close firmly around her upper arm, steadying her balance.

Once through the rocks, she glanced up at him. The glance became a short trance. He had her seventy-pound air tanks hooked over his shoulder, holding them with a couple of fingers through the harness as if they weighed no more than a sport jacket. He smiled, and she realized he'd said something. "W-what? I'm sorry, I didn't hear—"

His tone was easy. "I said, 'How did you meet him?'"

"Who?" She frowned at him; then her brow cleared. "Oh! Daniel. Well, I wanted something like this—" she raised the hand carrying the headset "—but I couldn't seem to find anyone who could make one. Then somebody mentioned Daniel."

"Who?" His interest still sounded casual.

"Someone who was interested in my work."

With a sideways glance, he saw her face take on the same fierceness it had when she'd said she'd had suspicions about who might have tried to break into the institute computer. It confirmed his suspicion that someone in the Navy department had had a hand in bringing Erin and Mathias together. If they couldn't directly control her work, they would have wanted at least arms'-length contact. He didn't think it had been an assignment. Mathias had been legitimately retired, but he wouldn't have been averse to letting them know if anyone else was pursuing Erin. "Did you know him long before you married him?"

Another glance, and he saw her face take on a thoughtful expression. "No, just a month or two, actually."

Christian stared down at her. Mathias must have known he was dying. Had he met Erin and seen the chance for a family, a bit of immortality? He had to admit that that was something else he was beginning to wonder about, too.

Erin returned to his original question. "The headset has a very limited range. Daniel was still working on it, trying to improve it, when he died. It picks up and transmits their half of the conversation to the computer, which translates it into English and sends it back through the earphones so I can hear it. I speak into the microphone—" she touched the metal wand that would be positioned in front of her mouth if she were wearing it "—and the computer translates that and transmits it back through this." She held up the microphone-like object hanging from her belt.

"You have a lot of equipment," he commented as they stepped up onto the dock.

Erin gave him a wry smile. "You mean a lot of expensive equipment."

He smiled, acknowledging her perception. "Does SOS pay for everything?"

"Everything. Phillip is an extremely persuasive fund-raiser," she added dryly as they walked the length of the floating dock.

"Then, too, he endowed SOS with a very large trust fund from his own personal fortune when he founded it."

Erin set down her equipment by the seaplane. A few yards away a small grayish-brown whale breached, then fell back into the water with a resounding belly flop. "Look! There's William, showing off, as usual."

Christian heard the fondness she had for the whale calf in her voice. "He's ready to play, all right." Automatically he bent with his hands on his knees so she could brace her back against his for balance while she put on her flippers. "Does SOS fund other research besides yours?"

Erin straightened and watched William swim around in circles, slapping his flippers on the water. His broad mouth opened with a stream of excited chatter. "A core-drilling project off the coast of South America and a sea-bed mapping expedition in the North Atlantic," she answered absently.

Christian supported the weight of the two aluminum air tanks while Erin slipped into the harness. "Damion made his money in oil, didn't he?"

"Oil exploration and development," she confirmed. "Some mining, too." She stepped away from him, flexing her shoulders to settle the tanks more comfortably.

Christian watched her buckle the weight belt around her waist. With the weight belt, air tanks and the suit, she had just about doubled her weight, yet she seemed to bear it more easily than most men would have. Her slim, beautifully proportioned body, he realized, disguised a remarkable strength.

Erin duck walked the few steps to the edge of the dock. She pulled the hood up and over her head, then started to position her face mask. Christian stayed her hand. Leaning down, he kissed the tip of her nose. "For luck."

"Did you kiss the guys for luck when you were a SEAL?" she asked, widening her eyes innocently.

"Only the ones with cute butts." He grinned and gave her fanny a friendly swat.

Giggling, Erin pulled her face mask into place. After securing the headset, she clamped the regulator between her teeth and pulled on her gloves. Christian looked down into her laughing sea-green eyes one last time, and she winked at him behind the glass, then turned and calmly stepped into a hundred feet of dark frigid water.

For several minutes Christian stood at the end of the dock. The surface of the bay had calmed considerably from the day before, and the dark green water had a thick, oily look. He watched a stream of bubbles stretching toward the middle of the bay and laughed softly. William must be talking nonstop, telling Erin of his adventures.

At last he turned back toward the beach. He shivered as the breeze seemed to cut through his jacket. Glancing up at the sky, he saw that the sun was shining a little more strongly, yet the day suddenly felt colder.

Instead of returning to the house, he climbed the slope behind the hut. He'd thought about trying out the fishing rod he'd found, but decided he wanted to be where he could keep an eye on Erin instead. Despite her seeming lack of fear about swimming with the whales, he felt uneasy. The belugas might be considered small, almost puny, when compared to others of their kind, but, compared to a human, they were giants. One careless flick of a tail and Erin's body could be broken as easily as a matchstick. Despite his smaller size, the young calf, William, was even more of a danger to her than the adult whales. Caught up in the exuberance of play, he could, like any small child, become too rough and break his toy.

He found a spot that was sheltered from the breeze by a small hummock but also afforded a clear view of the bay. Christian sat down on the lush grass, and for long minutes watched the small whale splash and play like a baby in a bathtub. Gradually more of the pod drifted over until Erin was surrounded.

Without the chilly wind, the pale sun had some heat, and Christian felt himself growing comfortably warm and a little drowsy. He scanned the bay below. The pale sunlight turned into dull spangles on the green water. Except for three whales off to one side who looked as if they might be feeding on a school of small fish, all the whales were now congregated around Erin. At a casual glance she might have been one of them, another calf. She and the infant Elizabeth were the same length, and the baby's brown color looked almost as dark as Erin's diving suit.

Except that the "baby" already weighed close to a quarter of a ton, he thought wryly. Erin said she had doubled her weight in just a week from the gallons of fat-rich milk her mother pumped into her. As he looked on, the calf's mother rolled onto her side, and Elizabeth moved close to suckle. The mother laid one of her short spatulate flippers over her child protectively. There goes another ten pounds, he thought laughingly as his body relaxed against the grassy hump behind him.

Idly he studied the whales. He identified William, his darker color already fading toward the white of adulthood, and two adolescent calves, which were near-white. All of them, the baby Elizabeth included, had the same broad head with the protruding forehead, chubby body and wide tail with an oddly elegant curve. As they talked with Erin, they nodded and turned their heads in an uncanny parody of human conversation. The warmth and his comfortable position had their effect. His eyelids felt heavier and heavier until they drifted closed.

He didn't know how long he had been asleep when suddenly he was wide awake. He didn't know what had awakened him, but he sat up, stretching his arms over his head, while he checked the bay. Everything looked the same—the bay was still calm; the whales were still gathered around Erin. The scene had a curiously pastoral peacefulness about it.

Slanting a look up at the sky, he checked the position of the sun. It had moved about ten or fifteen degrees closer to the horizon, indicating that he'd been asleep nearly an hour. She had enough air to stay down longer, but he knew Erin would be coming out soon. Even with the insulated suit, an hour was about all she would be able to take in the freezing water.

Standing up, Christian stretched again. He gave the bay one last look before starting back down so he could meet Erin when she came out of the water. He froze as he glanced toward the narrow mouth of the cove; then, with a hoarse cry, he began running. The belugas, busy playing with Erin, must have relaxed their careful monitoring of the sea around them. From his vantage point looking down on the bay, Christian had seen what they couldn't. Several tall black sails were cutting silently through the water. The killer whales had come back. This time there would be no escape for the belugas. And Erin was right in the middle of them.

Chapter 8

Although his legs were covering yards at a time, Christian felt as if his body were moving in agonizingly slow motion. Without slackening speed, his feet hit the broken rock Erin had stepped through so carefully an hour before. The loose surface shifted, and he started to go down. Training and superb reflexes took over automatically. His body tucked and rolled, and he was back on his feet, running, in one motion.

He wasn't aware that he had fallen. His attention—his entire being, mind, body and soul—had only one focus. Erin. He cursed the loss of his rifle. His only means of saving her now was the rubber raft, and as he leaped onto the dock, he prayed that there was enough gas left in the tank.

He had to untie the mooring lines, and he cursed the scant seconds it took. He didn't even have a lousy damn knife, he thought furiously as he jumped into the raft. He set the throttle and choke by touch, never taking his eyes off the bay. Nothing changed. Most of the pod was still gathered around Erin in the middle, while the few who were feeding had moved to browse in the shallower water near shore.

His hand faltered on the wooden handle of the starter rope. Had he seen what he'd thought he'd seen? The six tall dorsal fins could have been shadows from the clouds drifting overhead, a trick of the light on the water....

His question was answered in less than a heartbeat. The water in the middle of the bay suddenly exploded as a dozen killer whales broke through the surface. The orcas had run deep and silently like U-boats moving on a hapless convoy, and now they were closing in for the kill.

For an endless instant everything was suspended in time. The black and white orcas seemed etched against the sky as they breached. The belugas and Erin were motionless, as if the water in the bay had suddenly turned to ice, freezing them in place. Dimly Christian felt his lungs burning in his chest, demanding air, but he couldn't breathe. Then the orcas fell back as one with a tremendous smack that carried across the bay like a cannon shot, spraying up a sheet of silvery water.

Christian's hand convulsed on the starter handle, and the rope straightened, then broke from the pulley with the force of his yank. Fortunately the responsive engine had started, and he twisted the throttle wide open. Bent in an awkward crouch, he remained on his feet so he could see as much as possible. The belugas had galvanized immediately, grouping themselves so that Erin, Elizabeth and William were crowded into the middle, protected by a ring of white bodies. To Christian's puzzlement, the orcas seemed to be helping the belugas by circling the pod, as if urging them to pull closer together. Then, with a sick sense of horror, Christian understood what the killer whales were doing. They were rounding up their prey so it would be easier to control them. If any should be so foolish as to try to escape, the orcas could simply herd it back.

None tried to escape. The belugas, outnumbered and woefully outsized, closed ranks and tried to mount a defense, but, as Christian had thought once before, they didn't stand a chance. Their attackers were twice as long, three times as fast, four times as powerful and utterly without pity. One by one the dozen black and white demons feinted toward the line of small white defenders, swimming at top speed. The belugas staunchly held their positions even when it seemed certain the larger whales would overrun and crush them. At the last possible second each killer whale would turn aside and speed back to its place. The orcas each took a turn playing the one-sided game of chicken. They were taunting their victims, Christian realized, trying to increase their terror, feeding on it, enjoying it.

While the killer whales' attention was focused on the belugas in the middle of the bay, the two adults and the adolescent who had been feeding near the shore might have had a good chance of escaping, but they didn't take it. With a courage that was as valiant as it was useless, they tried a counterattack, ramming the orcas repeatedly with their only weapon, their humped foreheads. The black and white whales seemed as disturbed by the blows as a human might be by the buzzing of a pesky fly. Finally, though, as if annoyed by the nuisance, one of the orcas turned and swatted the charging youngster with its massive flipper. The white whale's body went still, the spasmodic twitching of its tail the only sign of life.

Other orcas nipped at the remaining two belugas almost playfully, herding them toward the main group. Christian saw that the flipper of one had been half torn away, and bright red streaks like garish war paint, ran down the side of the other. The belugas admitted their injured comrades to their circle, then closed ranks around them.

When Christian was less than a hundred yards from the orcas, they began swimming leisurely around the white whales, drawing the noose tighter. The belugas waited, tensed and motionless, for their enemies' next move. Desperately Christian willed more speed out of the already straining engine. He knew the orcas' next move as well as they did.

The baby Elizabeth was the first to die. One of the orcas dove suddenly, vanishing beneath the dark green water. Two more sounded behind the first. Before the flukes of the last two had completely disappeared, a tremendous geyser of water erupted in the middle of the belugas. The first orca rose up in the center of it, the body of the infant whale caught in its massive jaws.

Christian knew he would not forget what followed if he lived to be a thousand. The other two killer whales breached a few yards apart, and, with a soul-sickening horror, he watched the first whale toss the baby to the nearest of the other two. Like boys in a schoolyard playing a macabre game of keep away, the two killer whales took off across the bay, tossing the baby back and forth between them while the third one gave chase. Christian could hear the frantic screams of the mother over the racket of the outboard.

Equally frantic, Christian searched for Erin. She had been knocked underwater when the killer whale had snatched the infant, and now he couldn't see her in the chaos of boiling water and bodies. The scattered belugas were trying desperately to regroup, while the rest of the orcas, taking their cue from the first three, were moving among them, intent on cutting out another victim for their demonic play. The panicked whistles, squeals and mewlings of the belugas filled the air.

The killer whales paid no attention to him as he cut back on the throttle, shifted into neutral and let the raft drift. He didn't dare let the prop on the engine keep turning for fear Erin might not see it in the churned-up water. He shut his eyes for a second, trying to dispel the image of what would happen if she inadvertently came up under the cutting blades.

When he opened his eyes again, he saw her about a dozen yards away. She and an adult white whale, which he assumed was the calf's mother, were trying to protect William. Christian saw that she held the knife he'd strapped to her leg. He gunned the engine, aiming the raft straight toward her.

Christian was scant feet away, already reaching for her, when the raft rocked violently, almost capsizing. The only thing that saved him from pitching overboard was his death grip on the engine throttle. Knocked flat by the tremendous blow, Christian struggled to his knees in time to see the killer whale that had hit the raft bearing down on the calf, William. The mother whale threw her sturdy body into the orca's path, but the orca simply butted the minor irritant aside with its broad head. Then only Erin blocked its way to the small whale.

Fear knotted Christian's gut while he regained his feet. She looked so terrifyingly small and fragile as she faced a creature who could easily swallow her whole. Miraculously, the headset had somehow survived the violent dunking she'd had earlier, and he saw her lips moving while the regulator floated in the water by her shoulder, its air bubbling away uselessly. Erin had said that one problem with the headset was that she couldn't breathe and talk at the same time, he remembered inanely. He realized that she must be trying to warn the orca off, hoping that a few of her words would be understood by the huge animal. The killer whale pulled up less than a yard away from her, as if confused by the small black creature challenging it so boldly and so foolishly.

Erin felt no such confusion. In despairing horror, Christian watched her launch herself across the short space separating her and the orca, the arm holding the knife raised. She stabbed the knife down on the animal's snout, and the great beast actually flinched. He saw that she wasn't using the blade of the knife, but the weighted butt. Even in defense of the creatures she loved, Erin apparently couldn't bring herself to harm the demon.

Christian had no such compunction. Giving the engine a spurt of gas, he brought the twelve-foot raft along side the thirty-foot killer whale. His only weapons were the six-foot oars that were kept in the raft in case of engine failure. He raised one in both hands, then, putting all the force of his body behind it, he brought the broad blade down on the sensitive nostril on the back of the orca's head. The whale bellowed in a mixture of fury, surprise and pain, and whirled its mammoth body with frightening speed to snap at the cause of its hurt. Its sharp teeth pierced the tough rubber skin of the raft, and one section deflated with a loud hiss.

As Christian crouched to ride out the violent slewing of the craft, unexpected help arrived. The old whale Abner attacked from the rear. Like a hound harrying a bear, the ancient beluga nipped at the orca's tail, finally clamping his few worn teeth in one broad fluke. The orca thrashed its tail, trying to dislodge him, but the old whale hung on grimly as his frail body smashed again and again into the water. Finally, with a mighty slap of his powerful tail, the killer whale shook him off. Before the old whale could recover, the furious orca turned on him. Seizing Abner in its huge jaws, it gave him a vicious shake, then dropped him. As Abner hit the water, Christian saw that a ragged gash had been ripped down the length of the old beluga's left side.

The other two air chambers of the raft were unaffected, and it stabilized quickly. Ignoring the water slopping in over the flattened side, Christian stood and jabbed the oar toward the orca's nearest eye. In an instinctive reaction to protect itself, the whale retreated. For a split second it looked at him, and Christian's blood ran cold at the glitter of malevolent intelligence in the small black orb.

A quick glance behind him showed that the mother and her calf had made good their escape. He looked back to see that behind the mask, Erin's eyes were wide with horror and sorrow. Suddenly they narrowed fiercely, and she started after the retreating orca. With a vicious curse, Christian twisted the engine throttle open, and the raft shot forward. "Erin!" he roared. "Damn it! Come back here!"

Impossibly, over the sound of the engine and the panicked whistles and squeals of the belugas, she heard him. She turned her back on the killer whale, and he saw her look past him. Seeing that William and his mother were safe and noticing Abner's feeble movement, she began swimming strongly toward him.

Christian saw the blur of motion behind her. Whether the orca was bent on revenge for her part in the calf's escape, or whether it had decided that she would make a good substitute, he didn't know. All he knew was that the killer was attacking, and he was too far away to save her.

The whale reached her before Christian's shouted warning even left his throat. He watched the scene before him as if it were a movie advancing frame by frame, so that he could see all the horrifying details with exquisite clarity. He saw the huge black and white monster rising behind her with a deadly grace. He saw her arms and legs stroking with a steady strong rhythm, unaware of the danger behind her. He saw the trickle of red blood staining the white patch above the orca's eyes, seeping down from its bloody blowhole. And he saw every one of the large pointed teeth in the massive jaws that engulfed her. The whale gave her a playful shake, then dove, carrying Erin down with him.

"Erin-n-n!" His anguished cry of helpless rage and despair echoed across the water. With a litany of prayers and curses he didn't hear, Christian slowly circled the slick on the surface of the water caused by the orca's flukes when it had sounded. He scrubbed his forearm across his eyes, trying to clear them of an odd cloudiness, unaware that it was caused by tears blurring his vision. He fought a panic and terror unlike anything he'd ever known before. Not even when he'd heard the cocking of the gun behind him and known that he was betrayed had he felt so afraid and helpless. He had accepted that he was going to die with a calm fatalism. Dimly he understood that it was fear that soaked his body with icy sweat and caused a trembling so severe he could hardly stand. Not a fear that he had ever felt for himself, but fear for Erin, that he might lose her, and that was something he couldn't accept.

Unconsciously he had been counting the seconds since she had disappeared below the surface of the bay. He counted with a measured accuracy while a part of his mind refused to believe that so little time had passed. It had to be more than thirty seconds; it had to be minutes . . . hours. . . .

She'd had the regulator in her mouth, and he estimated that she should have about ten minutes of air left. It had appeared that the whale had been biting her air tanks, not her body, and Christian tried to tell himself that she was still unharmed, but, with each passing heartbeat during which she didn't reappear, his sense of dread increased. An orca could easily dive a hundred feet in a few seconds, and Erin's body couldn't withstand that. If the whale took her down more than seventy feet, she would need at least a ten minute stop part way back up to decompress so the nitrogen trapped in her body could escape, or she would have a deadly case of the bends.

He was starting to count off the second set of sixty seconds when he felt something bump the bottom of the raft. Throwing the engine into reverse, he backed up swiftly.

For a moment his heart almost failed him. Erin was face down in the sea. The hood of her diving suit was gone, her hair floating around her head like wet skeins of gold silk. The headset was gone, along with her face mask—and so were her air tanks. Either the harness had been ripped off by the force of the killer whale's jaws, or she'd slipped out of it to escape, Christian thought as he steered the Zodiac close beside her body.

She couldn't have been without air for more than a minute; her heart would still be beating. There was no sign of blood in the water around her, so she was probably uninjured. All he had to do was get her breathing again and she'd be all right, Christian reassured himself with a calm rationality as he reached over the side for her. He didn't hear his own hoarse, tear-choked voice desperately pleading for it to be true. "Oh, Erin...dear God, let her be all right...please...let her be...don't..."

More water poured into the raft as he leaned over the deflated edge, but he didn't notice. She was drifting faster than the raft, out of his reach. Even overextending his arm and shoulder muscles, his fingers barely touched the tips of her hair. They closed on a few strands, and he pulled carefully, afraid to pull too hard. Her body drifted backward slowly until he could wrap his fist in the heavy, wet mass; then he yanked as hard as he could and her body bumped into the side of the boat.

Easing his arms under her, he scooped her out of the water and gently laid her on the wooden floor of the raft. Her body was limp; she wasn't breathing, and her face was completely drained of color. There was a long rent in one sleeve of her diving suit, and vivid red showing beneath it. A bright drop of crimson oozed out and splashed on the bleached wood of the floor. She was so still, so white, he thought despairingly, almost as if she were— He refused to allow himself to think it as he knelt by her head. Forcing out his oddly reluctant hand, he felt for a pulse under her jaw and breathed a silent prayer of thanksgiving when he found it, beating slow and steady. He bent, repositioning her head as his mouth closed over hers, and he began to breathe life back into her.

With the ninth breath, he felt her body convulse; then she dragged in a deep ragged breath on her own. It was expelled in a wracking, retching cough as she struggled to sit up. Christian slipped an arm around her back, supporting her while she cleared her lungs.

Finally Erin lay back weakly against his arm. She looked up at Christian, absently noting the harsh new lines around his mouth, wondering at the residual dark shadows of fear in his light blue eyes. Raising a hand that felt as heavy as stone, she touched his cheek. "Thank you," she said in a raspy whisper. He captured her hand swiftly, turning his head to kiss the palm. It was still covered by the heavy glove, but Erin imagined she could feel the warmth of his mouth through the rubber.

Impatient with the cold dead feel of the rubber, Christian jerked off the glove with one hand, then laced her clammy fingers tightly through his. "Do you feel any paralysis, any numbness, any pain?" he asked intently.

"No." Her throat was raw from the salt water she'd swallowed. "I don't have the bends. He didn't take me down that far."

"How did you get away?"

Erin shook her head a little, trying to clear the lingering fuzziness in her mind. "I'm not sure. I think the harness on the tanks broke, but he tried to grab me back."

Her hair was plastered to her skull, and with a new chill of horror he realized the significance of her missing mask and headset when he saw the raw red scrapes on her scalp. "By the head?" His voice was as hoarse and raspy as hers.

She nodded. "He just grazed it, then let me go. He must have finally realized I wasn't one of the belugas." Erin clutched his jacket, trying to pull herself up to see over the side of the raft. "Christian, what about the whales?" she asked urgently. "Are they all right?"

Christian forced her gently back down before she could see the bay. His gaze swept rapidly around it. The pale sun still shone with a dull sparkle on the low waves; clouds still drifted slowly overhead. Only the bodies bobbing on the gentle swell gave grisly proof that it had not always been as peaceful as it was now. Although it had seemed like hours, incredibly the one-sided battle had lasted hardly more than five minutes, and then the killer whales had left as suddenly as they came.

For a minute he watched Elizabeth's mother, who was a few yards away. Repeatedly she pushed her dead child up to the surface with her broad beak, as if urging her to take a breath. Finally two other whales hovering nearby moved in. Gently they herded the mother away, escorting her toward the other side of the bay. He watched until the small brown body sank out of sight. "Elizabeth didn't make it," he told her as gently as he could. "And several others. William and his mother are all right."

The little bit of color her face had regained drained away again. "Abner?"

He shook his head. "I don't know. I don't see him." Still keeping her locked in his one-armed embrace, Christian reached back to the engine. It was still idling, probably running on fumes, he thought absently. He opened the throttle and headed back to the dock.

During the brief ride, Erin was quiet. He could feel the strong shudders that rippled through her periodically. They were partly from shock, Christian knew, and partly from cold. She had been in the icy water too long and lost too much body heat to warm up naturally. She needed a hot bath and some hot food inside her, and he intended to see that she got both as soon as they got back to the hut.

They reached the dock, and Christian eased his arm from around her, reluctant to release her even for the few minutes it would take to secure the raft. He felt the constant need to touch her so he could reassure himself that she was truly all right.

After tying up the raft, he reached down to help her out. He saw her eyes widen at the sight of the gashed side as she stepped over it, but she said nothing.

When he started to lead her over the rough wooden planks of the dock toward the beach, Erin rebelled. "I have to find Abner," she said, pulling away from him.

He held tight to her arm. "The raft is damaged, Erin. We can't take it out again."

"We can repair it," she insisted, trying to work free of the hand manacling her elbow. "I have a kit, and it will only take a few minutes. Then we can go out. He's hurt, Christian, because of me."

Christian ignored the plea in her voice and turned her arm over to show her the long tear that ran from the shoulder of the diving suit almost to the wrist. Blood oozed steadily now from the deep scratch in her arm. "You're hurt, too, Erin. You're chilled, and you've had a bad shock. The only place you're going is into the Jacuzzi to get warmed up. I'll go back out after I take care of you, and I'll look for him."

Erin stared stupidly at her arm. She hadn't even felt the wound. It must have been made by one of the orca's razor-sharp teeth. Now it began to burn, a fiery pain stretching the length of her arm. She ignored it. "No. I want to go now. My arm can wait, and I'm not that cold."

"Yes," Christian said implacably, watching her body shake with another strong shudder. He began to hustle her over the rough wooden planks of the dock.

"No!" Erin tried to dig in her heels, to no avail.

The argument was settled when they both heard the two-note whistle that was her name. The call was weak and came from the left. Christian had unconsciously relaxed his hold, and, with an unexpected twist, Erin wrenched away from him. She heard his hissed curse, then his feet pounding behind her, but surprise gave her just enough of an edge to beat him down to the beach.

Abner was a few yards offshore. The afternoon was lengthening into the bright twilight of early evening, and Erin could all too easily see the ugly red gash defiling the purity of his white skin. She ran out into the water, vaguely aware of Christian shouting behind her. Wading through chest-deep water, she reached the old whale's side.

The cold salt water had slowed the flow of blood from the wound to little more than a trickle, but Erin knew from the weak movement of his flipper as he tried to greet her that Abner had lost far too much blood and was very weak. The gash looked even worse on closer inspection. Beneath the layers of muscle and insulating blubber, Erin could see the dull white gleam of his ribs in too many places. Even more ominous was the fine pink mist coming from the nostril slit in the top of his head each time he exhaled a shallow, uneven breath. The terrible battering he'd suffered had caused severe internal injuries.

Erin looked down to see one milky blue-black eye watching her. Gently she rubbed his head and felt a small tremor under her hand. "Oh, Abner, I'm so sorry," she whispered past the tears clogging her throat.

"How is he?"

Erin turned at the sound of Christian's quiet question behind her. He was standing a yard or so away, the outgoing tide washing the tops of his knee-high Wellingtons. She shook her head, unable to speak.

"There's nothing you can do for him," Christian said gently.

Erin swallowed convulsively. "I—I know. I just want to stay with him for—for a little while . . . until . . ."

He nodded, and Erin turned back to the whale. He was resting quietly, seemingly in no pain, and Erin stroked the top and side of his head, giving what small comfort she could. She didn't know how long she had stood in the chest-deep water when suddenly one of her legs buckled under her, and she realized it had gone numb from the cold. Reluctantly she understood that she couldn't stay in the freezing water any longer. She wrapped her arms as far as she could around the whale's neck. "I have to go for a little while, Abner, but I'll be back," she whispered. He seemed to understand, giving an odd mewling sound as she pulled away.

Erin turned to see Christian wading through the surf toward her, heedless of the frigid water and his lack of protection. She took a few steps forward, but both legs buckled this time. Before she could fall, his strong arms came around her, and he lifted her clear of the sea. "I'll get you all wet," she admonished him weakly and heard him mutter something under his breath. He held her high against his chest, and Erin turned her face into his throat, unconsciously seeking his scent, the warm wonderful smell of life to dispel the cold ugly stench of death in her nostrils.

Too soon he put her down on the rocky beach, several yards above the high-tide line. Erin stared, mesmerized by the vision of heat and bright light in front of her. "How did you manage to build a fire?" she asked wonderingly. There was no driftwood on the beach, and she knew she hadn't any wood lying around.

One corner of his mouth jerked up in a thin smile. "I used the coffee table."

Erin frowned at the wood scraps piled nearby, waiting to feed the lovely warmth. She recognized several splintered pieces as part of the staves that had formed the spindle of the cable spool. He must have rolled the heavy wooden reel down to the beach, then managed somehow to smash it into firewood.

"Over here." He took her elbow and guided her to a folded piece of canvas tarp that she recognized as his makeshift poncho. Efficiently he stripped off the diving suit. "Sit down."

Christian reinforced his quiet command with a gentle pressure on her shoulder. She sank obediently to the tarp facing the fire, and he swiftly wrapped two blankets around her. He'd built the fire in front of one of the massive boulders littering the beach, knowing the heat from the fire would reflect off the rock and warm her back. It wasn't how he wanted to warm her up, but it was the best he could do. Intuitively, Christian knew Erin wouldn't leave Abner while he still lived. Without guilt, he prayed that the old whale's death would come soon.

Christian retrieved something from the edge of the fire and pressed it into Erin's hand. Gratefully, she wrapped her other chilled hand around the object's delightful heat.

"You're supposed to drink it, Erin."

Erin heard the thread of humor running through the careful patience in his voice. She looked down and saw that he had put a mug of something dark and thick-looking in her hands. "Oh," she said dumbly. "Of course." She raised the mug. Her nose told her it was beef broth. With the first sip her tongue told her that he had heated it up just as it came from the can, undiluted, but she liked the strong meaty, salty taste. She drank it down, savoring the feel of the soup's warmth coursing down her throat, through her chest and filling the empty pit of her stomach.

As soon as the mug was empty, Christian replaced it with another one. Erin took a sip of tea so strong and so sweet that she would have gagged on it normally, but tonight the extra caffeine and sugar were just what she needed, and she drank it down, too.

When the second mug was empty, Christian took that one, as well. He added more wood to the fire; then he came to sit behind her. Swiftly he removed the blankets he'd wrapped around her earlier and rewrapped them around them both. He wrapped his body around her, too. Raising his knees, he used his legs to swaddle her hips and thighs, his chest to sheathe her back, his arms to swathe her shoulders and breasts, enveloping her in a warmth that penetrated the deep chill at the center of her body. She relaxed into that warmth, and for long minutes she sat, silent, staring into the soaring flames.

"How much longer, do you think?" Christian asked softly.

"Not long. He's very weak," she said sadly.

Christian's arms tightened around her in silent comfort.

As soon as she opened her eyes, Erin realized that she must have fallen asleep. The sun, which had been well above the horizon, had started to set, darkening the beach with orange-tinted shadows. She was lying curled up under the blankets, alone. Rising to her knees, she looked around for Christian.

He was standing at the edge of the water, his back to her, looking out to sea. "I think it's about over," he said, then turned around and started toward her.

Again, some uncanny ability had told him that she was awake. Erin rose from the blankets, shivering a little in the cool air after the warmth of the wool. "I'll go to him." She reached for the diving suit, and he helped her to put it back on. The suit fit so closely that even the rip in the sleeve hadn't allowed much water to seep in, but even that little had spread itself equally, making the suit miserably cold and damp inside. She shut her mind against the frigid clamminess that immediately penetrated her thermal underwear. The old whale had been injured in her defense. She would go into the water without the suit at all before she would let him die alone.

She walked down the beach and into the water. Abner's eyes were open, but he seemed unaware of her approach until she touched the side of his head. He raised it slightly, then let it fall back as if even that were too much effort. Erin caressed his head as she had before, and he responded with the same mewling sound. She saw that the pink mist from his blowhole was bright red now, and the sound of his exhalations was rough and labored. She spoke to him, hoping he would hear the love and affection within the words he could not understand.

Just as the hazy sun dipped below the horizon, a terrible shudder shook the whale's huge body. His eyes, which had been dull and unfocused, suddenly burned brightly and fixed on her. There was one last rattling breath that turned into a sigh; then his body seemed to settle lower into the sea. The blue-black eye gradually glazed over, and Erin knew he was gone. For a long moment she rested her forehead against his. Finally she raised her head to look at him one last time. "Goodbye, Abner," she said softly.

Christian was waiting for her when she walked out of the sea. Without a word he wrapped her in the blankets, then held her tightly.

"He's gone." Her voice was muffled against his chest.

"I'm sorry." Christian realized he meant it. The whale had had a nobility that had seemed oddly human, and he regretted his passing.

"It was my fault." Her tone was flat and completely dispirited. The tears that might have eased the terrible ache she felt seemed to be frozen inside her.

"It wasn't your fault, Erin," he corrected her gently. "He was old and probably knew he was going to die soon. Instead of a slow, lingering death from age or disease, he died a warrior's death, protecting those he cared about. A man can't ask for much more than that." Neither of them thought his words were strange or inappropriate.

With a sigh she nodded once, then stepped back a little to look up at him. "The northwest Indians believed that a whale's bones must be returned to the sea, so that his spirit might be set free to live again."

Christian understood the silent plea in her eyes. Both of them knew what would happen to Abner's body if it stayed where it was. It would wash ashore on the next tide, and he knew she couldn't bear to see the gulls picking the brave creature's bones. "I'll take care of it," he promised quietly. He turned her against his side, and they climbed the hill to the lonely hut in silence.

The radio operator turned to the tall man pacing his small office. "I think maybe that message you were waiting for might be coming in, sir. It's from the Coast Guard station on Attu."

The man who had identified himself as Captain McBride reached out an impatient hand for the headset, and the operator gave it up without hesitation. Non-communications personnel were never supposed to touch the equipment, but what the hell. Maybe it would get the man out of his way that much sooner. The past two days he'd been haunting the office like a dark, silent ghost. Besides, he didn't look as if he'd take too kindly to being refused.

The message was coming in scrambled, which meant it was classified, and the radio man moved to turn on the descrambler. Somehow it didn't surprise him that this McBride, or whoever the hell he was, already knew which switches to press. He rearranged some paperwork, unobtrusively watching the man listen to the message coming through the earphones. He couldn't tell if it was good or bad news, because McBride's expression never changed from the grim mask he'd worn the past two days.

After about a minute and a half, McBride acknowledged the message and signed off. Silently he handed the headset back. "Good news, sir?" the radio man ventured.

To his astonishment, McBride smiled. Not a particularly friendly smile, it was true, and it only lasted about three seconds, but it was a smile all the same. He half expected the darkly handsome face to crack. "Yes, chief, it's good news."

As McBride shut the door behind him, the chief petty officer breathed a long sigh of relief. He wondered briefly at the words McBride had muttered softly as he went out the door. "I knew he'd get to her."

The chief promptly forgot them, laughing softly to himself. He would drive himself crazy if he tried to figure out all the classified messages he'd taken over the years.

Chapter 9

Leaning against the wall, Erin stared out the small window over her desk. For once, she thought absently, she wasn't sitting at the desk, slaving over the computer. It was very late, or rather, very early in the morning. She watched the withered flames of the fire dying on the beach. "You know, it's funny," she said suddenly. "I was wishing we could have a fire the other night, but I didn't have any wood." She looked vaguely at the spot the wooden cable reel had occupied. "Besides, there's no fireplace here," she added after a minute.

Christian watched her from his position on the couch. Those were the first words she'd spoken since coming out of the sea nearly two hours before. She'd taken the shower he'd started for her, stoically endured his treatment of the long deep scratch on her arm, eaten the scrambled eggs he'd cooked for her, then spent the rest of the time wandering aimlessly around the hut. She hadn't spoken—and she hadn't cried.

She stopped by the metal bookcase and meticulously arranged the haphazard assortment of books on one shelf. Christian knew tears were coming and, although he shared the same sense of helplessness most men felt at a woman's tears, he wanted them. They would ease the pain he knew she was feeling, the pain that was dulling her beautiful green eyes, making her face drawn and tight, and her normally graceful movements jerky and clumsy.

Erin had had her first experience with evil in its most amoral, conscienceless form. And the fact that the evil hadn't had a human form, he suspected, only made it worse. To find that it was just as universal as voice prints must have come close to shattering her.

The shelf was reorganized, and she moved on. When she passed in front of the couch again, Christian stretched out a long arm to block her way. "Sit down, Erin," he commanded softly.

He turned his hand slowly until it was palm up in silent invitation. Just as slowly, Erin put her hand in his. Despite the warmth of the hut, her hand was ice cold. He tugged gently in silent repetition of his command, and this time she followed it.

She clutched his strong, warm hand to her breast. The warmth of it traveled up her arm, through her body and into her heart, melting the tears frozen there. "They weren't even hungry," she whispered as they began to seep. "They just killed them for the fun of it."

Christian felt the warm tears splash on his wrist. He drew her limp body onto his lap and shifted, bracing his back against one arm of the sofa and stretching out his long legs on the seat. Cradling her against his chest, he silently offered his solace.

Her sobs intensified, hammering through her body and pounding into his. Gently he rocked her in his arms. "Cry it out, love. I'm here. I'll take care of you," Christian crooned quietly as he held her closer. His mouth brushed tenderly over her forehead, her hair, her wet cheeks.

Finally Erin lay still in the two strong arms sheltering her, exhausted, her grief spent. Her fists, which had been tightly balled against the pain, opened on his chest. He had changed into the sleeveless sweatshirt and too-big sweatpants, and she rubbed her fingers unconsciously over the soft fleece like a little child seeking the reassuring comfort of her security blanket.

His big hands stroked over her shoulders and back, kneading and loosening tight muscles. One hand glided up to her neck, to practice its magic touch there. Erin released a long shuddering sigh. Her arms stole around his neck as she shifted on his thighs, and her parted lips came to rest in the hollow of his throat. It seemed only right that she sample the tangy flavor and smooth texture of his skin. His pulse beat fast and steady against the tip of her tongue.

A slow shudder went through Christian's body as his fingers slid through her hair. He cupped the back of her head and tilted her mouth up to his. As they opened over hers, his lips were soft and soothing, making no demands. Her own lips parted, and his tongue eased inside. The callused fingertips of his other hand slipped inside the collar of the soft rose plaid flannel shirt she wore, massaging her shoulders, her sharp collarbones; then his hand spread, circling her throat.

Exhausted and drained by death, Erin's body began to reawaken and fill with life. Her hands crept beneath the ragged edges where the sleeves of the sweatshirt had been cut off, and her palms shaped the sculpted muscles of his shoulders, skimmed his warm, satiny smooth skin.

Christian's hand skated inside the open neck of her shirt, and his fingers closed lightly over her breast. His touch was gentle and curiously sexless, intended to comfort not arouse, but his palm grazed the hardening peak, and her mouth became more demanding, almost desperate, as her nails dug into his shoulders.

Erin grabbed at him convulsively when he abruptly broke off the kiss. He moved his hand back and tried to ease her head onto his shoulder, but Erin resisted. Raising her head, she looked up at him. "Tonight . . . if you asked me to share the bed . . . I wouldn't refuse," she whispered.

"Tonight I couldn't ask." His voice was harsh with rigid control. Christian knew that he could satisfy all the aches and fantasies he'd suffered while lying sleepless in that wide, soft bed, thinking of her just a few feet beyond the closed door. And he felt the same need she did to convince himself that she was safe and unharmed. The most convincing way would be to lose himself so deep inside her that there could be no doubts, for either of them.

But, for Erin, it would be for all the wrong reasons. He looked down into her eyes. They weren't heavy-lidded and slumberous with passion; they were wide and helplessly vulnerable, the clear sea-green color dulled by exhaustion, grief and desperation. Were the circumstances different, he would have granted her the comfort and forgetfulness that could be found in another warm and giving body. And not because he was such a selfless bastard, either, he thought derisively, but he didn't have the right to offer it, and, he admitted, he was being selfish, too. He didn't want the memory of their first time together to be tainted by the horror of this day. But, he resolved fiercely, he would have the right to make the offer—and soon.

"Please ... I need—"

He brushed an infinitely gentle kiss over her slightly swollen lips to stop her words. One corner of his hard mouth turned up in a small, bittersweet smile. "I've made so few noble gestures in my life, Erin. Please allow me this one."

The arms around her weren't the embrace of a lover, Erin finally realized, but the embrace of a caring, loving friend. It was enough, more than enough, and, with a sigh, she laid her head on his shoulder. She was so tired. Feeling warm and safe at last, she gave in to her exhaustion.

For a while Christian simply held her and watched her sleep. Her mouth was relaxed and soft, her lips slightly parted and moist. There were faint shadows under her eyes, and her lashes were darker shadows on her faintly flushed cheeks. She looked so young, so innocently trusting, and he felt his heart clench inside his chest. Comfortable on the old sofa and even more comfortable with the soft warmth in his arms, he let his thoughts drift.

A low keening sound brought him back to an awareness of his surroundings. As always, the speaker was turned on to broadcast anything picked up by the underwater microphones. Careful not to awaken her, Christian set Erin aside on the sofa, arranging her body comfortably before he rose and went to the bank of electronic equipment on the other side of the room.

Erin could add another to her catalog of voice patterns, he thought as he gave the knob on the speaker a vicious twist. The sound of grief was universal. He knew everything that was broadcast on the speaker was also recorded for future analysis. Not caring if he was destroying a summer's worth of work, Christian shut down every piece of equipment. She wasn't going to relive Elizabeth's and Abner's deaths and her own narrow escape whenever she listened to that damn tape, he decided grimly.

In the bedroom he pulled off his sweatshirt, then, without ceremony, swiped Oscar off the bed and peeled back the quilt and top sheet. With an affronted air, Oscar stalked off, and Christian followed him into the living room. Then he knelt by the sofa and cautiously slid his arms under Erin's shoulders and knees. His powerful thigh muscles drove him upward, bearing both their weights. He swayed a bit and cursed the lingering weakness in his body. After shifting her boneless body in his arms, he began walking toward the bedroom. Her head lolled back into the hollow of his shoulder, and her hair was a silken spill over his bicep.

Her breast pushed warm and firm at his bare chest, and he could feel the nipple rubbing and hardening through the soft flannel with each step. Her lashes fluttered once, a butterfly kiss against the bare skin of his shoulder while she settled deeper into his arms. A quiet sigh fanned across his chest, sending his own nipple into a tight pucker, and Christian laughed ruefully to himself. She was arousing him more asleep than the most practiced whore could wide awake and trying. What if she woke up, he fantasized, and touched her tongue to him, moved the hand down that was curled now against his belly...?

He ended the fantasy abruptly as he bent one knee to the bed and laid her down, taking care not to jostle her. For a moment he stared down at her. He should be the one to sleep on the sofa tonight, but his newfound nobility didn't extend quite that far, he discovered. He still had the need just to touch her, to be sure that he hadn't lost her.

Christian lay down beside her and covered them both with the quilt, then pulled her relaxed body back tightly against his. Their heads were sharing the same pillow, and he tucked the top of hers under his chin. He closed his eyes, and, content and at peace, he let sleep take him.

Eyes closed and still half asleep, Erin stretched out a hand. Frowning when it encountered empty space, she woke up the rest of the way and slowly opened her eyes. They focused on the dent in the pillow beside her head. Dimly she remembered waking up once, in the throes of a nightmare she couldn't remember now. She hadn't had to reach for him then, because he'd already been there, holding her securely, protecting her against the terrors of the night.

She came out of the bedroom a few minutes later dressed in corduroys and a lamb's wool sweater to see him sitting at the kitchen table reading an old newspaper, a cup of coffee with a lazy curl of steam rising from it by his elbow. The scene was so ordinary, what thousands of women saw every morning, that there was a curious lump in her throat.

He looked up from his paper with a smile. "Good morning, sleepyhead. I was beginning to think you were going to sleep your life away."

Erin smothered a yawn. "I feel like I almost did." When she opened her eyes after the yawn, she realized that the bright light filling the kitchen was natural. She looked toward the window. Pure yellow sunshine poured through the glass like a river of liquid gold. Oscar was lying in the bright pool where it fell on the floor, his body stretched out to an impossible length, as if he were determined to soak up every drop possible.

"The sun is shining," she said wonderingly. Looking back at Christian, she asked curiously, "How long was I asleep?"

He chuckled as he rose from the table and went to the stove. "Around the clock and a little more." He took the cover off a frying pan and released a mouth-watering smell of breakfast sausage. "Are you hungry?"

Her stomach answered his question with a loud rumble, and they both laughed. "No, actually I'm starving," she said with a wide grin.

She excused herself for a quick trip to the bathroom to wash up and comb her hair. When she came out he was dishing up sausage and several of the frozen waffles she'd had in the freezer. Usually they tasted like cardboard with maple syrup. This morning she was so hungry they tasted like ambrosia.

Christian sipped his coffee while he watched her wolf down her breakfast. She was still a little pale, and her voice was raspy with the remnants of weeping, but the dark shadows that had dulled her eyes were gone. She crossed the knife and fork on her empty plate. "How are you this morning?" he asked quietly.

"I'm fine," she answered with a soft smile. It wasn't a lie. With her long sleep had come an easing of the terrible ache in her heart. She would always mourn the loss of Abner, who in many ways had been her friend, but already the horrific memory of the killer whales' attack was fading.

Christian nodded, then stood up with a sudden briskness and began clearing the table. "If you don't have anything you have to do today, how about giving me a hand with my plane?"

He didn't need her hand or anyone else's, Erin decided an hour later. She sat cross-legged on the dock, watching him fashion a clever brace out of wire and a length of pipe for the bent pontoon bracket. His request had simply been an excuse to get her out of the hut so she wouldn't sit and brood over what had happened. She wouldn't have, but she was grateful that he had thought of it.

She'd noticed that the deflated air chamber in the raft had been repaired. She hadn't needed to look down the beach to know that he'd given Abner's body back to the sea, and she was grateful for that, too.

She was also grateful for being able to face him without any embarrassment this morning. He had rebuffed her offer last night with such delicacy that she didn't feel any shame. Erin watched him bend the pipe to fit with his bare hands. To find such sensitivity and gentleness in a man so strong and big seemed a paradox. Erin sensed depths in this man that she might plumb for a lifetime and never reach bottom. The idea of trying was exciting... and a little frightening.

Closing her eyes, she turned her face up to the sun and tried to think of nothing more complicated than its welcome warmth on her cheeks. It was the rarest of days in the Aleutians—a perfect summer day. The sky overhead was deep blue and devoid of a single cloud. The sun burned white-hot, as if to make up for all the days when it was little more than a pale spot in a dark cloud. Around the island the sea was a mirror reflecting the sapphire brilliance of the sky.

Erin opened her eyes to see that Christian had finished the job of bracing the crumpled strut. "Is your plane ready to fly?" she asked, trying to keep the fervid hope that it wasn't out of her voice.

"All but the flaps." Christian straightened and walked back along the ten-foot pontoon to examine a hinged section on the trailing edge of the right wing. There was a corresponding section on the other wing. Both raised or lowered according to how much lift was needed to get the plane airborne. Right now both were stuck in the fully retracted position, which meant the only way he would be able to take off would be into a stiff head-wind where he didn't need any extra lift.

"Will you be able to fix them, or will you have to have Sam fly in a part after all?"

He could fix them right now, with a couple of hours and a few tools. "I don't know yet. It may take a day or two." He turned around suddenly and surprised a pleased smile on her face.

Erin stood up. "Why don't you leave it for tomorrow?" she said lightly. "Today is too beautiful to waste working."

For a brief, magical time the barren, stormswept island had become a cool emerald Eden. The breeze was light and frivolous, carrying the scent of sweet grass instead of the strong smell of the sea. It teased at their hair as Erin and Christian explored hidden nooks and crannies, finding unexpected treasures. Small, perfect wildflowers poked their heads above the grass for a rare peek at the sun, and in a small bowl, sheltered from the relentless wind, they found wild strawberries.

Erin popped another of the tiny berries into her mouth, and there was an explosion of sweetness on her tongue.

"You know, if you weren't being such a pig, we might have enough of these for dinner," Christian noted mildly.

"You're just jealous because I found more than you," Erin retorted with a grin, "but to show what a good person I am, I'll share." On her knees, she inched forward to give him her last few strawberries.

Instead of taking them from her, Christian wrapped his fingers around her wrist and raised her hand to his mouth. It took her a second to understand what he wanted; then slowly she placed a berry at his lips. His eyes holding hers, he opened his mouth, and she moved forward. His tongue flicked the tip of her thumb as he drew the strawberry into his mouth.

The tiny touch on her finger tingled up her arm. One after the other she fed him the rest of the berries. When they were gone, still holding her gaze, he took her fingers into his mouth one at a time to lick off the sweet, sticky juice. His tongue curled around each finger, and Erin felt a corresponding curl of sensation deep inside her.

When her fingers were clean, he placed her arm around his neck. Her other arm joined it as his mouth met hers in a long, leisurely kiss. Her eyes drifted closed, and Erin tasted the strawberries again, infinitely sweeter this time.

The kiss ended as slowly as it had begun. They drew a breath apart, and Erin saw that he was smiling at her with that peculiar gentleness again. Wordlessly he helped her to her feet, and, hand in hand, they started back toward the hut.

Hours later Erin was wishing she had saved the strawberries for dinner. "Darn it," she muttered as she set the table. "Why couldn't I have brought some wine, or maybe a few candles?" Such a perfect day deserved a perfect meal, and she feared theirs would be far from it. In the afternoon Christian had tried the fishing rod, with success, and she had dug a bucket of butter clams across the island on the only sand beach. But even

with a salad and the small loaf of sourdough bread she'd discovered at the bottom of the freezer and the frozen chocolate
cake, it would still be a simple meal.

She was tuning the shortwave radio for a Russian channel
that she'd discovered played classical music at night when
Christian came into the living room. His hair was still damp
from his shower, and he'd used one of her disposable razors.
Erin was almost sorry he'd shaved. She'd gotten used to him
looking a little bit rough and untamed; then she realized that he
still did. "I thought we'd have a little dinner music," she said
as the quiet strains of Chopin came through the radio. "Although I'm afraid the dinner isn't very much. At least it isn't
out of a can, though."

Christian watched her turn a small bouquet of wildflowers
in a juice glass a few degrees one way, then turn it back. Then
she fiddled with the placement of the cheap salt and pepper
shakers on the cracked tabletop. He found her nervousness
oddly endearing. "I'm sure it will be perfect," he told her and
was rewarded with a dazzling smile.

Considering the limited menu and her even more limited
skill, the dinner turned out surprisingly well, Erin decided.
Oscar, bribed with a fish all his own, even behaved himself for
a change. After clearing away their plates, she brought the
chocolate cake and fresh coffee to the table for dessert.

Christian swiped a bit of the frosting before she could cut the
cake. He winked at her frown as he licked his finger. "Mmm.
Good."

She laughed shyly. "This is my birthday cake."

His hand froze in the act of pouring them each more coffee.
"When is your birthday, Erin?"

She gave him a crooked grin. "Yesterday. I slept right
through it, didn't I?" The stark memory of why she had been
asleep tried to intrude, but Erin refused to admit it. "I'm glad
you're here. I would have had to eat it all by myself."

"I'm glad I'm here, too, Erin. No one should be alone on
their birthday," he said quietly, remembering the times when
he had been. He raised her hand from where it lay on the table

between them and pressed a soft kiss into her palm. "Happy birthday."

They finished the meal in comfortable silence. When they had taken care of the few dishes, Christian took a blue windbreaker off a hook by the door and held it open for her. "It's such a beautiful night, let's go outside and enjoy it."

Erin slipped into the jacket. Even with the sunshine, the day hadn't warmed much over sixty degrees, and she knew it would be chilly outside. Christian wore only his black sweater, but, as Erin already knew, he seemed impervious to cold.

She was starting to move away to zip the windbreaker when he turned her around and gently pushed her hands out of the way. The zipper was stubborn. His knuckles rubbed against the front of her jeans as he worked to connect it at the bottom. Erin felt every light brush as a sharp tingle deep in her belly. Finally the zipper cooperated, and he slid it up smoothly. His fingertips skimmed the valley between her breasts, and Erin almost moaned. He arranged her collar, then leaned down to give her a quick kiss. "Let's go."

The summer solstice had passed, so the sun was staying longer below the horizon each night. Tonight the sky was almost dark enough for the stars to show. Two brighter planets were visible in the deep lavender western sky.

By silent consent they climbed the short hill behind the Quonset hut. When they reached the summit, Erin gasped softly. "Oh, how beautiful!" Against the midnight-blue northern sky hung a curtain of red, blue, green and purple lights. The curtain rippled as if in a breeze that made the colors shift like the patterns in a kaleidoscope, never stopping, ever changing.

"The aurora borealis," Christian murmured beside her.

"The northern lights," Erin affirmed. Secretly she preferred the less scientific, more romantic name for one of nature's most spectacular shows. "I've never seen them this time of year before." The unusual appearance of the lights only added to the magic of the day.

"Look."

Reluctantly Erin tore her eyes away from the fantastic light show to follow his soft command and gasped again. "Oh, they're back!" After the orcas' attack, the belugas had disappeared from the bay, and Erin had despaired of seeing them again. But now, below, in the calm, dark waters of the bay, the pod moved in a silent ballet choreographed to the music of the sea. Arching and diving, they danced through the water, leaving swirls of green luminescence in their wake. Silent, she and Christian watched until they disappeared behind the headland that overshadowed the mouth of the bay.

Unconsciously Erin raised her eyes to the crest where she had first seen the wolf the summer before. A mist, too light to be considered fog, eddied around the rock, and Erin almost fancied that the gray vapor was curling itself into the form of a wolf tonight. She turned to the blue-eyed wolf beside her.

He was watching her with the intensity she had become used to. She wasn't sure who reached for whom first. One hand resting at his waist, she placed the other on his square jaw, her thumb rubbing over the slight roughness of his skin. The light wind that blew her hair back ruffled his. One of his hands fitted itself to the small of her back, while the other cupped her cheek, his long fingers sliding into her hair. His expression was sober as they stared at each other for a long moment without speaking. Then he lowered his head. His eyes shut as his mouth touched hers, and Erin's eyes closed, too.

The kiss was unlike any of the others they'd shared. His tongue took her mouth immediately and plunged deep, as if it were his exclusive right, yet there was nothing hurried or rushed about the kiss. In return her mouth claimed his just as completely. It was a consummation, as if an important matter had been discussed and decided and was now being carried out.

And Erin knew that was exactly what was about to happen. She'd known it all through this magical day, had known it, she realized at last, since the night the sea had brought him to her. From that night they had been moving inexorably toward a consummation of the sexual pull between them. She had resisted it, but finally she understood that the little thrill of panic she felt every time he was near wasn't because she was afraid of his overwhelming masculinity and virility. She was afraid of her response to it. He drew her as surely as a moth to a flame, but, unlike the mindless moth, she had recognized her danger, had been afraid that she might be burned up in his fire.

She was still afraid, she admitted honestly, but she was more afraid of missing the fire altogether. There was far more than mere sexual attraction between them. Erin sensed an intelligence that complemented her own. He seemed to understand and perhaps even share, as no one else ever had, her feeling for the whales and her desire to understand them. She didn't fully understand him and knew that she might never have the chance to, but she wouldn't think of that tonight. They had already experienced more in a few days than many couples did in a lifetime of living together. They had defeated death together; now it was time to celebrate life. If the celebration was short, if all she could have was one night of his fire, then so be it. She wouldn't hope for more, only that it would burn hot enough to keep her warm for the rest of her life.

When his head lifted, the expression in his eyes was unreadable. He smiled faintly and, taking her hand, led her down the hill.

The radio was playing Mozart when they came through the inner door of the air lock. His head cocked, listening to the stately music, Christian helped her off with her windbreaker. When Erin turned back to him after hanging it up, he smiled at her, then bowed slightly and held out his hands in a perfectly pantomimed invitation to dance. Erin stepped into his arms, and he led her into the classic rhythms of a slow waltz. Their bodies were perfectly attuned to the music and each other with never a misstep as he turned her slowly around the floor. Erin laid her cheek on his shoulder and closed her eyes. They should both be in powdered wigs and brocade and dancing on marble under crystal chandeliers, she thought whimsically, instead of wearing old jeans and sweaters and dancing on warped wooden planks under a dangling light bulb. But the magic was still the same.

They danced slower and slower, to their own beat now. The inside of his thigh brushed the inside of hers as he turned her one last time, and the music went on without them. Their tongues took up where their feet left off, slow dancing to rhythms far more ancient than those of the music.

His mouth left hers, and Erin slowly opened her eyes when she felt him step back. To her surprise, they were in the bedroom. Deftly his large hands undid the three buttons at the neck of her sweater. Automatically Erin raised her arms, and he pulled it over her head. As she lowered them, he unclasped her bra with equal adroitness and drew it over her arms. Something else he has a facility for, a tiny voice whispered impishly inside her. A small jolt of pleasure shivered through her when his fingers undid the button of her jeans and brushed the bare skin of her stomach.

Christian felt her flinch, and, holding her eyes, he deliberately brushed his rough fingertips over the smooth soft skin of her belly again. He got the same helpless response, and he saw her eyes widen and turn dark. He lowered the zipper of her jeans slowly, then reached inside to palm her hips. Dropping to his knees, he drew the soft denim down, his hands trailing down the backs of her thighs, her knees, her calves, stopping at her ankles. He felt her sway, and she locked her hands on his shoulders to brace herself. Reaching up, he hooked his thumbs in the fragile wisp of lace and silk that was all she had left and drew it down with equal slowness. As he removed her shoes and socks, he felt the fine tremor that was rhythmically running through her. At his light touch on the backs of her ankles, she stepped out of her jeans and panties.

Grasping her hands, he stood up, then held her away from him to look at her. His eyes traveled leisurely down the length of her naked body, here shadowed, there highlighted in the glow of light from the other room. They roved back up, pausing on the golden fluff at the juncture of her thighs and again on her full breasts, all in shadow except the dark rose tips, which budded under his long, feasting look. He pulled her close for a brief kiss, then, releasing her hands, stepped back.

Erin knew by his easy relaxed stance that he wanted her to return the favor and undress him. She managed to pull off his sweater, but then her fingers fumbled on the clasp of his pants.

The hard warm ridge straining beneath the black fabric brushed her fingers, and they became even clumsier. "I guess I'm better at this when you're unconscious," she whispered with a small nervous laugh. His hands closed over hers, and she glanced up.

He was smiling at her softly. "I'll take care of it this time." He stripped off the rest of his clothes matter-of-factly, then pulled down the quilt and sheet. Erin's eyes flickered over him, refreshing her memory of his magnificent body. There was a touch of apprehension in her shiver of anticipation when she saw the essence of his manhood rising powerfully from the thick, dark gold thatch at his groin.

Christian saw her flicker of fear. Taking her hand, he carried it down and closed her fingers around him. "There's no more than you can handle, love," he assured her gently. After a moment, her hand moved hesitantly, and he threw back his head, gritting his teeth as he felt her fingers' delicate explorations.

It was like a living thing in her hand, Erin thought dazedly, soft velvet and steel hard. Daniel had never encouraged her to touch him, so she'd been reluctant to initiate anything on her own. Fascinated by Christian's lively response, her hand moved more surely, measuring him, caressing, until she heard the hiss of his indrawn breath and a muttered curse. His hand clamped over her wrist, and Erin tried to snatch her own hand back guiltily.

His hoarse laugh was rueful. "We'd better save that for later, sweetheart, or I'll explode right now." Christian noticed her anxious look. She might have been married, he thought, but she was innocent of the pleasure she could give a man. "It's all right, Erin," he reassured her softly. "I want you to touch me, but I like it a little too much, and I want to take it as slow as we can this first time." Her look of anxiety dissolved into a shyly sexy smile that was oddly thoughtful, and Christian laughed wryly to himself. He should have known that she would realize instantly the newfound power she had. He decided just as instantly that she would exercise that power only on him.

He lifted her, then set her in the middle of the bed. She had made it that morning with fresh linens, and Erin felt the cool, unwrinkled smoothness of the cotton sheet against her back. She opened her arms in mute entreaty.

Christian followed her down, and her mouth reached up with gratifying eagerness for his, hotly demanding his taste in exchange for her own. He met her demands and subtly raised them. He ran his hands slowly over her slim, sleek body, savoring the unexpected lushness of her hips and breasts, learning her body, stroking, petting, touching, always touching. His callused fingers feathered over one breast, drawing ever smaller circles until they found pebbled flesh. He felt her small restless squirmings and smiled against her mouth. Her responses were untried; most of them, he suspected, were new to her. Pulling back, he blew his warm, damp breath against her breast and watched the nipple draw tighter. Watching her face, he brushed his thumb over the rosy bud. She whimpered a little. He did it again and yet again, drawing a small cry from her each time. He alternated the rhythm by raking the blunt edge of his nail over the ultrasensitive point. She moaned, and her eyes fluttered closed.

Her breast was achingly tight, pleading for release from the torturing pleasure. "Christian, please," she begged, her voice husky with need. A wet, hungry warmth captured the bursting nipple, and he suckled strongly. Erin felt the pull deep in her womb and cried out. His hunger was hers, searing deeply into her like a hot brand, and her body began to smolder. Her hands dug through his hair to his skull, clamping convulsively as he drew more of her into his scorchingly hot mouth.

She tasted even sweeter than he had imagined. Christian smoothed a hand across her concave stomach and over the curve of her hip. He trailed it down the outside of her thigh, then back up the inside, his fingertips gliding over taut, quivering flesh. His long forefinger traced the crease between her thigh and her belly, up, then down, and he felt her uncontrollable shudder. His hand brushed over her ruff of hair, and he followed the opposite groove, eliciting another shudder. As he raked his fingers lightly through the soft tangle, his palm shaped itself to the small mound between her thighs.

Erin's hands twisted into the sheet, and a long, quivering groan was torn from her as his hand set up a throbbing beat. She had a need to be taken that was purely physical, purely delicious and purely frustrating, because she couldn't do anything about it. She wanted to wrap herself around him, pull him deep inside her to fill this awful emptiness, until there weren't two separate bodies anymore, only one, but she couldn't. It was all she could do to breathe.

One long finger probed and teased, and she arched helplessly against his hand. Flames began licking at her body. She couldn't be feeling this impossible pleasure; it was like nothing she had ever experienced, nothing she had ever even imagined. His thumb slipped over the sensitive button, and she ground her head into the pillow, her neck arching. "No, no," she whimpered. She sensed some impending cataclysm, and suddenly she was afraid to let him continue . . . yet desperate that he might stop.

"Yes, Erin, yes. Let go, love. Let go for me." He scattered hot damp kisses down her throat and over her breasts between his husky words. Her body arched again. He slowed the rhythm, pausing between strokes, letting her anticipation build before the next one, and long shudders began to convulse her body. "That's it. Let it happen. Let it happen, Erin."

Gasping and shaking, Erin felt the flames dying down. She'd just undergone the most terrifying, glorious experience of her life . . . yet still something had been missing. A second later she knew what it had been.

Blanketing her body with his, Christian slid inside her, filling her in one smooth, powerful thrust. The sensation was so exquisite that she thought she might die.

For a timeless moment they stared into each other's eyes. Hers shimmered brightly as his body took possession of hers. His were glazed with disbelieving pleasure. Her strength matched with his created a physical tension that was exquisite and almost unbearable.

Erin felt the fire within her burn higher again. Her hands stroked over his back, following the flexing and contracting of his powerful muscles as his body stroked hers with a slow, deep rhythm. Wearing an expression of agonized pleasure, his face was taut above hers, the skin pulled tight over his cheekbones, evidence of the control he was exerting over himself.

She didn't want control; she wanted the fire. Her hands clenching on his hips, she arched upward. With a low growl, his control snapped, and they were both caught up in a frenzied, pile-driving rhythm that fanned the flames higher and higher. The sparks ignited her blood, and wildfire blazed through her. A last bit of rationality told her dispassionately that she was going to be burned alive, but she didn't hear. Her body writhed in the flames in an agony of delight. Dimly she heard a long scream, then Christian's hoarse cry, and she knew he had gone with her into the fire. Their bodies were burned together, their souls scorched.

For long minutes they drifted, like bits of ash on the wind. Their exhausted, sweat-slicked bodies were still anchored together in a tangle of arms and legs. Christian sprawled heavily over Erin. He knew he must be crushing her, but he couldn't bring himself to move. Small jets of pleasure still pulsed through him, making him weak.

A long sigh trembled through her body into his. He levered himself onto his elbows and looked down into the wide stunned eyes below him. Tears were drying at the corners. Unembarrassed, he reached up to wipe away a similar wetness on his own cheeks; then his head bent, and he sipped away her salty tears. Her hands languidly caressed his shoulders and neck while he whispered feather-light kisses and wordless murmurs of wonder and appreciation over her cheeks and chin and throat.

At last he began to ease away. Erin's hands tightened convulsively on his shoulders. "Please stay...."

"...inside you?" Her smile was a little shy and radiantly beautiful. "It would be my pleasure, love." Forever. That's all he wanted—forever. And tonight he would let himself pretend that he could have it.

Chapter 10

Christian came awake slowly, breaking a habit that had developed years ago when his life had sometimes depended on his ability to awaken instantly, preferably on his feet and running. There was a concentrated patch of weight and warmth near his knee that told him Oscar had managed to wedge himself between them again. Sitting up, he reached down and lifted the cat out of the nest he'd made for himself and set him gently down on the other side of the bed. "You're going to have to learn to share her, cat," he whispered.

He settled back on one elbow to look at his woman sleeping next to him. Erin lay on her stomach, the sheet twisted around her waist, exposing the beautiful line of her back and shoulders. She had one knee drawn up, and her hand tucked under the pillow beneath her cheek. Her hair spread over the pillow in a tangle. Tangled mostly by his hands, he thought wryly. He remembered one point when they'd been making love. Was it the second time or the third? He'd gathered up handfuls of it and rubbed it over his chest and belly as if he were bathing in its fragrant silkiness.

His woman. The curve of her breast was visible under her
arm. He reached out to trace it with a blunt fingertip, his touch
feather-light so he wouldn't waken her. She needed to sleep;
there were pale lavender bruises of exhaustion under her long
dark lashes. He needed to sleep, too. His body was sated and
bone-tired, yet he wanted her again, Christian thought ruefully. A small smile curved her mouth. Was she dreaming of
him? Giving in to temptation, he lowered his head to press a
kiss on her sleep-soft mouth. She stirred, and he eased down to
cradle her body against his. She turned into him, fitting herself to him automatically. Her arm wrapped around his waist,
her full breast nestled against his chest, and her knee slid up,
tucked between his thighs.

His woman. His mouth curved unconsciously in a sardonic
smile. He had arrogantly assumed that he would awaken her
sexually, teach her the delights of her body, and he had. But he
had learned something, too. He knew all about physical grati-
fication, but he had discovered that there was a part of himself that had been unawakened, too, a part he hadn't even
known existed. It was as if there had been an empty place
waiting inside him that only she could fill. In return, he'd given
a part of himself that he knew he had never given to anyone
else. It hadn't been just the physical ecstasy of climax that he
had felt. It had been the joining of two hearts, two souls, two
minds, a blending of the two of them into a whole that was
somehow greater than the two halves. Love?

He had given up on the idea of love when he had given up the
other foolish dreams of youth. And love was supposed to make
people noble and self-sacrificing, wasn't it? His one "noble"
gesture hadn't lasted very long, he reminded himself caustically. If this was love, it had made him greedy and selfish. His
arms tightened reflexively. Erin whimpered in her sleep, and he
forced himself to relax his hold. She was his woman, and he was
unwilling to sacrifice any of the incredible joy he had just experienced. He was glad this night had happened. He knew she
hadn't given herself to him lightly, and her response had been
fantastic. She was bound to him now, and that would give him
an advantage when he told her the truth. That wasn't noble,

either, but he would use any edge he could find, he thought as he drifted into sleep. She was his, and he wasn't going to lose her.

Erin. Where are you? Answer. Answer now.

I am here.

Erin didn't need a translation to hear the alarm and warning in Martha's voice.

Danger for you. Great disturbance coming. You and man leave now.

" 'Great disturbance' is how they describe an earthquake," Erin murmured to Christian, who had come to stand beside her. She typed in her response.

You leave, too?

Others gone. I go now. You, too. Go now, Erin.

The speaker and printer went dead at the same time; then she heard Christian's quiet question.

"Is there any chance that she's wrong?"

"Virtually none. Whales live in such close harmony with their environment that they sense even the tiniest changes, more accurately than the best seismic-detection equipment we have." She didn't need an earthquake this morning, Erin thought a little hysterically, not when just last night she'd experienced one of cataclysmic proportions. She looked at him quickly, then away. He'd been asleep when Martha called. He'd taken the time to pull on his pants, but he'd zipped them only part way. They rode low on his lean hips, and she could see the line of fine silky hair her fingers had investigated so thoroughly last night.

She turned away, and her body protested the sudden move. Hugging her arms around herself, she stood in the middle of the floor. She wasn't cold; actually, she felt a little too warm, but she'd only thrown on a shirt, and she felt very exposed.

"Why did they leave?"

She glanced at him. He was leaning against the desk now, his arms folded across his chest, staring at the walls and roof as if trying to judge their strength. "They seem to know whether the quake is going to be a large one or just a tremor," she said absently. "If it's going to be large, they get away from land, because they could be washed ashore and stranded if there's any kind of tidal wave."

He pushed himself away from the desk and came toward her. "What are you going to do?" He'd already decided what she was going to do, but it would be easier on both of them if she made the same decision.

"I'm going to take their advice and leave. That is—" she smiled crookedly "—if your plane's available for hire."

"I imagine we can come to terms," he said gravely; then his tone became brisk. "I'll get the plane ready, then come back up for you." He caught her chin in his hand and kissed her, hard. "Be ready to go in twenty minutes."

He had on his sweater and boots and was out the door in less than sixty seconds. Erin dressed rapidly in a pair of corduroy jeans, sneakers and a flannel shirt over a silk turtleneck. Then she ran to the computer and started making copies on floppy disks of everything stored in its hard-disk memory. Perhaps she should be grateful for the distraction of an earthquake, she thought, feeding another disk into the machine. When Martha called, she had been lying awake, wondering if she had the courage to face him when he woke up. She'd been wishing desperately that there was someplace on the island where he couldn't find her, so that she could try to come to terms with the startling discoveries she had made about herself during the night. She had wanted to experience his fire; what she hadn't guessed was that there was a corresponding fire in her. He had fed it, encouraged it to burn out of control, and a lifetime of thinking of herself as a reserved, self-controlled woman hadn't prepared her to handle the wildly primitive responses he had provoked.

She felt her cheeks color. She remembered writhing and straining against him, pleading for—*demanding*—still more of his mouth, his hands, his body. Her voice had been low and rough, like the growl of a hungry animal. He'd met her demands, and her moaning cries echoed in her memory with excruciating clarity. It should frighten her to know that he could draw those responses from her so easily, that he had that kind of power over her, Erin thought, and it did. It embarrassed her a little, too, that she had been so...so wanton. But her fear and embarrassment weren't enough to keep her from wanting to burn with that fire again.

The floor shifted subtly beneath her feet, and the dishes and pots and pans rattled in the kitchen as a small tremor suddenly shook the Quonset hut. It was followed almost immediately by a second, a little stronger. She hadn't resolved her conflict this morning lying beside him, and she wasn't going to have a chance to resolve it now, either, she realized.

Christian worked the control to see if the flaps were responding. The threat of an earthquake provided the solution to two problems. He'd wanted to contact Eisley to have him check out a couple of things, but had been unable to do so from here. He'd also wished there was a way to get her off the island, short of tying her up and throwing her onto the plane. She was too vulnerable here. He wanted her somewhere safer, and he knew just the place.

He climbed out of the plane and glanced at the sky. The sunshine and light breezes of yesterday seemed like an illusion now. A thick layer of clouds obscured the sun, and the breeze had become a near gale. He looked up to see Erin hurrying down the dock with just a small waterproof box and a pet carrier. Above the whine of the wind, he could hear Oscar loudly expressing his opinion of his confinement.

"What's in the box?" he asked as he took it from her and stowed it in the plane.

"Copies of all the information I had in the computer here." She looked at the wrench in his hand. "Is your plane ready to fly?"

"It better be," he said tersely. "I've jury-rigged the flaps, and everything else checks out okay." He raised an eyebrow as he reached for the cat carrier. "Where are your clothes?"

"They can wait. I'd like to take some of my equipment. The re—"

They both heard the rumble, like that of a distant freight train, at the same time. A wave of motion began at the crest of the hill behind the Quonset hut. It rippled downward through the long grass, and the hut appeared to shift on its foundation. Then the rocks on the beach began skittering and jumping like drops of water on a hot griddle. The dock rose and fell, as if a heavy swell had passed beneath it.

Erin turned to watch the wave travel across the bay. "That was a pretty strong one," she said, her voice tight with worry.

"Come on." He seized her hand and started for the beach. "If you want your equipment, we'd better hurry. I don't think we have much time left."

"Christian, no!" She tried to hold him back.

He snapped around to look at her questioningly.

"No," she said more quietly. "I don't think we should take the chance. The equipment doesn't matter." Erin spared a fleeting thought for the thousands of dollars' worth of electronics she was abandoning. "I've already got the most important things—Oscar and the language disks." And you, she added silently. "Let's go."

He didn't argue. Still holding her hand, he steadied her when she stepped onto the pontoon, then freed her hand to hold the door open against the wind.

Erin paused for a moment to look back at the Quonset hut. A significant part of her life had been spent here, she thought, not in terms of time, but events. She glanced at the man beside her. Perhaps the most significant part.

Christian saw her mouth tremble; then her jaw clenched as she took a last look at the Quonset hut. "I'm ready," she said in a steady voice and climbed aboard.

With his hand at the small of her back, he gave her a boost. After casting off the mooring lines, he climbed in after her and settled into his seat. "Strap yourself in," he reminded her as he fastened his own seat belt.

For the next few minutes he was occupied with taxiing away from the dock and to the opposite end of the bay, so they could take off into the wind. Surreptitiously, Erin watched him. His large, strong hands controlled the airplane with the same sureness he had used to control her body the night before. The Cessna bounced over the choppy waves, building up speed, until it was barely skimming the whitecaps. He pulled back on the stick, and they rose smoothly.

He banked and turned the plane in a full circle over the island, as if saying farewell. Resolutely, Erin kept her eyes straight ahead, resisting the temptation to look down. Only when she felt the plane level and straighten out did she realize that she had been sitting bolt upright, her body tensed and her fingers knotted together.

Christian's hand closed over both of hers. "How are you doing?"

Even with the engine noise and the rushing wind, Erin could hear the gentle concern in his voice. She looked over at him with a smile. "I'm doing fine." She forced herself to relax and sit back. Her fingers loosened and curled around his. She hadn't been tense because she had worried about his ability to fly the small plane—she had never doubted it. She'd been trying to absorb the unexpectedly sharp pain she'd felt at leaving the island. Her smile turned a little ragged around the edges. "You know—" she tried to laugh, but her voice caught and the laugh came out sounding like a sob "—that old hut, awful as it was, was the closest thing I had to a home."

In his eyes she saw regret and compassion and another emotion she couldn't quite read. His hand slipped up her arm, and he laid the back of his fingers against her cheek, then stroked her skin in a gentle caress. She caught his hand in hers, holding it still for a moment; then, knowing he needed both hands to handle the plane in the shifting winds, she laid it gently back on the controls.

After a few minutes his mouth quirked into a wry grimace. "It's probably a little late to ask now, but you don't get airsick, do you?"

From the tone of his voice she knew that he was fervently hoping she didn't. She shook her head, her laughter genuine this time. "No, I don't get airsick."

It was a good thing she didn't, Erin thought half an hour later, because if she did, by now she'd be heaving her guts out, as her grandfather had always so elegantly put it. The weather seemed to deteriorate the farther they flew, but the tough little plane took it in stride. Gathering up his charts and maps again after hitting yet another air pocket, Erin said, "Why don't you let me navigate?"

After satisfying himself that she knew how to read the complicated maps and how to chart a course, he turned the job over to her. "Where are we headed? Adak?" she asked.

"No," Christian said briefly. "Anchorage." At her look of obvious surprise, he added casually, "I carry extra fuel for long-distance flying, so there's no need to stop. Also, if the whales are right, this whole area is going to be unstable. We could easily find ourselves in the same trouble on Adak as we were on your island." And there was no need to take the chance of running into Sam Akiachak.

Erin accepted that and began plotting a course toward Anchorage.

Even without any solid evidence, Christian knew it was the Aleut pilot who had sabotaged his plane. He'd had the opportunity and the knowledge, and Christian was fairly sure of Akiachak's motive. Not just the motive for sabotaging the plane—which was to keep Erin isolated—but his motive for being involved in the plot to keep Erin isolated. He would have Eisley check that out, too. The person interested in making sure Erin stayed unprotected would know soon enough that she was no longer on the island, because he knew that as soon as Akiachak thought up another excuse, he would be back to make sure the stranger had left. And now, when word reached Adak of the earthquakes in Erin's area, he would have a better reason than flying several hundred miles out of his way to deliver a couple of letters, Christian thought sardonically. Akiachak would know Erin must have left with her unexpected guest and would report accordingly, but by then Christian would have taken her to the one place where he could be certain she'd be safe—his own island. He was sure he could find an argument that would convince her to stay with him for the few days it would take Eisley to confirm the identity of Akiachak's boss and deal with him. He glanced at the blond head bent over a map. It was convincing her to stay longer that was going to be hard.

The only consolation to be found in the rotten weather, Erin decided, was the tail wind they picked up over the Bering Sea. It blew them into Anchorage early in the afternoon, and she directed Christian to a small seaplane port on the outskirts of the city. "There it is," she said, pointing to a sign advertising the available services painted on the roof of a long, ramshackle building beside the dock. She had to raise her voice over Oscar's; he had been stridently reminding them for the past hour that somebody had forgotten to put any food in his carrier.

The building beside the dock housed a café and small store. While Christian refueled the plane, she went inside to find something to stave off Oscar's imminent starvation. There was no pet food, but she found tuna and took a can to the counter along with an opener she'd found in another aisle. Only when the clerk had rung up her purchases did she realize that she had no money. In the rush of leaving, she hadn't thought to get the expense money she kept to pay Sam for the groceries he brought. Then she remembered that Christian didn't have any, either, and he was filling his plane with gallons and gallons of fuel!

She was starting a mumbled, incoherent explanation to the clerk when Christian walked in and laid several bills on the counter, along with a chit for the fuel. "That, too," he said to the clerk, pointing to the tuna and the opener.

"Where did you get the money?" Erin asked almost accusingly. "You didn't have any when I found you."

"I keep my wallet in the console when I'm flying. It's uncomfortable to sit on," he said equably, accepting his change. He put the bills in a plain black leather wallet, which he tucked in his back pocket, then dropped the few coins in a charity container on the counter, picked up Erin's purchases and took her by the arm.

Feeling suddenly numb, Erin let him lead her outside. My God, this is goodbye, she realized. She would have to wait here in Anchorage to find out conditions in the area around the island, then make arrangements to go back as soon as they stabilized. He would naturally be anxious to go home—and she would never see him again, never laugh and talk and tease with him again, never again know that mind-shattering joy that had been hers too briefly, never tell him that she had fallen . . .

She wanted to scream at the unfairness of it. Instead, in silent misery, she watched him cross the dock after leaving her in front of the café next to the store. He'd said something to her, but she hadn't heard it. He disappeared inside the plane, then climbed back out a couple of minutes later without the tuna. He spent several more minutes checking the brace on the pontoon strut and something on the back edge of the wing. He was already anxious to leave, she thought. He was probably trying to think of a graceful way to say goodbye that wouldn't embarrass either of them. Eventually she and their past few days together and all that had happened to them would take on the unreal quality of a dream—if he ever thought of her at all. Erin knew she would never forget him.

Maybe he would—no. Erin stopped that wild hope before it could fully form. After his experience, he wouldn't want to wait around to fly her back out to the island. Her island was the last place he would want to go. He came walking toward her, and Erin tried to brace herself.

"Do you want to get something to eat here—" Christian nodded toward the café behind her "—or look for someplace—Erin? What's the matter?" He took her chin with his hand and turned her face up to his. It was pale, her eyes wide and unhappy. "Are you sick? Did that rough ride get to you?"

She realized that he must have seen something of what she was suffering in her face, and she tried to school her features to impassivity. "N-no."

His forehead furrowed with bewilderment. "Then what is it?"

She tried to pull away from him, but he simply tightened his grip, and she saw impatience beginning to edge into his puzzlement. "Look, I know you must be wanting to get back to your farm as soon as possible." Erin was proud of the steadiness of her voice. "I'll just wait here in Anchorage until I can go back to the island. There's no need for you to—"

"You won't be going back, Erin," he interrupted. He released her chin and curled his hand behind her neck.

She stared at him. "What do you mean?"

"The kid pumping gas has a radio on. I heard a news bulletin reporting that a volcano in the Russian Aleutians erupted without warning. It's putting out a lot of ash, and it's drifting eastward, so the area west of Adak has been closed, and everyone but military personnel has been evacuated. They seem to think it's going to continue erupting, so you won't be able to go back for a while. I thought you'd probably want to just go on back to Vancouver with me," he added with deliberate offhandedness. The look of misery on her face changed almost instantly to one of happiness before she managed to blank it over. She'd been unhappy because she'd had the mistaken idea that they were going to separate, he thought, and he felt an intense satisfaction.

"Yes, that would probably be best," Erin agreed, trying to match his casualness.

"Well, now that that's settled—" the hand on her neck tilted her mouth up for his kiss, then slid around her shoulders companionably, turning her into his side "—what do you want to do about lunch?"

They ate at the café on the dock and were airborne again less than an hour later. From Anchorage Christian turned southeast, and Erin mapped out a course for Ketchican, a small city at the tip of the finger of Alaska that extended down into Canada. The weather was worse than ever, and Erin remained quiet, knowing that Christian needed his full concentration to fly the plane. She didn't mind the lack of conversation, because she had something to concentrate on, too.

She completed the thought that she had started on the dock. She had fallen in love with him. Exactly when, she didn't know. Maybe it had happened when she found him on the beach, maybe when he was so caring the night Abner died, maybe.... It didn't matter when, only that it had. It wasn't until she had panicked when she thought that they were going to part that she

had realized it. Or admitted it. That didn't matter, either. What
mattered was what she was going to do about it.

She had no illusions that he would feel as if a piece of his
heart was being torn out when they eventually did part. When
she had made love with him, she had promised herself that she
would live with that decision without regret or recrimination,
no matter what happened. But after the pain she'd felt today,
she knew she had already broken part of that promise. She'd
felt regret, mind-numbing, heartbreaking, body-aching regret.
And it was right that she had, Erin thought, for how genuine
could a love be that felt no pain at the prospect of parting? And
it would only get worse the longer they were together. Was she
strong enough to bear it? Erin realized that she would have to
be, because she was too weak to deny herself the joy of being
with him.

They flew out of the storm about a hundred miles north of
Ketchican. One minute they were in a cloud with nothing to see
out the windows but gray mist, and the next the cockpit was
flooded with brilliant orange light from the setting sun. They
were too far south now for a true "midnight sun," but the sun
still set late, lingering on the western horizon to paint the sky
with every shade imaginable between the lavender at the top to
the line of molten white-gold on the horizon. The sun began its
slow slide over the edge of the world, and the sea below them
turned blood red.

Christian looked at Erin, and, as if she sensed his gaze, she
turned toward him. She smiled without saying anything, then
turned back to the beautiful sunset. That was one of the things
he liked about her, Christian realized suddenly. She didn't seem
to feel a need to fill the silences between them with chatter.
They were comfortable silences; he didn't feel a need to fill
them, either. He could talk to her, and, perhaps even more important, not talk to her. She was leaning her head back against
the seat as she looked out the window, and it wasn't long before he realized she was asleep. If the seats had been closer together, he thought wistfully, she could have laid her head in his
lap.

She didn't wake up until he was making a landing in a small inlet choked with fishing boats and other seaplanes. She sat up, pushing her hair out of her face, to peer out the window beside her. "Ketchikan?"

Her voice had the huskiness of sleep, he realized as he nodded. He'd heard that same huskiness in her voice last night, but she hadn't been sleeping then. "I thought we'd look for a place to eat, then find a hotel."

"Okay." Her response was muffled as she covered a wide yawn.

They found a coffee shop that was still open just a block from the dock. The shop catered to the crews of the fishing boats, so the food was plain and filling. Erin found she was surprisingly hungry, considering that she had spent most of the day sitting. From the waitress Christian got directions to a motel two blocks away. Erin saw the woman's surreptitious glance at their ringless hands and waited for the knowing smirk or look of censure. Instead she saw a wistfulness on the woman's face when she looked back at Christian. Too late, he's mine, Erin told her silently, then almost laughed out loud when she realized what she was thinking. She had never felt that kind of possessiveness before, and she found she rather liked it. After knowing Christian, she had begun to understand what instincts drove lionesses to fight over the right to the favors of the dominant male. As she had thought the night she'd found him, Christian Dekker would dominate any situation, not because he was loud or aggressive, but simply because it was obvious that he was an exceptional man. The woman who had him would fight to keep him.

Erin didn't see whether he used one last name or two when he registered them at the motel. She did note that the clerk handed over only one key and that he didn't seem disturbed by their lack of luggage, or that they'd arrived on foot. He might have been upset had he seen the cat carrier, she thought with secret amusement, but Christian had judiciously set Oscar down outside, out of sight of the big front office window, before they'd come in.

Back outside, he retrieved the carrier from behind a bush, both of them giggling like conspiratorial children and shushing Oscar frantically when he complained bitterly about having been abandoned. Erin suspected that they were both a little punchy from fatigue. They walked down the sidewalk in front of the numbered doors until Christian drew her to a stop. "This is it. Number 19."

He opened the door and snapped on the light. Erin could see that the room had nothing to recommend it beyond the fact that it was clean, but that was enough. The surge of energy she'd felt after dinner was already sputtering, and when Christian offered her the shower first, she didn't argue.

The motel bathroom was stocked with complimentary packets of shampoo and conditioner. She was careful to use only half of each and only one of the two bath towels, although hand towel might have been a more accurate description, Erin decided as she tried to wrap it around herself. It wouldn't reach more than two-thirds of the way, and finally she gave up and just stood naked on the bathmat, drying her hair with one of the smaller towels and wishing she had a comb. She was about to open the door a crack and ask Christian if he had one in his wallet when the door opened anyway.

Erin turned around with a gasp, reflexively trying to cover herself with the towel, then realized the foolishness of it. She dropped the towel and stood facing him. She saw the pupils of his eyes narrow as he lookcd her over slowly. Erin found nothing insulting in his thorough look; instead, she felt proud that her body seemed to please him.

"Turn around," he said, his voice raspier than usual.

Erin complied.

"Hold your arms out to the side."

She did and heard his rough sigh. Then she felt him at her back, and his arms came around her, locking across her collarbones. His sweater sleeves brushed her nipples. They were sensitive after his hungry mouth and hands the night before, and the soft wool rubbing over them instantly tightened them into hard little nubs. Erin moaned softly, then moaned again when he dropped one arm to splay his hand over her belly. His palm was scaldingly hot on her cool damp skin. He pressed her hips back, fitting her bottom against him, and she moaned a third time when she felt his arousal, hard and hot through the rough cloth.

His mouth nuzzled through her damp hair to her ear, and she felt the warm blast of his breath. "I shouldn't be touching you when you're so clean and smell so sweet," he whispered, "and I'm dirty and smell like a goat." He rotated his hand over her belly, rubbing her hips against his.

Erin wanted to tell him that he wasn't dirty and he smelled wonderful, but her throat was too tight to talk. She tried to turn in his embrace, but the arm across her chest tightened, keeping her in place.

"If you turn around, I'll never get a shower." His husky voice was full of rueful laughter. "I only came in to give you these."

He stepped back, and she felt him take her limp hand and put something in it. She looked down and saw a wide-toothed comb like the one she'd had at the hut, two toothbrushes and a tube of toothpaste. He must have gone out and found a store while she was taking a shower. She turned around to thank him for his thoughtfulness and found herself facing the closed door. She leaned her forehead on it until her momentary weakness passed. Once again he'd aroused her almost instantly, calling forth this newfound sensuality that she still wasn't certain how to deal with.

She entered the bedroom a few minutes later. "Thank you for the toothbrush and stuff," she said softly. She'd put her shirt back on, feeling a little reluctant to be naked in front of him now.

"You're welcome." He brushed a kiss over her forehead on his way into the bathroom.

Twenty minutes later Christian looked down at Erin and laughed softly. He'd been afraid that she would be asleep, he thought with wry regret. And apparently he'd been right. She was lying on her back, and her eyes were closed. The sheet over her breasts was rising and falling evenly. He snapped off the dim light on the nightstand and slid naked under the sheet beside her. As he started to ease her bare body back into his arms, she rolled over and wrapped her arms around his neck.

"What took you so long?" she whispered as she pulled his mouth down to hers.

Chapter 11

I've always thought these were the most beautiful islands in the world.'' They were following the Strait of Georgia between Vancouver Island and mainland British Columbia, and Christian was flying low enough that Erin could see each individual evergreen on the islands below. The deep blue water and steep coastlines could have been lifted from a Norwegian fjord.

Christian banked slightly to the left to pass over the northernmost of the Gulf Islands. Those were the first words she'd said in an hour, he thought. She hadn't started the flight in silence. They'd left Ketchican late, because neither of them had wanted to get out of bed. Christian smiled to himself. He would always have a particular fondness for the number nineteen. She'd talked almost nonstop once they were airborne. Chattered, he thought, laughing soundlessly as he remembered his thoughts yesterday about their comfortable silences. The chatter had been comfortable, too, and he'd been talking almost as much as she had. They'd shared childhood memories, compared notes on places they'd been, discovered they both had a secret passion for oatmeal cookies with butterscotch morsels and hated potato chips. Neither of them saw many movies or watched much television, but they both read a lot, and she'd confessed to being a hard-core detective novel junkie. He wondered what she'd say when she saw his paperback detective novels cramming his bookcase. Then, about an hour ago, she'd stopped talking.

He made a half turn over Salt Spring Island and headed east. He knew precisely when she'd stopped—when they'd flown over the northern tip of Vancouver Island, a sign that the trip was almost over. She had kept the conversation away from any talk of what they would do then, but he knew she expected them to go their separate ways. The fact that she was obviously depressed by that thought made him happy as hell.

The time was fast coming when she would find out just how much pain she could bear, Erin thought. What would he say when they landed? *Well, so long. It's been fun.* She could suggest that they see each other again, but what would they do? Go to a movie? Go out for dinner? *Date,* for God's sake? After what they'd been through together, the idea of dressing up and meeting in some restaurant to make polite dinner conversation seemed so absurd that she almost laughed out loud. She didn't, though, because she knew it wouldn't be a laugh that came out.

Finally she roused herself from her misery long enough to see that they were just passing over the distinctive saddlebags shape of Orcas Island in the San Juans. The Gulf Islands and the San Juans were all part of the same cluster of islands between Vancouver Island and the mainland, but their ownership was divided between Canada and the U.S., so each country had given their portion a different name. Orcas was on the American side—and about fifty miles south of Vancouver. "Christian, where are we going?" she asked quietly.

"Home," he said simply.

"Your home?" Even as she asked, Erin knew it was a stupid question. She didn't have a home, unless one counted that impersonal two-room apartment at the institute.

He nodded.

"I thought . . . Why?"

Because I want to see you sitting in my den with your feet up reading a detective novel, taking oatmeal cookies out of the oven in my kitchen, lying in my bed. "I thought I'd return your hospitality, show you my island," he said lightly. He glanced over at her. "You don't have to go to the institute right away, do you? After all that's happened, we both could use a couple days' R and R."

Another reprieve. Should she take it or get the execution over with? An inconsequential memory popped into her head suddenly. When she was a little girl, she and her mother used to roast marshmallows in the fireplace. Her mother would always tell her not to eat hers when they were right out of the fire, but to let them cool. But they had seemed so much sweeter when they were hot, so she'd tried to judge the exact moment when the marshmallow would have cooled enough to be bearable, but still have that supersweet taste. At least half the time she'd ended up with a scorched mouth, but the brief burst of sweetness had been worth it. Perhaps the memory wasn't so inconsequential, after all. Would another brief sweet taste be worth the pain this time? "I really should . . . no, I don't have to go back right away. I could stay . . . for a few days."

"Good," was all he said.

She looked down at the sea below them. He was circling an island, dropping steadily in altitude. The island was roughly circular and looked to be about a hundred acres in area. Most of the surface was covered with towering evergreens that marched down to the white sand beaches or to the edges of craggy gray cliffs. Through the largest gap in the trees, she saw an orchard of fruit trees about ten acres in size. Through another gap she saw a house.

Of weathered gray wood, it rambled along the top of a sheer cliff. She knew, without seeing it, that the view from the veranda running along the front would be magnificent. A wooden stairway traversed the face of the cliff, leading down to the beach below. A dock and what seemed to be a large boat house jutted out from the narrow strip of sand. As the seaplane came out of another turn, he pointed the nose straight toward the beach.

She had seen no other houses on the island when he'd flown over it. He was obviously the sole occupant and just as obviously the sole owner. Land like this was at a premium, and if anyone else had owned a piece of his island, they would have a summer home on it, at the very least.

Erin rapidly adjusted her estimation of his financial situation upward and by a considerable amount. She had assumed he lived rather modestly on a military pension, supplemented by occasional charters and the income from his apple orchard. The trees she had glimpsed looked either very old or very young, and she imagined he realized little, if any, profit from them. A one-man air-charter business, even full-time, brought in enough money to cover upkeep on the plane, provide the basic necessities of life and little else, and by his own admission, Christian didn't work at it full-time. Neither, judging by the size of Daniel's Navy pension, would his pension cover the expense of buying a plane, much less an entire island. The obvious conclusion was that he had another source of income, one he hadn't told her about.

She had considered the possibility that he might have inherited his wealth, but she discarded the notion. For one thing, nothing he had told her this morning about his childhood indicated a moneyed background. What was more significant was that nothing about him said he had ever known a life of privileged ease, even as a child. He was too tough, too resourceful. What he had, she knew instinctively, he had earned, and he had to have earned it in the years since he'd retired from the SEALs. Did those skills account for his mysterious income? And the scar on his belly? How had he "earned" that? She hadn't worked up the courage to ask him how he had acquired the scar, perhaps, she realized, because she really didn't want to know.

He brought the plane down in a perfect landing on the mirror-smooth water, then taxied toward the dock. The boat house, she realized, was an aircraft hangar. She watched him press what looked like an electronic door opener mounted on the instrument panel, and the front of the hangar glided upward. He drove the plane inside, pressed the switch again and cut the engine.

The sudden silence seemed almost unnatural. All Erin heard was the soft lapping of the water on the dock and a few popping noises from the airplane engine as it cooled.

Christian turned to her. "We're home," he announced quietly.

While he tied up the plane and performed a few post-flight tasks, Erin explored the hangar. She discovered that it was longer than it appeared from the air, and that it did house a boat after all. A sixteen-foot runabout was moored in front of the plane. She imagined he used it for traveling back and forth to the mainland or the larger islands for supplies, since it would be better than the plane for relatively short trips.

When she walked back down the dock, he was waiting for her. "Here." He handed her the box containing the language disks, then picked up Oscar's carrier and led the way through a small side door.

Outside, Christian paused on the dock as he always did when he came back home. He slowly scanned the beach, the forest behind it, the cliff and lastly the house at the top of it. He wasn't sure if he did it to make sure everything was the same as when he'd left it, or simply because he liked looking at it and taking pleasure in the knowledge that this beautiful place was his. A little of both, he suspected.

He turned to Erin, who had been waiting quietly beside him while he completed his little ritual. "This is Mary's Island, although," he added with a wry grin, "nobody seems to know who Mary was. The former owners think she might—" He broke off when he saw that she was looking at something beyond him. A split second later he heard a jingling sound.

"Hey, Clancy!"

Setting down Oscar, he whistled, then called to the large, reddish-gold dog bounding down the wooden staircase toward them. Within seconds the dog was galloping down the dock, the metal tags on his leather collar jingling cheerfully. As soon as he reached his master's feet, he dropped to a sitting position. His tail wagging madly, he barked excitedly in welcome. Christian hunkered in front of him and roughed up the dog's floppy ears with gentle affection. "Hey, boy. Did you miss me?"

The dog's behind wriggled in delight, and Christian laughed. Again, Erin had a glimpse of him as a boy, and she smiled unconsciously. The dog looked to be part Irish setter and part fence jumper. Or island hopper, she amended with a silent laugh. His fur was longish, wavy and shining with health. The feathers on his tail and front legs were free from tangles, and his coat was well-brushed.

Christian reached up and took one of Erin's hands, tugging her down beside him. Keeping her hand in his, he presented it to the dog. "Clancy, this is Erin. She belongs here now," he said quietly.

Erin waited while the dog sniffed at her hand delicately, learning her scent, then gave it a friendly lick with a long pink tongue. "Hi, Clancy," she said softly, cautiously scratching the silky fur behind the dog's ears. "You're a good boy, aren't you?" she crooned as he laid his big head on her knee.

"Good. He's accepted you," Christian said with quiet satisfaction. "He doesn't know many women, and I wasn't sure what his reaction to you would be."

"Who takes care of him when you're gone?" she asked, petting the head resting heavily on her leg. She was surprised by the keenness of the disappointment she felt that someone else lived on the island, too. She had wanted them to be alone.

"The couple next door, Ted and Nora Ryan."

Erin glanced in the direction he'd indicated, wondering how she'd missed seeing the other house. Then she laughed softly. "Next door" was across two miles of open water. She could see a scattering of weathered cottages on an island about twice the size of Christian's.

"They're semiretired and work as caretakers for the summer homes over there. They keep an eye on things when I'm away and take care of Clancy." After standing, Christian helped her to her feet, then walked over and picked up Oscar's carrier. "I think I'll save Clancy's introduction to Oscar until we get up top, where the trees are handier for climbing." He laughed ruefully. "I don't know what his reaction to a cat is going to be."

He reached for her hand and Erin quickly put it in his. Together, they started up the dock toward the beach. She glanced back to see Clancy still sitting behind them. She hadn't seen any signals or heard Christian give a command to the dog. Obviously he was extremely well-trained. Christian whistled a three-note combination, and Clancy leaped up to race after them. As soon as he reached Christian's side, he slowed to a sedate trot. Erin could hear Oscar's low growl, but the dog seemed oblivious to him.

"He's a beautiful dog. How old is he?"

"Around three and a half. He washed up on the Ryans' beach one day three winters ago, more dead than alive. There were two other puppies that washed up with him, both dead. Ted figured somebody had gotten rid of a litter they didn't want. He and Nora already had a dog, so they gave him to me."

Erin gasped softly. "How could somebody just dump them out in the ocean like that? That's hideous."

She was looking at him and saw his eyes suddenly turn bleak and empty. "Sometimes people do things that are even more hideous."

Feeling guilty for destroying the happy mood by bringing up what she suspected were difficult memories, Erin changed the subject. "How come he doesn't know many women?"

Christian stopped at the foot of the stairway leading to his house. He turned and kissed her mouth softly. "Because you're the first one I've ever brought here."

Erin savored that revelation all the way up the long climb to the top of the cliff. The stairway ended at one end of the veranda. "Oh, Christian, this is magnificent," she breathed as she stepped onto the grayed planks of the porch. The view of islands and water was unmatched by any she had ever seen, and she had spent the past twelve years of her life on coastlines all over the world.

"Wait until you see the inside."

She heard the trace of smugness in his voice and thought of a small boy showing off his treasures.

"Well, here goes. Clancy, meet Oscar."

Erin turned around to see him opening the door of the pet carrier. He didn't attempt to force Oscar to come out, just left the door open for the cat to make up his own mind. Cautiously, he stepped over the sill. He eyed the large red dog with obvious disdain, then, tail in the air, stalked slowly down the porch to look things over. Clancy, undaunted by the cat's unfriendly attitude, followed to sniff at him inquiringly. Oscar, aghast at the stranger's rude familiarity, jerked around to face him. Fur bristling, ears laid back, he swiped a paw across the dog's black nose to teach him better manners. Erin noticed, though, that he had his claws sheathed. Satisfied, Oscar turned back to resume his inspection. Clancy, looking properly abashed, followed meekly behind.

Erin turned at the short burst of astonished laughter beside her.

"Well, I'll be damned. I never figured that." Christian laughed again, shaking his head. "I thought we'd end up having to rescue Oscar from some pine tree."

Erin laughed with him. "Oscar will keep Clancy in line. He's an old street fighter from way back." She took his hand and led him over to a door in the back of the house. "Show me the inside," she said.

Two doors opened off the veranda. He unlocked the nearest one, a French door, and Erin took a few steps inside, then stopped short in surprise. "Oh, I thought this would be the living room."

Christian stood beside her, smiling slightly. "It is unusual for a bedroom to have an outside door, but the original owner built the house this way," he explained. "He did it for the view, I imagine, or for a shortcut to the porch. Whatever his reason, I'm glad he did." He looked down at her. "I like it."

"I do, too," Erin murmured, walking farther into the room. The focal point was an alcove bed, faced with oak panels carved with an elegantly simple pattern of twining leaves. A lighted bookcase formed the headboard. The bed was large, king-size at least, but the closet-like construction made it seem cozy. Erin could imagine lying in it on a stormy night, a fire in the little tile stove across the way, and feeling that nothing in the world could ever harm you. The rest of the furniture was functional and simply designed, some of it modern, some of it, like the settee placed diagonally in front of the windows, antique. There were no frills; it was an eloquently masculine room. "How long did it take you to get this bed?" she asked wonderingly.

"I made it. I worked on it off and on for about a year."

His shrug was indifferent, but there was an unmistakable pride in his voice. And well there should be, Erin thought as he showed her the rest of the house. There were two more bedrooms, both with alcove beds, also. One, with rows of drawers beneath the boxed bed, had the definite look of a child's bedroom.

"The house had been abandoned for about ten years when I bought it four years ago," he said, showing her into the kitchen. Erin drew a quick breath at the sight of the carved pine table in the eating nook, the golden pine cabinetry, the plain white tile counters and the gleaming chrome appliances. "The frame was still solid, but I had to gut the place down to the studs." He looked around the room with obvious satisfaction. "It took four years and a hell of a lot of work, but it was worth it."

"Yes, it was. You have the most beautiful house I've ever seen," Erin said sincerely, and she felt a vicious stab of jealousy for the woman who would eventually get to live in it. For it was obvious he had built the house with a wife and family in mind.

After a few days, she began to entertain the cautious hope that that woman might be her. She knew it was foolish and dangerous and could only lead to even worse heartbreak, but she was too human not to hope. He said nothing about her leaving, and when she had tentatively brought the subject up on the third day, he'd simply brushed it aside and begun telling her about the family of sea otters that lived in a cave on the north side of the island.

On her island, their togetherness had been enforced by the fact that there was no one else around. He could have talked to her, kissed her, made love to her, because she was the only entertainment available, Erin had told herself brutally, but they were back in civilization now, with other women available, and he showed no desire for anyone else's company. Her hope, like a tiny tree growing in the shade of a huge boulder, grew slowly out of the darkness and toward the sun.

The afternoon of their arrival, Erin had asked about a telephone.

"I don't have one. The underwater cable runs right by the island, but I've never bothered to have a line run here." He smiled at her. "I guess I better, though. Why do you want a phone?" he added.

"I really should let someone at the institute know where I am. When they hear about the earthquake and the evacuation, they're going to wonder what happened to me."

Rapidly Christian considered his choices. He could make up some lame excuse about the boat not running right now, but then she might insist on taking the plane. Although it made him vaguely uneasy, he decided there could be no harm in letting her call. She was well-protected here; no one could get to her. In fact, the more he thought about it, Christian decided it might be a good idea for her to call. Akiachak's boss had probably already traced his name through the registry of pilot licenses and knew where he lived. If the man did a little more checking in the right places, he would realize that it was no accident that Erin was with him, and it might prompt him into doing something rash. And he himself needed to get in touch with Eisley, anyway.

"All right. Let's go over to Orcas. You can make a call from there, and—" he grinned at her "—maybe add a little variety to your wardrobe."

Looking down at herself, Erin considered the clothes she'd been wearing for days. "Well, I suppose I could get another pair of socks," she said, straight-faced.

The powerful runabout made the trip to Orcas in less than half an hour. They tied up at the public dock, and, as they walked to town, several men hailed Christian by name. He returned their greetings but didn't stop to talk. Erin knew she was the object of several speculative looks and felt a satisfaction almost as intense as when he had told her that she was the first woman he'd ever brought home. If the men on the dock were used to seeing him with a woman, she reasoned, they wouldn't be so interested in her.

They climbed up the hill to town, and Christian led her into the first store they came to. Once they were inside, she realized it wasn't a store at all, but the entrance to a group of small shops and restaurants clustered around an open square. The layout and the steep-roofed, painted clapboard buildings were reminiscent of a New England fishing village.

"There are several public phones here," Christian said, taking her arm to guide her around a corner to a bank of telephones. He gave her a quarter and took the phone at the other end of the row for himself. Erin inserted the coin, then paused to stare at him thoughtfully. Had he gone to the other end to give her privacy for her call, or because he wanted privacy for his own? He, too, put in a quarter, then rapidly punched more buttons than were necessary for a local call. She waited, but he didn't put in any more money. The number he was calling rang for what seemed like a very long time before he began speaking. She could tell that the call was serious by the sober, almost grim, expression on his face. He spoke rapidly, listened for a minute or so, then shook his head forcefully and began speaking again.

The recorded voice in her ear was insisting that she either dial a number or hang up, and Erin hastily punched the button for the operator. He came on the line, and she gave him her credit-card number, which she had memorized, and Phillip Damion's private number. The line was busy, and the operator came back on the line. Did she want to try another number?

Absently Erin gave the public number for the institute. Christian was listening again, frowning now, as if he didn't like what he was hearing. A loud beep in her ear startled her, and Erin pulled the phone away to stare at it; then she understood that she had heard the beep on the phone machine. It must be the weekend, she realized. On the island she always lost track of the date because it simply wasn't important. Quickly Erin began to speak, feeling awkward, as she always did, when she had to talk to a machine. "This is Erin Mathias. I've left the island because of the eruption. I'm staying with a—a friend on Mary's Island, one of the San Juans. There's no phone so if you—"

The machine cut her off, and she heard the dial tone. Erin hung up and looked down the row. Christian was gone. She looked around, but she didn't see him anywhere. After standing by the phones for a minute, she decided to go into the first shop. It looked like it sold clothes, and she would be able to see Christian through the wide window if he passed by.

Erin riffled through a rack of shorts. Who had he been talking to? He hadn't been having a friendly conversation with someone; it had almost looked as if he were making some kind of report. She felt a slight uneasiness tickle up her spine, and it reminded her that there were still some very large gaps in what she knew about him.

The uneasiness she felt wasn't because she was concerned for herself. She felt a sense of security with him that she'd never known with any other human being. She was concerned for him. From chance remarks that she'd overheard between Daniel and his friend Quinn Eisley, she knew that several of the men they'd worked with had become private mercenaries. Was that what Christian Dekker was? His SEAL training would have made him a prime candidate for that kind of work, and it could explain the scar and his money.

The idea chilled her; then she thought of the house she'd just seen. He'd said it had taken him four years to rebuild it. She knew it must have been four years of full-time work, not weekend puttering. And she'd seen all the new young trees in the orchard they'd flown over. He couldn't have been working at anything else. If he had been a mercenary, he hadn't been one for the past four years. And anyway, she told herself, his past was his own; it was his present that mattered. The phone call had undoubtedly been something innocent, like a call to the agricultural agent about tree borers or something, she decided wryly.

"I think those would be a little big, don't you?"

Erin turned around quickly at the sound of his deep raspy voice behind her. She smiled, then asked, "What?"

"Those shorts." He reached past her, and Erin turned to follow his hand. She saw that she was holding a pair of size sixteen shorts and realized she'd been paying no attention at all. He reached back and pulled out two pairs, one khaki, the other navy blue. He held them up. "Here. These are more your size."

Erin took the hangers from him, glancing at the tags. He had judged her size exactly. She felt her cheeks color. He hadn't measured them by sight, but by touch. The skin on her hips tingled just as it did when he closed his big hands around her when they made love. She could almost feel them now, his long blunt fingers pressing into her flesh, his thumbs rotating over her hip bones. Her face grew hotter as she remembered the things he did then. She glanced up and saw that the pupils of his eyes had narrowed to pinpoints, the ice-blue color almost incandescent, as he stared down at her. He was remembering, too, and a hot ribbon of excitement curled in the pit of her stomach.

He shoved his hands into his pockets and spun on his heel. She heard him clear his throat, but his voice still came out a little hoarse. "Why don't you try those on?"

Erin found an older saleslady, who gave her rumpled corduroys and flannel shirt a pitying look and promptly escorted her to a dressing room. They fit perfectly, of course. She glanced at the price tags, then decided to take both pairs anyway. She could afford to splurge a little.

She was zipping her corduroys when the saleslady discreetly pulled aside the curtain and handed in two shirts. "Your husband said to try these, too," she said, adding, "he has very good taste."

Erin took the red and white striped terry top and the soft, silky island print in bright pastels. They were both the right size. "Yes, he does," she said in a thin voice. Of course the lady would mistakenly think he was her husband. They were together, and he was buying her clothes. Erin couldn't see the point of correcting her.

And he really was going to have to buy her clothes, she realized. She had no money, and no way to get any without some kind of identification. "I'll take these," she said and followed the saleslady out.

"Christian, I don't have any money," she murmured under her breath when she was standing beside him again.

"I know," he said. He was looking through a rack of tank tops. He pulled one out, held it up to her, looked at it critically, then shook his head and put it back.

"How did you know?" she asked, noticing a top in a soft rose that she secretly coveted.

He gave her corduroy jeans a dry look. "Erin, the way those pants fit, I'd know if you had a dime in your pocket, let alone a wallet." He held the rose top under her chin, nodded and laid it over his arm. That was when Erin noticed the white clam diggers underneath them.

"Christian, that's enough," she said firmly.

"Why? We can afford it, dear." His tone was innocent.

The saleslady must have referred to her as his wife. She ignored the pang in her heart that wished it was true. "Yes, I can afford it." She put emphasis on the "I." "That's not the point. I already owe you for half the motel room, and for my meals. I should help pay for the fuel for your plane, too, and I don't like owing money."

Christian started to laugh, then realized that she was serious. He put his hand over his mouth to cover his smile. "I know you're good for it, Erin," he said solemnly.

She gave him a sharp look and was starting to say something else when the saleslady returned. She was carrying several sundresses, and Erin groaned inside. The woman obviously thought she had a hot prospect.

Ignoring her, the saleslady addressed Christian. "One of these would look very nice on your wife," she said with what Erin thought was just a touch too much simper.

Christian shook his head. "I don't think so," he said decisively. "I think that one, over there on the mannequin, would be better."

Erin and the other woman turned automatically in the direction he was pointing. Erin knew immediately which dress he meant, although there were several mannequins in that general direction. It was a halter style made up in a soft sea-green georgette with yards and yards of filmy skirt. Damn, why did he have to be right?

Apparently the saleslady knew which dress he meant and thought he was right, too. "A much better choice, sir," she said, already crossing the store.

"Christian!" Erin said furiously under her breath.

"It's a gift, Erin. Consider it a late birthday present. Besides—" he wove his hand into her hair, rubbing his thumb at the corner of her mouth "—how often do you find a dress that's the same exact color as your eyes?"

His thumb teased a smile from her reluctant lips. "Not very often," she agreed softly. "Thank you."

The saleslady returned with the dress on a padded hanger. "Anything else?" she asked brightly.

"Yes, I need some underwear," Erin said, giving Christian a look that defied him to pick that out, too. He didn't, stepping down to the end of the counter, and quickly Erin picked out a couple of bras and some panties. As an afterthought she added a pair of white leather sandals. They would go with the shorts, yet be dressy enough for the sea-green dress.

The saleslady was totalling up her purchases when Christian came back to stand beside her.

"What about a swimsuit?"

"I don't need one," she said stubbornly.

She felt his lips brush her ear. "Good. I prefer skinny-dipping, too," he murmured seductively. "Ted Ryan will like it, too. He's got a good telescope."

Erin jerked her head away to glare at him; then her mouth started to twitch. He was waggling his eyebrows at her in a leer so outrageous that she couldn't possibly take offense. Laughing, she leaned weakly on his chest. "All right. I give up. I'll get a swimsuit, but that's it. No more!"

To her surprise, the swimsuit he picked off the rack was not a bikini or a one-piece cut to the waist, top and bottom. He chose a plain black racing suit with a conservative cut—exactly the one she would have chosen if she'd seen it first. In fact, all his selections reflected her taste, she thought, and felt touched that he had given them so much consideration.

After leaving the shop, they found a grocery store, then headed back to the island. It was just sunset when they returned. Erin watched him perform the same small ritual he had when they'd first arrived, turning in a slow circle in the middle of the dock to look over his island home. She could understand why he did it. The specialness of this place almost demanded a ceremony to honor it. She waited beside him, silently celebrating the peaceful beauty of his home.

When he had finished, they walked down the dock and across the strip of beach to the steps. As she was starting to climb, he touched her shoulder. "Look," he said quietly, lifting his hand to point to a small island between his and the Ryans'. The island was hardly bigger than the average-sized house. There was one lone tree on it, a snag silhouetted against the brilliant sunset. The top had an odd, mushroomed appearance, and when Erin saw movement there, she realized it was a nest. A large bird launched itself from the nest and became a black shadow swooping across the setting sun. It glided toward their island and headed for a pair of gulls feeding on a fish down the beach. The bird made no sound, but the gulls leaped up suddenly and flapped away, squawking. The big bird extended its feet and snatched the fish up in its talons; then its wings beat strongly, and it swept upward.

"It's an eagle," she cried delightedly.

"A bald eagle," Christian confirmed. "There's a pair of them." Erin looked up and saw that there was another bird moving in the nest. "They came the year I did. They migrate every fall, then return in the spring to raise another chick."

As they watched, the adult eagle returned to the nest, and Erin saw a flurry of movement, then heard a thin chittering cry drift over the water. She looked back to the man standing beside her. He was watching the eagles, a soft smile lighting his face. He turned to her, and his smile became softer, sweeter. Erin was glad he didn't say anything. Words would have been intrusive. He just wrapped his arm around her shoulders, and, together, they walked up the cliff to his house.

As they had done on her island, they prepared dinner together: steaks, salads, French rolls and the most enormous baked potatoes Erin had ever seen. Christian ate his, and most of hers, too. He inhaled food, Erin thought, but then, he was a big man. Still, it amazed her that there wasn't even a molecule of fat on his lean, hard body.

After dinner, they carried their glasses of wine out to the veranda to watch the stars come out. Erin had pulled her hair up into a loose knot and was wearing the sea-green dress. Christian had changed into bleached denim jeans and a soft cream knit shirt. He sat down in an oversize wicker chair, and she started to take the chair on the other side. As she stepped in front of him, he reached up and caught her waist, pulling her down onto his lap. He snugged her between his thighs, her back against his chest, and, settling back in the chair, he stretched one leg out, bracing his foot on the railing. Erin kicked off her sandals and stretched out her legs, too, resting her bare heels on the railing.

There was a soft breeze blowing the sweet scent of Spanish broom to them and tinkling the wind chimes hung over their heads. Idly Erin stroked her hand over the soft denim covering his thigh. "I bet you were glad to finally have something else to wear besides that sweater and pants."

"Uh-huh. I can't decide whether to burn them or have them bronzed. Those clothes have a lot of history."

Her soft laughter joined his in the darkness; then they were quiet, content to watch the stars twinkle and shine in the midnight-blue sky. Far across the water Erin could see a few lights, but it was so dark around them that they could have been the only two people in the world. Supremely happy and feeling marvelously lazy, Erin rested her head on his shoulder to watch the ocean glimmer under the moonlight. Then she looked at the sky for a while, before turning back to the ocean.

Slowly she sat forward. "Christian, what is that?"

He heard the astonishment and wonder in her voice. He had had his eyes closed, savoring the warmth of her body seeping into his, filling all the cold dark places. When she moved, he opened his eyes. "It's a mirage. We have a lot of them here."

"It looks so real," she murmured. About a mile from shore a city rose out of the sea. It glowed with an ethereal light, shimmering as if diamond dust had been scattered over it. The buildings' walls merged with one another so that there were no gaps between them. The roofs rose at different elevations, with sections of the dark star-scattered sky framed between them. "You've seen it before?" Erin whispered, almost afraid that even the sound of a normal voice might destroy it.

He spoke softly, too. "A few times. It's always a little different. There's another one that looks like a forest. I've seen that several times, too."

They watched the magical city in silence until the breeze quickened. The city glowed more brightly for an instant; then the mirage seemed to dissolve, blown away by the wind. Erin felt his sigh merge with hers.

His hand brushed up her bare arm and across her shoulder to the halter of her gown. It slipped over the hollow at the base of her throat, but his fingers didn't trespass under the fabric on the other side. Instead his hand glided down to close over her breast. His palm cupped it, and Erin felt it grow full and heavy. A heavy fullness began to grow gradually in her lower body, too, while his long fingers shaped the nipple through the fabric, bringing it to an aching hardness. Somehow the fabric between them made it more arousing than if his hand had been under her dress on bare skin. The material had just a hint of stiffness, and she found the slight scratchiness rubbing and sliding over the ultrasensitive nipple incredibly erotic.

Her head arched back slowly against his shoulder while he strung soft, biting kisses along her throat. She turned and captured his mouth in a hot, slow kiss. Their tongues stroked with the same easy rhythm as his hand on her breast. Gradually his knee rose, and her hand slipped to the inside of his thigh, rubbing up and down, heating the soft denim with the friction of her palm. Her knuckles brushed the growing hardness between his thighs, and she heard him growl softly deep in his throat. Erin no longer feared the power he had to raise that wildfire response in her, because she had learned that she had the same power over him.

His other hand dropped to her lap. Her legs shifted languidly, and his fingers searched through the soft fabric until they closed over the small mound he was seeking. The heel of his hand began a gentle grinding motion that generated a heat deep inside her. Her hand stroked higher; his answering growl was deeper. The sensations produced by making love with their clothes on were delicious, but after a time their bodies wanted both less—and less restriction and more—the even more delicious feel of bare skin on bare skin.

Christian slid one arm under Erin's knees and the other around her back. He stood easily with her in his arms and carried her down the veranda to the last door. He paused, and she reached out to turn the knob. After nudging the door open with his shoulder, he carried her through, leaving the door open to the soft breeze.

He set her on her feet by the alcove bed, and they played the game of undressing each other. First he loosened the few pins holding her hair, drawing them out one at a time until her hair cascaded down over his hands, shining palely in the moonlight. He reached behind her neck and unfastened the halter, then drew the dress up a handful at a time, enjoying her shiver of anticipation. Finally he pulled it over her head, leaving her clad only in lacy panties. Erin slid her hands under his shirt and raked her nails delicately around his waist, enjoying his small shudder. She gripped the shirt and worked it slowly over his shoulders and head. It joined her dress on the settee. Taking her time, she unfastened the button at his waist, then pulled the zipper down millimeter by millimeter. Her hands slid inside his pants and tugged them slowly down over his hips and long muscled legs. He stepped out of them, wearing only his white briefs, and they landed atop the growing pile of discarded clothing.

When Erin stood up, he pulled her into his gentle embrace. She wrapped her arms around his waist, pressing her cheek against his strong heartbeat. The warm breeze was soft on their naked skin, and for a few moments they were happy just to hold each other, enjoying the simple pleasure of being together.

At last he pulled down the quilt and sheet and eased Erin back on the bed. He slid her panties down her legs, pushed off his briefs and joined her on the mattress. They began kissing again, clinging, incredibly soft kisses. Their hands on each other became more curious, their touches longer and more demanding, but the pace of their lovemaking remained unhurried, in tune with the soft rhythms of the night and the whispering ebb and flow of the sea below.

His blunt fingertips gently traced the puckered tip of her breast; then his hard palm rubbed down the cool, smooth flesh of her stomach. He paused to circle her navel and discovered that the tip of his little finger exactly filled it. His hand traveled lower, his fingers seeking her warmth, exploring shallowly at first, then gradually deeper.

Her fingernails scratched lightly down his ribs and across his belly, making him suck in his breath. Erin laughed softly; then the laugh caught in her throat, becoming a moan as his fingers turned slowly. Her hand curled around him, stroking with light, airy motions, feeling him grow stronger while he sighed letting out a long ragged breath.

They shifted as one, and he entered her as easily as slipping into a warm pool. He pulled her closer, and they lay still while her gentle inner pulsings wrapped them both in soft sensation.

He felt her quiver gently once, then began slowly rotating his hips. His hands drew her thighs around him then moved up to caress her breast. He looked down into her eyes as his body caressed hers with a slow, steady beat. Her smile blurred, and her eyes drifted shut.

They moved in a concert of unity where each seemed to know what the other wanted. She tightened her legs around his hips and raked the backs of his thighs lightly with her toes. His measured pace became more ragged and faster, like their breathing. He cupped her buttocks, pressing himself deeper, and he heard her soft cry of pleasure. Arching above her, he drove deep, and she accepted him joyfully; the elemental force that had been building in both of them was now forcing them to speed. It burst free, and Erin cried out his name in a long, choking moan. Dimly she heard his hoarse shout of ecstasy.

She fell asleep almost immediately. Christian gathered her to him and rolled onto his side. His arms and heart full, he, too slept.

Chapter 12

Slowly, Erin opened her eyes. She shut them again. She didn't want to wake up, didn't want to move, didn't want to do anything that would disturb this wonderful feeling of sated slothfulness. It was the fifth morning she had woken up in this marvelous bed, and she still couldn't quite believe she was here. Sometimes she wondered if she weren't living in the mirage she'd seen that first night.

Finally she forced her eyes to open again. The bed beside her was empty, and she could smell coffee. She really should get up, she thought guiltily. But she didn't. Instead she lay on her stomach, her chin on her arms, laughing at the sight of Oscar washing Clancy's face where the two of them lay by the French door. The two animals had worked out a friendly, if rather strange, relationship.

A movement near the door caught her eye, and she rolled over to see Christian coming toward her carrying two mugs of coffee, wearing just a smile. He was, she had learned, completely unself-conscious about his nudity. She hadn't quite reached that stage yet, she thought wryly as she pulled the sheet higher over her breasts. Rising up on one elbow, she enjoyed his approach.

"What are you grinning about?"

She gave him a look of wicked innocence. "Oh, I was just thinking what cute legs you have." She had never realized how much fun this kind of bedroom teasing could be, but then, she had never been relaxed and comfortable enough in a bedroom—or anyplace else—to try it.

Deliberately Christian set the two mugs on the bookcase; then, his arms held out wide and his fingers hooked like claws, he advanced on her like a big blond bear. Gasping in mock horror, Erin cowered in the corner. Her gasps dissolved into helpless giggles as he fell on her and pretended to gnaw on her neck, growling ferociously as he rubbed his stubbled jaw over her throat. She struggled, not very hard, until she was too weak with laughter to move.

Christian shoved himself up and glared down at her. "Behave, or you don't get any coffee, and I've noticed—" he gave her indolently sprawled body a significant look "—that you can't seem to get moving without it." She made a rude face, and he laughed, leaning down to give her nose a quick bite that made her giggle again. Rolling off her, he reached for the mugs. He passed one to Erin, then relaxed against the pillows with his own. He had never felt so happy and at peace, he marveled. And all because of the woman beside him.

She completed his home. These past four years he'd unconsciously been building a nest, he thought humorously, like some male bird, waiting for a female to hop by and like it well enough to settle in. All that time, although it amazed him to admit it, he'd wanted to be domesticated. He'd wanted someone to share the house with, someone to have children with . . . someone to spend his life with. And now he'd found her.

Eisley had thought he would have the information they needed by today, and then they could take action. Afterward, he would explain everything to Erin, but even as mellow as he was feeling right now, Christian thought sardonically, he couldn't fool himself into thinking that she would be a good sport about it. She was going to be mad as hell. But he had to believe that she would eventually forgive him; then he was going to ask her to share the house and his life. She needed a home, and he had one to offer. He knew she loved the island, and, unless he was misinterpreting that soft light in her eyes, she loved him, too. Surely that would be enough.

He glanced over and saw her watching him with a hazy smile on her face. He took her empty mug out of her hand and set it down with his. Wrapping her in his arms, he pulled her to him for a long good-morning kiss. They rolled across the bed lazily, with Erin ending up sprawled on top of him.

Erin rubbed her nose in the hollow between his shoulder and strong neck. She smelled the clean salt tang that was uniquely his own and the darker, earthier scent that reminded her of how they had spent a good part of the night. If you could bottle that, women would be causing riots in stores everywhere, she thought with a secret smile. He nudged her with his chin and caught her mouth in another long, lazy kiss. His tongue tasted her thoroughly, and Erin closed her eyes to concentrate on the splinters of delight piercing her so sweetly.

His mouth left hers reluctantly, and Christian framed her face in his hands. "How do you feel about going diving again?" he said quietly. She had gone swimming with him in the shallows near the dock, but she hadn't mentioned diving again. Christian suspected that while her conscious memory of the killer whale attacking her was fading, her subconscious hadn't forgotten it at all. He'd seen similar reactions in men who had survived shark attacks and knew that if she didn't get back in the water soon, she might never dive again.

"Scared," she said honestly.

He searched her eyes and saw her fear. "That's understandable." He paused for a moment. "Will you come with me this morning? I have tanks, masks, all the necessary equipment."

He was putting subtle pressure on her, but she recognized the wisdom behind it. Applying the same principle of getting right back on after falling off a horse, she needed to dive again to dispel her irrational fear of another attack. "I'll come," she said quietly.

He didn't give her a chance to change her mind, Erin thought wryly. Immediately he pulled her from his cozy bed, and fifteen minutes later they were in the runabout, heading for a shallow lagoon on the other side of the island. From the speed with which he had organized their equipment, Erin knew that this hadn't been a spur-of-the moment offer, but something he'd planned in advance.

It was a beautiful morning, with a clear sky and a soft, warm breeze that fanned them as they traveled. Christian tied up to a marker buoy at the mouth of the lagoon. At high tide, Erin estimated that the evergreen-shrouded pond would be about twelve or fifteen feet deep. The tide was changing now, and much of the floor was exposed, the sand flats carpeted with brown, white and black sand dollars. The small channels that cut through the flats were running only a foot or two deep, with long strands of seaweed waving in the current like a mermaid's hair.

Christian knew the water was warm enough that they could dive comfortably for a short time without wet suits. Silently he passed Erin a face mask, a single air tank and a pair of his flippers that he'd cut down to fit her. He watched her put on her equipment, shoving the face mask up on top of her head. She'd spent a few hours each day just lazing in the sun, and her skin was tanned to a warm honey gold. The new color in her face made her eyes flow like misty emeralds, and her long sexy legs looked even longer and sexier. She glanced up with a small tight smile, then stepped over the stern of the boat to climb down the short ladder beside the engine.

They waded through the shallow rivulets of seawater crisscrossing the sand flats, disturbing crabs and small fish hiding under the long seaweed, which had been laid flat by the rushing tide. They surprised the otter family he had told her about raiding a dense patch of seaweed. From a few feet away, they watched the sleek little animals dive and come up with a mouthful of crab. The otters ate furiously, trying to avoid the wicked pincers of their breakfast.

While Erin was busy laughing at their antics, Christian led her into gradually deepening water. When the water lapped her chin, she felt a small scurry of panic. Her eyes flew to him, and he smiled encouragingly, then pulled his face mask into place and arranged the mouthpiece for his air tank. He disappeared under the surface, and Erin followed a trail of bubbles leading into ever deeper water. The trail stopped at the mouth of the lagoon, and she knew he was waiting for her. After a moment's hesitation, she pulled down her mask and bit down on the mouthpiece. Taking a deep breath, Erin let herself sink beneath the water.

The tide pushed her like a tailwind as it rushed out of the lagoon. The water was crystal clear, and she found Christian easily. As she approached, he began swimming again. Erin swam behind him, feeling more secure in following his lead. She had admired his coordination and agility many times, but never so much as now. He moved through the water as if he'd been born in it. He was clad only in brief trunks, and she could see the powerful muscles of his legs working sinuously as he kicked through the water. He stopped, suspended in the ocean, and pointed downward. About ten feet below Erin saw a brilliant patchwork of orange, purple and raspberry-colored starfish clustered around bright lime-green anemones. Without giving herself time to think about it, she jackknifed and dove straight down.

She surfaced a minute later with a two-foot-wide purple sunflower starfish in her hand. She waved it triumphantly, grinning at him through her mask. The many arms of the starfish waved, too, and Christian laughed, giving her a thumbs-up sign. She dove again to replace the starfish, and he watched her pat it back into place on the bottom.

The belugas had told her that she swam like a rock. Perhaps, compared to them, she did, but she was the most graceful human being he had ever seen in the water, Christian thought. The black swimsuit she wore emphasized the suppleness of her body as she moved almost as fluidly as the water around her. She resurfaced beside him, flashed a smile and took the lead farther out into the open sea.

He saw the dark shapes swimming below them before she did. Moving up beside her, he waited to see what she would do.

They were pilot whales, swimming about twenty feet below them in seventy or eighty feet of water. He knew the exact moment she saw them by the sudden clumsy movement of her body. She stopped and watched the passage of the fifty or so blackfish. The largest were about twenty-five feet long, but the pod included a number of smaller juveniles and calves. He touched her arm to let her know he was there if she needed him, but did not take her hand. In order to conquer her fear, he knew, she would have to face it on her own.

Three of the smaller whales swam up and hung vertically in the water about ten feet away. Christian could hear their chatter as they discussed these two-legged intruders into their domain. Very slowly Erin extended her hand to them. None of the three whales shied away, so she swam forward a foot. The larger two whales immediately retreated, turning and swimming rapidly after their disappearing pod. The smallest hesitated, then swam toward Erin. As Christian watched, the pilot whale touched Erin's outstretched hand with its bulbous head. She scratched the youngster's forehead, then patted it. A piercing whistle penetrated the underwater silence, and the small whale turned away slowly, as if reluctant to leave. The whistle sounded again, and the whale began swimming after the pod. It stopped twice, each time turning to look at them before going on again.

Erin watched them until they disappeared, then pointed to the surface and kicked upward. Christian angled upward toward her, surfacing at the same time she did. "Did you see that?" Her eyes were shining with excitement. "Oh, I wish I had my equipment set up here! I could have talked to them."

"I saw it," he said, realizing he had another powerful inducement that he could offer her to stay with him.

"I studied them before I did the belugas, you know, but I couldn't do much with their language then. What I've discovered about the beluga language can be applied to theirs, though, and now I could." Too excited to stay still, she began swimming toward the mouth of the lagoon five hundred yards away. When she reached the boat she resumed the conversation as if there hadn't been a ten-minute gap, looking in the direction they had just come from. "It would be so much easier to study whales that didn't migrate as much as the belugas do,'' she said wistfully.

She shrugged out of the harness to load it into the boat, and Christian took the weight of the tank from her. ''It would be easier to study some that you didn't have to live out in the middle of nowhere to find, too, I imagine,'' he said blandly. He lifted both tanks over the side of the boat. Pulling off his mask, he enjoyed the view as she climbed up the short diving ladder set over the transom.

As soon as he stepped into the boat, she tossed him one of the towels to dry off. He gave his body a quick swipe, then rubbed the towel carelessly over his head. Suddenly Erin was in his arms.

''Thank you,'' she whispered, hugging him tightly. ''If you hadn't come with me, I don't know if I would have had the courage to dive again.''

''You would have found it,'' he said lightly. He looked down into her shining eyes. She had a courage and strength that humbled him, and he wondered if he could ever love her more than he did right then. Smoothing her damp hair away from her face, he brushed off a few glistening diamonds of water with his thumbs, then kissed her soft mouth. ''Mm.'' Pulling back slightly, he licked her lips and grinned down at her. ''You taste salty.''

Erin reached up and nibbled lightly on his bottom lip. ''So do you,'' she murmured.

It was a purely natural gesture, and it thrilled him. As her reserve and inhibition gradually faded, she was responding to him more and more freely, even, to his delight, occasionally taking the initiative. The second time they'd made love last night had been at her instigation, and his body began to heat at the memory of her eager hands and mouth, and the feel of her silky hair sweeping slowly over his belly and thighs. His arms tightening around her, he bent to capture her mouth.

She slipped free with a laugh. ''I'm starving. Take me home and feed me,'' she commanded, giving him a little push. ''I want waffles and bacon, lots of bacon,'' she decided.

He laughed silently. And she was learning to tease. "Okay, I'll take you home," he said agreeably, pulling her down onto the seat beside him. Her automatic reference to his house as home thrilled him even more. "But—" he slanted her a look as he started the engine "—I get to choose dessert."

Her eyes promised that it would be worth the wait.

Erin closed the mystery she'd been reading with a satisfied snap. Propping her feet up on the veranda railing, she rested her head on the back of the chair. She had done nothing more strenuous than turn the pages of a book all afternoon. Christian had gone to Orcas to get his mail, as he did most afternoons, but she'd been in the middle of the second chapter by then and already hooked, so he'd gone alone. He usually did; she'd only been off the island once since their shopping trip, and then only because she had wanted to try to contact Phillip Damion again. She was happy to stay behind and explore the island with Clancy, or beachcomb or putter in the kitchen. One afternoon she'd tried her hand at baking and produced a batch of acceptable oatmeal cookies. She smiled at the memory. She guessed they were acceptable. He'd eaten the whole batch except for the one small one she'd managed to snatch.

Today, though, she'd stayed because she wanted a little time to herself to try to decide how long this idyll could last. Erin closed her eyes tiredly. But she hadn't decided anything. She'd escaped into the pages of a book instead. As much as she wanted to stay here forever, she knew she had to leave... and soon. The peace and beauty of his home were seducing her in a way that had nothing to do with the nights they spent steeped in sensuality. She had found a place where she could happily spend the rest of her life... and she had to give it up. To stay much longer would be to risk a heartbreak from which she knew she would never recover.

Erin opened her eyes, staring vacantly at the distant eagle family. She needed to get back to work. Even in the short time she'd spent on the Aleutian island, she'd made important discoveries in understanding the whales' language, and the data should be entered into the institute computer as soon as possi-

ble. Her research had been the greatest source of satisfaction
and joy in her life. It would still bring her satisfaction and joy,
Erin knew, still be a vitally important and necessary part of her
life, but no longer the sum total. Christian Dekker had shown
her that there was much more to life than work. There was
passion, desire . . . and love.

One of the eagles stepped onto the rim of the nest, spread its
long wings and soared into the empty blue sky. Vancouver was
only an hour away by plane, she thought. He could fly up; they
would still see each other. Erin was trying to ignore her dismal
lack of conviction in that hope when she heard the sound of a
powerboat. She jumped up and looked down toward the dock,
expecting to see Christian's blue and white runabout. Instead
she saw an unfamiliar green boat. Clancy, who had been lying
at her feet, had already started down the steps leading to the
beach, and she followed him.

As Erin stepped onto the dock, the boat bumped against the
tire fenders at the far end. She could see two men, one seated
at the controls and a second one standing, looking as if he were
preparing to jump onto the dock. He never did make the jump.
To her utter amazement, friendly, well-behaved Clancy suddenly went berserk. Snarling rabidly, he lunged and snapped at
the man, who wisely made no further attempt to leave the boat.

She ran down the dock, calling to Clancy to stop. Not until
she reached the end of the dock did the dog quiet down. Then
he positioned himself between her and the men in the boat.
When the standing man made a move, as if he were thinking
about jumping onto the dock again, Clancy growled a low
warning and lunged again. When Erin saw who the man was,
she received another surprise.

"Mason! What are you doing here?" Mason Charles was
Phillip Damion's personal assistant. Erin had never cared for
the man, feeling that he had about as much personality as a
jellyfish, but he did seem devoted to Phillip. A small, thin, sal-
low man, he was dressed in his usual three-piece suit. Erin saw
by the sign painted on the side of the green boat that it was a
water taxi from Orcas, and she surmised that Mason had taken

a ferry from Victoria to Orcas, then hired someone to drive him over.

"I came to see you, Dr. Mathias." The tone of his high-pitched, nasal voice suggested that she had inconvenienced him greatly by being out on some island instead of at the institute, where she belonged. "Can't you call off the dog?" he added in a near whine.

Erin spoke quietly, patting the dog's shoulders. "Clancy, it's all right, boy. Let the man get out." Clancy looked around at her, wagging his tail, but when Mason Charles again tried to leave the boat, he stiffened and growled again. Privately Erin thought he showed remarkable perception. "I'm sorry, Mason, I can't. What do you want?"

"Phillip wanted to make sure you were all right. He'd never heard of this Christian Dekker you're staying with, and he was worried about you." Mason managed to include both accusation and snide insinuation in his aggrieved tone.

Erin decided that she'd had enough of the man. "If Phillip had been in either time I called, he could have heard all about him," she said crisply. "Where has he been?"

"Oh, he has a special project he's working on," Mason said vaguely. "He just came back last night."

"Well, tell him I'll come in Monday." Erin felt a sudden desolation as she realized that she had just decreed the end of the idyll; but, perhaps that was for the best. Subconsciously, at least, she had realized that she couldn't live in a mirage indefinitely. It was time to face reality, and now reality was only three days away. That was all the time she had left with Christian.

"Why don't you come back with me now? Phillip's very anxious to talk to you." Mason tried an ingratiating tone that was even more annoying.

"He can talk to me on Monday, Mason," she repeated shortly. She saw that Mason seemed to be looking at something over her shoulder and turned to see what. She got her third surprise in as many minutes when she saw the man a few yards behind her on the dock. She hadn't heard him approaching, and Clancy hadn't given a warning either. Where had he come from?

Even when he was less than six feet away, Erin couldn't hear
the sound of his footsteps. He was a stocky man, about her
height, with grizzled hair cut very short and a face that showed
he hadn't lived an easy life. Erin judged him to be about fifty,
although what she could see of his body beneath his dark T-
shirt, windbreaker and jeans could have belonged to a man
fifteen years younger.

"You heard Dr. Mathias. She said she'd be there Monday."

His voice was low and almost as deep as Christian's as he
stopped a little in front of her. Positioning himself just like
Clancy, Erin realized suddenly. The dog gave him a brief look,
wagging his tail in greeting.

"Are—are you Dekker?" Mason blustered.

"No, but I'm a friend of his."

Mason tried the ploy of staring the man down and with-
stood the stranger's implacable gaze for all of two seconds.
"All right," he addressed Erin truculently. "I'll tell Phillip
you'll see him Monday." He made an abrupt gesture to the man
at the controls, who'd been a very interested bystander. The
man started the engine, and Mason sat down stiffly without
bothering to say goodbye.

Erin turned to the stranger as soon as the water taxi had left
the dock. Since Clancy so obviously considered him a friend,
she wasn't afraid of him, but his abrupt appearance had startled her, to say the least, and raised some interesting questions. "If you don't mind my asking," she said politely, "who
are you?"

"Ted Ryan," he answered immediately. "Christian asked me
to keep an eye on things until he got back. I saw the boat
heading your way and came over."

Erin blinked at him. She'd somehow gotten the impression
that Ted Ryan was an elderly man, everybody's idea of a
grandfather. This man was not elderly, and, although he was
old enough to be a grandfather, he wouldn't fit anyone's image of the typical grandpa. "How did you get here?"

He nodded. "My boat is around the corner. I took a shortcut through the trees."

Erin glanced in the direction he indicated and saw that he'd come from the section of the beach where the trees grew down almost to water's edge. That explained how he had seemed to appear as if out of nowhere. She began walking toward the house, and he walked with her. "Can you stay, Mr. Ryan? Christian should be back soon, and I'm sure he'd like to thank you for keeping an eye on me," she said blandly.

He chuckled ruefully, acknowledging that the "things" he was supposed to keep an eye on was her. "He just wanted to be sure you were all right while he was gone, Erin." He saw her sudden frown. "I'm sorry. I didn't mean to be familiar, Dr. Mathias. Christian refers to you as Erin, and that's how I think of you."

Erin waved away his apology. "No, please—call me Erin." Absently she frowned at him. "I was just wondering how Mason knew Christian's name. The message I left only mentioned where I was staying, not with whom."

"Be sure to tell Christian when he gets back," Ted Ryan instructed as they had reached the end of the dock. He took her hand briefly. "I'm happy to meet you, Erin. I'd like to stay, but I promised my wife I'd take her to San Juan this afternoon. I'll bring her over soon to meet you, too." He smiled, and Erin had the feeling he didn't do that very often. "I think you'll like each other." With that he turned, took a few steps up the beach and melted into the trees.

Erin stared after him until she heard the distant sound of an engine starting up. She felt as if reality had suddenly shifted a few degrees, almost like another earthquake. Ted Ryan had said that Christian referred to her as Erin, implying that Christian had talked to him about her more than once. Each time that he left her alone, Christian must have stopped at the Ryans'. Why did Christian think it was necessary to have Ted Ryan keep watch over her when he was gone? And why had Ted landed out of sight and snuck through the trees instead of simply coming in to the dock? And she was certain that the bulge she'd seen in the small of his back when his jacket pulled tight for a second was a gun.

She felt Clancy nudge her knee, as if he wondered why she was just standing there, doing nothing. Absentmindedly, she gave his head a pat. She felt as if she were acting in a play where everyone knew their part except her. Slowly she started up the beach, the large red-gold dog trotting at her heels.

Christian frowned at the book lying on the seat of the chair on the veranda. He called Erin's name, then rapidly searched the house when he got no response. He was starting back through the empty house at a run when he caught a glimpse of color through the kitchen window. The window overlooked a different part of the beach, and the color he saw was her shirt. She was walking along the edge of the surf, with Clancy following faithfully.

Only part of his tension relaxed. Eisley had missed their meeting, and when he'd stopped to check with Ted Ryan on his way back, he'd learned of Erin's visitor. Even if Erin hadn't left a message at the institute saying where she'd be, he had been sure that Damion would track her down as fast as he could, but sending someone to verify that she was with him was a surprise. Ted had caught only the last part of the conversation, but he had heard Erin address the man as Mason. That would be Mason Charles, Damion's toadie. He had been trying to convince Erin to go back with him because Damion was "anxious" to talk with her. He'd damned well bet Damion was anxious, Christian thought grimly. Ted had said that Erin had refused, but promised to come up to the institute on Monday. Christian felt a momentary bleakness. Had she been planning all along to leave then?

Christian shoved both the question and his feelings aside. He had no time for them now. He suspected that things were beginning to move very fast, and he was stuck on a treadmill, because Eisley hadn't shown up in San Juan. He raised his head suddenly at the sound of an approaching aircraft. Maybe Eisley hadn't missed the meeting after all. He glanced down at the figure on the beach. It would take at least an hour to walk back, and Eisley should be gone by then.

A few minutes later, Christian gestured the dark man toward one of the wicker chairs on the veranda and took one for himself. "What have you got?" he asked, indicating the plain manila envelope in Eisley's hand.

"Confirmation of what you suspected. Most of it would be hard to prove, but the Canadian government is sure they can get him on the tax-evasion angle, if nothing else." Eisley studied the big blond man going over the pages of information with a look of fierce satisfaction. Dekker had been the best agent he'd ever worked with, the only one he'd really trusted—as much as he could trust anyone. Dekker had been the complete professional, impersonal, cold-blooded. He'd worked the same way after leaving Damage Control—just earning more for it. Eisley sensed that this time he was not impersonal *or* cold-blooded, and he was taking no money for the job. "You're doing this for the woman, aren't you?" Eisley asked curiously.

"Yes," Christian agreed softly.

"She knows who you are?"

"Not yet," Christian said without expression. "When this is over."

Erin heard the two voices as she slipped into the house through the kitchen door. She had heard a plane fly over the island earlier and suspected it had landed when the sound of the engine had ceased abruptly instead of gradually fading. After Mason Charles's unexpected visit and learning of Christian's inexplicable request that Ted Ryan keep watch over her while he was gone, she had been extremely interested to know who was on that plane. Striking out across the island instead of returning by the beach, she had managed to get back before whoever it was had left.

Soundlessly she crossed the living room to stand in the open doorway. She looked at the two men standing together on the veranda, one very blond, the other dark. Now she realized why Christian Dekker had reminded her of Quinn Eisley. They were both tall, though Christian was a little taller and more muscular, but she was looking at light and dark versions of the same man. They had the same stance—as if they were ready to

pounce in any direction—and there was the same aura of
something dangerous about them. "Hello, Quinn." Both men
turned at the sound of her voice. And there was the same
empty, guarded look in their eyes, she added silently.

Neither of them showed any sign of being startled, and that,
she knew, was due to their training. Eisley glanced from her
white face to Christian's suddenly grim one.

"I should have guessed." Erin's voice was low and harsh.
"Everything about you said agent, but I fell for your apple-
farmer story anyway." She swallowed hard, trying to fight
down a wave a nausea from the obscene taste of humiliation
and self-disgust in her mouth. Her hand made a grand sweeping gesture around the veranda. "Is this one of Damage Control's infamous safe houses?"

"This is my home. I haven't worked for Damage Control for
four years," he said quietly. Neither of them gave any notice to
Eisley's silent departure.

"I see. You just pimp for them on a free-lance basis now."
The words sounded as if they had been torn raw and bleeding
from her throat. "That was the plan, wasn't it? That you'd
keep me drunk on sex until I gave you access to my research?"
As hard and condemnatory as her words for him were, her
words for herself were infinitely more bitter. "Well, you should
have just asked. I was so far gone I would have given you
any—" Her voice broke. "Anything."

"That's enough, Erin," he said in a clipped tone. He could
see fine tremors beginning to shake her body. "I'm not after
your research. I'm trying to save it. And I never pimped for
anybody," he added deliberately.

Her short, disbelieving laugh sounded like fingernails on a
blackboard. "You certainly give your work your all." The
tremors were getting worse; she was visibly shaking now, and
rubbing her hands up and down her arms as if trying to wipe
away something filthy. "Tell me, is lovemaking always that wild
for you, or were you exerting more effort than usual because
the stakes were higher? Only I suppose I shouldn't call it making love, should I? I should call it—"

"Don't say it, Erin," he warned, his voice soft and deadly as he saw her lips begin to form the word that would turn the most profound, soul-enriching experiences of his life into an obscenity.

"Why not?" she practically screamed at him. "That's all it was to you!" Beneath the pain and fury of betrayal, he heard her desperate plea for him to tell her that it wasn't true. Suddenly she trembled violently, and her knees buckled. Christian lunged forward and caught her before she stumbled to the floor. Her strong, slim body strained against his hands, and her flailing fists struck at him, hard, hurtful blows that he made no attempt to dodge. "Let me go! Don't touch me! Don't—" Her body suddenly convulsed in a terrible racking sob, and she went limp against him. "Why, Christian? Why?" she whispered as the sobs became continuous.

Dropping into the nearest chair, Christian cradled her in his arms until her heartbreaking weeping eased. Then he answered her question.

Christian leaned back against the railing, feeling as exhausted and battered as if he'd been in a vicious fight. Erin sat in the chair alone now, her hands clasped in her lap, staring sightlessly past him. She had, he thought, the slightly out-of-focus, concussed look of a disaster victim. The file Eisley had brought lay in her lap. She had reviewed the contents, expressing no surprise at the information on herself.

"Why didn't you just tell me who you were?"

Her raspy voice had a lifeless quality. They were the first words she had spoken since she'd stopped weeping and, considering the shocking contents of the file, not the words he would have expected. "As I said, I wasn't sure at first that the sabotage on my plane hadn't been directed solely at me. I couldn't see any point in alarming you unnecessarily," he said neutrally.

"But you could have told me later." A dull red flush tinted the skin drawn tighter than usual over his cheekbones, and enlightenment dawned. "You were embarrassed to tell me." Her disbelief was obvious, bringing some animation back into her voice.

His short bark of laughter was bitter. "You have to admit there would have been a certain irony in thanking you for saving my life in one breath, then telling you I had come to protect yours in the next."

Her furious gesture denied that excuse. "I don't believe that. You're the strongest, most self-reliant man I've ever met." Her own disillusionment and anger blinded her to the dried salt in the corners of his eyes and the spasm of emotion that briefly crossed his face. "You just chose the easiest way to manipulate me into doing what you wanted." The unrelenting memory of how willingly she had made his job easier sickened her again. Erin rose from the chair abruptly in a futile attempt to escape her pain.

Christian watched her pace the wide porch, moving like a marionette with a palsied puppeteer jerking her strings. He spoke a dozen languages, he thought derisively, but he couldn't find the words in even one to justify his lie.

She turned suddenly, staring at him. "You must have given thanks for the earthquake, coming when it did. It gave you the perfect opportunity to get me here, in your house, in your bed, where you could really keep me under your thumb," she said scathingly. He didn't deny it, and she felt a physical pain so severe it almost drove her to her knees. "Is Ted Ryan one of you, too?"

"He was in something similar," Christian said expressionlessly. "He got out about twelve years ago."

They would of course have recognized each other for what they had been, Erin thought bleakly. She found she could keep the pain at bay with her anger, so she fed it, nourished it. "What did you plan to do when the job was over? Ask me to stay on for a few more nights of fun and games?"

"No, I planned to ask you to stay on permanently, to live with me," he said in a tone almost as cutting as hers. He saw by the tortured anguish in her eyes before she closed them that the answer would have been yes, and the agony that tore through him almost made him cry out.

Erin turned away from the pain in his eyes before she believed it. He was saying his lovemaking wasn't a lie, but you couldn't believe anything a liar said, she reminded herself bitterly.

When he could trust himself to speak, he asked tonelessly, "Do you believe the information on Damion?"

Erin forced herself to look at him. He was leaning against the railing, stone still, as he had been since leaving the chair where he had held her while she wept and raged at him. She wanted to scream at the memory, but she was suddenly too exhausted, and she realized that she had indulged her own selfishness long enough. There would be time later, years of it, to chastise herself for her weakness, for the recriminations she had promised herself she wouldn't have. There was something much more important at stake here than her own self-respect. Whatever she thought of the man personally, Daniel had chosen well when he had chosen Christian Dekker. Like it or not, she was going to need his help to be sure her research was not perverted into the nightmare she feared.

"Despite recent evidence to the contrary, I'm not completely stupid." Rubbing the dull ache forming in the middle of her forehead, she gave him a faint smile that was more sad than bitter. "Yes, I believe it. When Daniel first told me that he didn't think Phillip was as altruistic as everyone believed, I put it down to paranoia developed after all his years in your business. Then I began to think a little for myself. Just as you noticed—" she pointed to the discarded file envelope "—all the SOS-sponsored research, with the exception of mine, involves deep-sea drilling and mapping—the same kind of exploration oil companies do. And oil was how Phillip made his fortune. I began to wonder if perhaps he wasn't using the SOS contributions to fund oil exploration for himself, but I couldn't figure out why he would need to. His fortune is enormous. He's the third-richest man in Canada."

She turned and faced the apple orchard, folding her arms around her middle as if in pain. "There were rumors that his financial situation had suffered badly because of the oil glut and poor investments." She laughed mirthlessly. "But I didn't listen. I still thought Daniel was being paranoid. Then, last fall, just after he died, I heard a very vague rumor that Phillip was trying to break the trust he'd set up to finance SOS. I couldn't confirm it, although—'' she glanced over her shoulder at the file, then at Christian ''—I see you were able to.''

Erin began pacing again, passing in front of Christian, taking excruciating care not to touch him. ''I began to suspect that perhaps Phillip's only purpose for setting up SOS all those years ago was as a tax dodge, and that now, when he needed money, he would use whatever assets SOS had to get it, including my work.'' She stopped at the opposite end of the veranda, and her voice took on a cutting edge as she sent him a sharp look. ''A number of people, including the ones you worked for, would be willing to pay a great deal for my research. Daniel had coded all of my research up to the time of his death, and I did the same after that, using three-layer codes and changing them for each section of new material. The only way Phillip can get it is by getting the codes from me.''

He finally pushed himself from the railing. It was the first clumsy move she'd ever seen him make. ''So what are you planning to do?'' His question was very quiet as he stood facing her.

She answered in a calm, cool voice that cost her every ounce of self-control she had. ''You said Eisley thinks the Canadian government will have gathered enough evidence to put Phillip under arrest within a few days. Until then, I'll stay here. You're a liar and a cheat, but I know I can trust you to keep me safe, so I'll stay until Phillip is arrested.'' She didn't hear the paradox in her words. ''Then I never want to see you again.''

She turned toward the door leading to the living room. In the doorway she paused to look at him one more time, and Christian heard her last words, cold and flat and ugly. ''I think you should take the check Quinn left in the folder. You've more than earned it.''

To aid in the creation of a thoroughly dreary atmosphere, the day that had been so sunny and warm became gray and rainy toward evening. Forced inside, Erin stared out one of the wide living-room windows at the dismal scene outside. Rain ran like tears down the glass. The leaden, uncomfortable silence in the house was a bitter reminder of how easily they had laughed and talked before, how relaxed they had been with each other. Erin wandered the room without purpose while Christian sat in a leather easy chair in front of another window, his long, jeans-clad legs stretched out onto a matching hassock. She knew he was watching her in that silent unnerving way, making no pretense of reading the book on his lap. He had fixed dinner alone tonight. Working together in the kitchen, cheerfully getting in each other's way, was no way to preserve the purely imper-sonal business arrangements that were all she wanted now.

Erin pulled her flannel shirt closed across her chest and but-toned it. Using the coolness of the evening as an excuse, she'd changed back into the corduroy jeans, silk turtleneck and flannel shirt she'd worn down from the Aleutians; she'd even changed her panties. She knew the weather wasn't the real rea-son she'd chosen those clothes. She hadn't wanted to wear anything he'd bought her.

She stopped in front of the massive stone fireplace. Uncon-sciously she rubbed her cold arms. It would be nice to have a fire, she thought absently. He had built one the night of Ab-ner's death....

Ruthlessly Erin repressed the insidious memory of his ten-der caring that night. They had experienced so much in their short time together, lived so intensely, and the knowledge that it had been a lie made his betrayal all the more unforgivable. She resolutely turned away from the fireplace and searched for something with which to occupy herself until it was late enough that she could go to bed without appearing to be hiding from him.

The Seattle newspaper he had brought back with him was lying on the oak coffee table. Erin picked it up and settled on the overstuffed tweed sofa. Clancy lay down at her feet. He had been looking worriedly from her to Christian all evening. Os-car, she noted sourly, had ensconced himself on the hassock beside Christian's feet.

Quickly Erin scanned the paper, looking for any mention of the volcanic eruption in the Aleutians. If the seismic disturbances had settled, she might be able to leave here, go straight back to Alaska when she left. At least she could salvage her equipment. On the seventh page of the first section she found a two-column article. The news wasn't promising. The volcano was continuing to erupt regularly, spewing ash and gases, and the geologists monitoring it didn't predict an end anytime soon. The area from the volcano west to Adak Island was still closed.

Christian watched her continue to leaf through the paper, reading news items here and there with desultory interest. What a difference a few minutes could make, he thought caustically. A few more minutes on a remote Aleutian beach, and he would have frozen to death. A few more minutes in the water after the orca attack, and she would have drowned. A few more minutes, and Eisley would have been gone. The true irony was that he had planned to give her the file and explain who he was soon as she had returned from her walk this afternoon. He laughed mirthlessly to himself. A self-confessed liar always earned forgiveness for his sin, but he hadn't had the chance to confess, and because of her own honesty, his lies were all the more abhorrent. The words that might have earned him forgiveness were words he couldn't say now. She would think they were the ultimate lie.

He watched her turn to the second section of the paper. She was scanning the first page with as little interest as the others when suddenly he saw her face turn white as the newsprint.

"Oh, my God, no," Erin moaned softly.

"Erin! What is it?"

He sat down beside her, but she didn't look up. Her attention was riveted on a quarter-column article in the middle of the page. Quickly Christian read the few lines over her shoulder. The article described the stranding of a small pod of beluga whales on the coast of Alaska, near Bethel. Unable to save them, men from a nearby Inuit village had shot the whales to end their misery.

Crushing the paper in her hands, Erin raised her head. Christian saw the look of horror in her eyes. "Do you know what this means?" she whispered.

He shook his head silently.

"Belugas don't strand themselves. Other whales do, but not belugas. And even if they did, it wouldn't have been in this area."

The location of the alleged stranding had been niggling at the back of his mind, and suddenly he made the connection. "That's Akiachak's village, isn't it?" Her stricken look was his answer.

Erin had accepted the evidence against Phillip Damion, but she had refused to believe that Akiachak had sabotaged Christian's plane, even though it appeared that a dummy corporation traced back to Damion was the mysterious new financial benefactor the pilot had said he'd found for his village. "Why wouldn't the belugas have been in this area? Didn't you study them there a few summers ago?"

She nodded woodenly. "Yes, I did, but I had to pay Sam's village to do it. They have a permit, you see, to hunt a certain number of belugas a year. I paid them what the whales would have been worth not to, but even then, the whales were reluctant to come in when I called them. Since I didn't study at the village the past two years, they've gone back to hunting them. The whales wouldn't have gone anywhere near there—unless they were called."

Flinging aside the paper, as if she'd suddenly discovered it was crawling with spiders, Erin jumped to her feet. Christian rose after her. He knew what she was going to say. He'd probably even thought of it a split second before she did, but only because he'd had more experience with the unthinkable.

She took a few clumsy steps away from him, then turned back to give him a stark look. "Phillip found someone to break the computer codes on my research. Most of that pod would remember me and remember my call. If they heard it, they would think it was safe and come in close to the village. The traditional Inuit way of hunting small whales is to circle behind them in boats, then drive them up onto the beach. It appears as if the whales have stranded themselves, but they haven't.'' Her eyes had a haunted look as her voice dropped to an agonized whisper. ''I can imagine how bewildered they must have been when the men started chasing them.'' Her voice clogged with tears. ''I can hear them crying out to me, asking me why I called them so men could kill them.''

Her body was hunched, as if wracked by pain. Christian ached to take her in his arms and try to ease the hurt, but she showed no sign of wanting any comfort from him.

''Phillip was gone last week. He must have been up at Sam's village, supervising the hunt,'' she said dully. ''Although I don't understand why he would use my research like that.'' She laughed harshly. ''There's no profit in killing a few belugas.''

''No, but he could have been giving any potential buyers a demonstration of what he could do,'' Christian said quietly. ''I'll see if Eisley can find out if there were any strangers in the area.''

''I wonder if Phillip's sold it yet.'' Erin could hardly force the words out.

''We'll find out and take care of things, Erin,'' he promised.

She appeared not to have heard him as she walked into the spare bedroom and closed the door.

The house was dark when Erin opened the door again. She vaguely remembered hearing Christian go into his bedroom hours ago. She'd lain in the dark, feeling the tentacles of despair and anger wrapping tighter and tighter around her until she couldn't breathe. Moving through the silent house, she reached the kitchen. Briefly she considered fixing some cocoa, but wandered away before she made up her mind. She crossed the living room to see if the rain had stopped. Perhaps she could breathe better outside, she thought.

''Erin.''

Christian's voice came out of the darkness. She turned slowly and saw him materialize out of the shadows, and suddenly she knew what she wanted.

Blindly, she groped for his hand. His found hers, and he tugged, drawing her to him. Erin went willingly. He closed her within the circle of his arms, and she lay against him, absorbing the heat and strength of his body. Tomorrow he would still be the same man who had lied to her, hurt her more than she would ever have thought possible, but tonight he was the only one who could give her comfort from her sorrow and pain.

He was naked, and Erin slid her hands up his back, then down over his lean flanks, feeling the play of muscle under her hands. "Please . . . make love with me," she whispered.

For an answer she felt his hands on her waist, easing her away for a moment; then the flannel shirt that was all she'd been wearing was gone. He lifted her effortlessly in his arms and carried her back to his bed, laying her on the cool sheet.

Christian knew this solved nothing, but she needed him, and he needed her. To hell with nobility. This might well be all he would ever have of her, and he was too selfish to give up the chance.

They made love silently, as if words might spoil the understanding between them. As he lay down beside her, her hands smoothed over his chest, finding the small points of his nipples. Her fingertips teased them into tiny hard nubs; then her wet, rough tongue curled around each one in turn. Sensing what she wanted, he lay back, his arms spread at his sides, his body open and vulnerable. Kneeling over him, Erin savored the salty taste of his skin as her mouth moved lower. She followed the silky ribbon of baby-soft hair down to his navel with tiny wet kisses; then her tongue stopped to probe and tease. Her fingers sought out the unexpectedly soft places on his hard body, the inside of his elbow, the back of his knee. In the hollow below his hipbone she found one of the softest, and Christian knotted his hands in the sheet as her tongue sampled it. She slipped her hand up the inside of his thigh, her touch tantalizingly light as she began to stroke him. A long shudder shot through him when he felt the first soft searchings of her mouth.

He slid his fingers into her hair and held her head away from him. Her eyes met his in the dark, and he saw her slow smile. Gradually he forced her backward on the bed until their positions were reversed. He began to explore her beautifully strong body with soft touches, her breasts, her belly, her thighs. Erin felt the whispers of heat building as his mouth lingered at her breast. His hand mirrored the earlier motion of hers, sliding up her inner thigh to stroke and fondle and madden. When she thought she could stand it no longer, he shifted between her knees, nudging them wide apart, then penetrated the heat of her body with his. For excruciatingly long moments he slowly increased the heat until Erin felt she was suffocating as it seared through her, burning up the oxygen she needed to breathe. With a frantic hunger, she pulled him down to her and, like paper in fire, they burned each other up.

When Erin awoke at dawn, the bed beside her was empty and cold. She didn't need to think hard about where he had gone, and she wasn't surprised when, a few minutes later, she got down to the dock and found that the runabout was missing. She was certain he was meeting Eisley, and that the two of them were trying to decide how to contain the damage Phillip Damion might have done. After all, she thought humorlessly, that was the mission of Damage Control. She knew Christian was trying to protect her, but it was her research that had done the damage, and it was her responsibility to try to undo it.

Taking a waterproof bag from the boat house, Erin ran back up to the house. She put on her swimsuit, then rapidly packed a change of clothes and her sandals into the bag. Realizing suddenly that she had no money, she dug through the pockets of the shorts she'd been wearing on her second trip to San Juan. Christian had give her a twenty-dollar bill for a few personal purchases, and she had stuffed the change in her pocket and forgotten about it. She found the crumpled bills and scattered change, added them to her bag, then ran down the long stairway. He might have thought he had isolated her by taking the boat, Erin thought as she waded into the water, but he had forgotten that she had spent nearly as much of her life in the sea as he had, and the nearest ferry stop was on an island only two miles away.

An hour and a half later Erin was taking a seat on the ferry and trying to control her impatience. The boat had only one more stop, then would dock at Victoria, on the tip of Vancouver Island. From there, she would buy another ticket for the ferry that traveled up the western shore. The second stop would put her off only a quarter mile from the institute.

It was barely noon when Erin climbed the steep winding road leading to the gray stone building that housed the SOS offices and research institute. It was a Saturday, and she knew the building would be deserted. She had no keys with her, but when she had moved into the apartment at the back, she had hidden an apartment key in case she ever locked herself out. She reached up and felt the ledge over the door, and her fingers came in contact with cool metal.

Once inside, Erin found her spare key to the Institute's office and went straight for the main computer that housed all her research. She had no way of knowing if Phillip had found a hacker who had managed to crack all the codes or just the ones on the first block of information. That would have given him enough knowledge to call the whales, but little else. She wanted to eliminate any chance that he might gain access to the research he didn't already have. The main computer was never shut down, and Erin methodically began feeding the machine the codes for each file, followed by the command to erase them. The disks she had left at Christian's house would now be the only record of her research.

The computer whirred softly as it carried out her orders. The silence of the big building was eerie, and Erin felt the hair on the back of her neck rising at the random sounds that reached her. She was giving the command to erase the last file when she heard a sound behind her that was definitely not random. It was the unmistakable sound of a revolver being cocked. Slowly she turned around.

Erin had always thought that with his wavy silver hair and big, soft features, Phillip Damion looked more like an overworked diplomat than an oil magnate. Certainly he didn't look like a murderer, even with the nasty-looking black pistol in his hand. "Hello, Phillip," she said coolly.

"Erin," he replied, as if they were greeting each other at a cocktail party. "Mason said you wouldn't be in until Monday."

Silently, Erin cursed her carelessness at not checking to see if any cars had been parked in front of the building. She nodded at the box at his feet. "Did you find something else to steal, Phillip?"

He gave the box an absent glance. "That's just my personal papers. How do you know?" he asked curiously.

"Daniel never trusted you. Before he died, he arranged for Christian Dekker to protect me from you. They served together in the U.S. Navy. Christian found you out. The Canadian government knows about your scam now, too," she said with satisfaction.

Phillip shrugged as if that were only a minor irritation. "What are you doing here, Erin?"

"When I read about the supposed whale strandings near Sam's village, I knew you had used my research to call them in so they could be—" her voice broke "—slaughtered. Tell me," she asked conversationally, "did you break all the codes on my work?"

Phillip sighed. "Regrettably, no, only about half. And I imagine you just made sure we couldn't get the rest of it, didn't you?"

"Yes."

"But you have copies," he guessed shrewdly. "I know you, Erin. You wouldn't destroy your life's work so cavalierly." He raised the gun a little higher to point at the middle of her chest. "I'm going to need those copies, Erin. The deal I made was for all your research. Where are they? At Dekker's?"

"I'll never tell you, Phillip," she said, mostly to distract him. An inch at a time, she began edging toward the side door. If she could put another foot between them, she would take her chances that he wasn't a good enough shot to hit a running target.

"Oh, I'm afraid you must, my dear." His tone was regretful. "I've accepted a great deal of money for your work on the basis of that little demonstration. The people who paid me expect to get the full package. Now, you wouldn't want me to have to disappoint them, would you?"

Erin fought back the sick misery she felt at his assertion that the destruction of a dozen intelligent, loving creatures had been a "little demonstration." "I'm afraid you're going to have to," she said almost cheerfully, stealing another inch. "Just out of curiosity, who did you sell my work to?" She added two more inches.

"You needn't concern yourself about it, my dear," he said benignly, raising the gun and pointing it at the middle of her chest. "You won't have to worry about feeling guilty. Now, why don't you just tell me where those disks are?" he coaxed.

Erin forced her knees to stiffen and slid her feet one more agonizingly slow inch. "If you're going to shoot me anyway, why should I tell you, Phillip?" She was pleased with the calm tone that belied the mounting terror she felt.

"Because maybe I'll let Dekker live if you do."

Erin's laughter was completely spontaneous. "You wouldn't stand a chance against him, Phillip. You might as well give up right now." She sidled the last inch, and her body tightened, readying itself for the life-or-death dash she was about to make.

Phillip started to say something else, but she didn't wait to hear it. Drawing a breath, she whirled suddenly and began to run for the door. Too late she saw, out of the corner of her eye, the arm swinging down; then her skull exploded in a shower of colored lights.

Eisley's curse startled Christian, not because it was an unusual expression—it wasn't—but because it was so out of character. Eisley never cursed. A man had to feel something—anger, hate, fear, surprise—to curse, and Eisley was the most emotionless man he'd ever known. Eisley repeated the obscenity, then added, "Where the hell is she?"

"Take a wild guess." Christian was already starting back down the steps to the beach.

He heard Eisley's voice right behind him. "The SOS Institute?"

"Right the first time."

"But how the hell did she get off the island?"

Christian spared him a glance as he ran inside the hangar and pressed the switch that raised the front door. "She swam," he said laconically.

Eisley looked momentarily stunned; then he saw Christian climbing into the seaplane. His own was moored outside. "I'll alert the Canadian government and meet you there," he yelled above the roar of the small plane's engine.

Erin awoke to a hideous throbbing in her head and the metallic taste of blood in her mouth. She tried to raise her hand to her head, then realized her hands and feet were bound, and that she was gagged and lying in the back seat of Phillip's large Mercedes. Struggling against the nausea the pain in her head generated, she managed to sit up and peer out the window. What she saw did not reassure her.

The Mercedes was parked at the bottom of the hill below the institute, close to the dock where the SOS research vessels were moored. Right now the only vessel there was a seaplane with a stylized raven painted on the nose. As she watched, she saw Mason Charles and Sam Akiachak walk rapidly down the dock and climb into the plane. Which one of them had hit her? Erin wondered muzzily. Probably Mason. Sneakiness was his style. Then she saw Phillip Damion approaching the Mercedes, still with his nasty gun in his hand. Then her eyes widened.

Emerging from the scrub pine behind Phillip was Christian, silently stalking the other man, who kept walking toward the Mercedes, unaware of the danger at his back. Erin forced herself to watch Phillip so she wouldn't inadvertently alert him. As he opened the driver's door, Erin heard the deep, rumbly rasp she knew so well.

"Drop the gun and stand away from the car, Damion."

For a split second the older man seemed to hesitate; then, to Erin's horror, she saw him turn and raise his gun, and she heard the deafening report of the bullet discharging down the short barrel. Her scream was muffled against her gag as she twisted desperately to see out the window.

Christian was rolling on the ground. She watched for several heart-stopping seconds until he came up in a crouch, seemingly unharmed. Then Erin realized that she was moving, that the whole car was moving, in fact. At first she thought Phillip had jumped in and was driving away, but then she saw him standing outside. Still dazed, it took her a minute to realize that he must have shoved the car out of gear while she was watching Christian, then given it a little push to get it rolling—over the cliff and straight down to the sea.

She heard the engine of the seaplane fire up, then saw Mason Charles, armed and running back up the dock toward them. Frantic, she strained against her bonds, not feeling the rope cutting into her wrists as she tried to free her hands so she could tear away the gag and warn Christian of this new danger.

He had already seen it. Christian snapped off a shot that sent Mason diving over the side of the dock into the water. "Drop the gun, Damion," he ordered again. He advanced on the silver-haired man, fighting a sense of panic as the car with Erin inside picked up speed.

Phillip Damion began backing away from the car and toward the dock and escape. "You won't shoot me in cold blood, Dekker," he shouted triumphantly. "You're going to have to let me go to save the woman."

Christian looked at the terrified face staring out the window of the rapidly rolling car, then turned to the fleeing man. You're wrong, Damion, he thought as he raised his gun. Deliberately, he fired twice, then began running after the Mercedes.

To Erin, everything seemed to happen at once. She saw Phillip Damion fall at the same time that Christian grabbed the open door of the Mercedes. Simultaneously, Sam Akiachak's seaplane began to taxi away from the dock, and a helicopter appeared over the tree tops. The helicopter dropped, hovering over the seaplane, herding it back toward the beach until it ran aground. Then, movement on the periphery of her vision drew her attention and, horror-stricken, she saw Phillip Damion rise to one knee, gun in hand. He took aim and fired as Christian vaulted into the car. She heard his grunt of pain, saw the red blossom of blood on his thigh, and watched his fingers begin to lose their grip on the metal frame of the door. The edge of the cliff was rapidly coming closer, and she screamed against the gag for him to jump, to save himself. Instead, with a superhuman effort, he lurched onto the seat. His foot miraculously found the brake pedal, and the Mercedes jerked to a sudden stop. Erin was thrown against the front seat, jarring her aching head, and colored lights exploded again inside her skull.

She regained consciousness as a pair of strong hands reached in to lift her out of the back seat. Those same hands removed the gag from her mouth, then gently laid her on the ground and began to untie her hands and feet.

"Christian!" she cried urgently, then recognized the owner of the hands. "Quinn! Where is Christian?"

"Hold still, damn it! Let me untie you." Then, more gently, when he saw the terrified expression on her face, he said, "He's being taken care of, Erin."

As soon as Quinn had the ropes off and had helped her to her feet, Erin threw off his restraining arm and dashed over to two men squatting beside a prone body. Dimly she noted that the front wheels of the Mercedes had stopped a scant inch or two from the edge of the drop-off.

She reached the men working over the man lying on the litter. A soft cry escaped her as she saw how dead white Christian's normally tanned skin was. Blood was seeping steadily from under the pressure bandage on his thigh, and she knew without being told that the bullet had nicked, if not severed, the femoral artery. She reached for his hand, lying limp on the bright green sea grass, and moaned when she felt how cold it was. The medics ignored her; one was already busy setting up a plasma IV, while the other maintained pressure on the bandage.

As Erin clasped his clammy hand in both of hers, she saw his eyelashes flutter weakly; then his eyes opened, still bright and clear. She saw his lips working, and she bent close to hear, unaware of the tears streaming steadily down her face.

"You should have waited for me," he whispered raspily.

Erin nodded dumbly. "I know. I'm so sorry. Please for—"

"I'm sorry, miss. You'll have to move. We need to load him now."

Not understanding for a moment, Erin fought against the hands trying to take her away from Christian. Then she scrambled to her feet and tore after the two men carrying the litter toward the waiting helicopter. Grabbing Christian's hand, she felt his fingers grip hers strongly.

"Miss, I'm sorry, there's no more room."

Erin looked up dazedly. Glancing into the helicopter, she saw that it was already crowded. There were several Canadian marines, as well as Sam Akiachak and Mason Charles, who were handcuffed and crowded into the tail section. And there was another litter on the floor, holding Phillip Damion. Erin could see a blood-soaked bandage on his shoulder, but his eyes were open and semi-alert.

The medic spoke to her again, more sharply. "Miss, move back. There's no room for you."

She was roughly shoved aside, and she realized that she had been blocking the door, preventing Christian from being loaded aboard. The medics swung the litter aboard, then scrambled in after it, taking the last bit of floor space. Erin felt a tug on her hand and looked down to see that, impossibly, she still had Christian's hand locked in hers. She glanced up and saw that his eyes, burning brightly, were on her. "I love you!" she cried urgently.

His eyes burned brighter for a second; then his eyelids fluttered down. She thought she heard him whisper, "I know," and then his fingers relaxed in hers. The door was closing, and, unable to reach his mouth, Erin brushed a hasty kiss over his knuckles, then tucked his hand beside him on the litter as the door slid shut.

Quinn Eisley appeared at her side. He signaled the chopper pilot to take off, then drew her back out of the mini-hurricane created by the blades. She glanced up at the tall dark man by her side and, for the first time in all the years she'd known him, she saw emotion in his eyes. It was anguished regret. As soon as the helicopter was airborne, she stepped away from him and began waving a goodbye that she knew Christian wouldn't see.

Gritting his teeth against the agony in his left leg and fighting the black mist clouding his consciousness, Christian tried to raise himself to look out the Plexiglas door. Seeing him, one of the medics tried to force him gently back down. A curse burning through his clenched teeth, Christian fought the man off.

Finally understanding what he wanted, the medic slipped a brawny arm around him and raised his shoulders. "I don't blame you, buddy. I wouldn't want to leave her behind, either," he murmured appreciatively.

Christian ignored the man, concentrating all his awareness on the lonely figure below, one arm raised in farewell. She grew rapidly smaller as the helicopter gained altitude, and at last she disappeared. Christian sagged back against the medic's arm and let oblivion take him.

The helicopter was only a dot in the sky when Erin finally lowered her arm. She turned to Quinn Eisley, standing a few yards away, watching her silently. "You'd better get out of here, too, Quinn. Someone's bound to have reported the gunfire and all the commotion, and the local police are going to be crawling all over here in a few minutes." She gave him a faint smile. "Now that the marines have left, you might have a little trouble explaining what the U.S. Navy was doing landing on a Canadian beach."

He led her in the direction of the beach, where Christian's green and white seaplane bobbed a few yards offshore. For a moment he wondered what it would be like to have a woman look at him the way Erin Mathias had just looked at Dekker. Only once before had he seen that look of total love and devotion on a woman's face. It had been on Sarah Weston's as she'd watched her husband, Matthew, finally coming home to her after three long years. He put his arm around Erin's shoulders and gave her a very rare grin. "Who's going to tell them?"

Chapter 13

"You miss her, too, don't you, guys?"

Christian laughed ruefully as he got a soft whine and a curt meow for answers. It seemed impossible to believe that Erin had been in his house for only six short days. He felt her presence so strongly that he caught himself turning around to tell her something, looking for her to show her something special. Just now he'd almost called to her to come watch the eagle chick getting ready for its first flight.

He was sitting in the leather easy chair before one of the living-room windows, his legs stretched out, feet propped on the hassock, just being lazy. Clancy lay on the floor beside him. Oscar jumped and laid himself out on his right thigh, revving up his chain-saw purr. The cat carefully avoided his left leg, although the time was fast approaching when he wouldn't have to. The leg was healing well; another week, the doctor said, and he would be able to get rid of his cane.

It had been six weeks since he'd been wounded, a month since he'd been home...a lifetime since he'd last seen Erin. She had followed him to the hospital, he knew; Eisley had brought her, and he'd said she hadn't left his bedside for three days, not until the doctors had assured her that he was out of danger. He'd been drifting in and out of consciousness, and he couldn't be sure which of the times that he'd seen her she had been real and which times he had imagined her.

Since then he had seen her only on television and in the newspapers. Damion wouldn't admit who had bought her research, so she had gone public with her work, saying that the only way to safeguard the whales from exploitation was to allow as many people as possible to have access to her research. She had been in great demand, traveling, delivering papers, holding seminars.

He hadn't heard from her in all that time, but then, he hadn't really expected to. What had to be settled between them had to be settled in person—not with a phone call or a glib note.

The faint sound of a boat engine drifted through the open door off the veranda. After setting aside the cat, Christian rose from the chair, curious to see who his visitor was. He wasn't expecting anyone, although Eisley had mentioned that he'd be dropping by. There was still the matter of a three-hundred-thousand-dollar check to dispose of. He imagined Erin could put it to good use.

Christian looked over the railing in time to see a green water taxi pulling away from the dock. There was no sign of whoever it had delivered. He grabbed the cane leaning against the wall and started down the steps.

Even with the cane, he was walking almost without a limp. When she'd last seen him, with the black thread lattice holding his thigh together, she had despaired that he would ever walk normally again. Now, after unconsciously completing the little ritual she had seen him perform, turning a slow circle in the middle of the dock to celebrate the peaceful loveliness of his island, Erin walked slowly forward to meet him.

The sunlight formed a nimbus around his hair, throwing his face into shadow, hiding his expression from her. His hair was longer, almost shaggy, and he was dressed casually in an open blue work shirt and faded jeans. He looked a little thinner, but his tan was as dark as ever. "I see the eagle chick is learning to fly," she said when only a few feet separated them. She wanted to throw herself into his arms, beg him to hold her and never let her go, but the expression on his face held her back. It was somber, almost grave, and suddenly her terrible nervousness increased tenfold. She had been so horribly torn, sitting hour after endless hour beside him in the hospital. She wanted so badly to stay and take care of him, but she'd had a responsibility to the whales that she had unwittingly put in danger. He had proved his love for her without ever stating it by showing that he was willing to lose his life for her. She had told him that she loved him, but she hadn't stayed around to prove it. Did he understand that the choice she'd had to make didn't mean she loved him any less?

"You're walking well," she said, hearing the too-quick, inane words and despising them.

His voice was quiet and even. "The doctor says I can throw away the cane next week."

Instead of leading her up the steps to his house, he turned up the beach, and Erin had no choice but to follow. Maybe he doesn't want me in his home anymore, she thought, and the unutterable sadness of that caused tears to prick at the back of her eyes. She blinked them away rapidly and said with forced cheerfulness, "I'm glad it's so beautiful here today. I was in Tokyo yesterday, and the weather was miserable, rainy and cold."

He didn't answer, only stopped at a natural stone formation on the beach. Smoothed by centuries of waves flung over its surface, the boulder had been weathered into a miniature haystack with just room enough for two people to lean on it. Erin paused beside him, not quite touching, sensing his solid warmth. He was leaning against the rock, hands in his pockets, eyes on the endless action of the waves on the sand. "I had to go. I didn't want to. I wanted to stay with you, but Phillip wouldn't reveal who he'd sold the tapes to." Erin knew she was explaining badly. "I had to protect—"

"I understand," he interrupted quietly, turning his head to look at her. She was dressed simply in slacks and a sweater, and she looked tired, and much too thin and pale. He wanted to take her in his arms and coax one of those golden, breathtaking smiles from her, but that would be too easy, and would settle nothing. "You trusted the wrong people." His brief, self-mocking smile included himself.

She nodded, lowering her gaze against the sadness and naked pain in his eyes. The realization of vulnerability in a man so strong came with a poignancy that tightened her throat and made it impossible for her to speak. Her gaze fell on the cane propped beside him. *And I didn't trust one enough,* she thought.

After a moment of silence, her chin came up with a hint of determination. "I'm thinking of shifting my focus to the pilot whales around here," she began with a glance at his impassive face. The tension wound tighter inside her. She felt like a poker player guarding her hand while trying to make the other player show his. "I could live on one of the islands, commute to the Institute when I needed to. Of course, I'd need a permanent h—site so I wouldn't have to change the study group once I got established."

"You'd want an island without many people on it. That can be lonely."

"I don't need a lot of people." *Just you,* she added silently.

"How long would you plan to stay?" His tone was almost disinterested.

"As long as necessary to accomplish everything I want to do." *Building a life together, children.* "Probably fifty or sixty years." He merely nodded, and Erin took a deep breath, then laid all her cards on the table. "You said once that you had planned to ask me to stay here permanently, to live with you. Is that offer still open?"

"No," he said quietly, and she died a little inside. "I have another one now."

She waited to hear it, without allowing herself to hope.

A hint of that peculiarly sweet, gentle smile slightly softened the harsh set of his mouth. "Marry me, Erin."

He watched her answering smile form slowly. First the corners of her mouth began to turn up; then her lips curved, and her eyes lit with an inner fire that rivaled the sun's, and suddenly she was in his arms.

"I take it that's a yes?"

The words were light, but there was an undertone of uncertainty in them. Erin pulled back, and her smile disappeared as they searched each others' eyes down to their souls, finding understanding and forgiveness, trust and love. "Yes," she said, and her smile returned with a brilliance that dazzled him. She took his mouth with a hungry kiss. "Yes. Yes. Yes."

Hours later, he propped his head on his hand and looked down at her. She looked sleepy and satisfied and exactly right in his bed. His other hand traced down the center of her body from her throat to her waist. "You haven't asked me to say it," he said quietly.

"It isn't necessary," she said just as quietly, reaching up to touch his beloved face.

He took her hand in his, pressing a gentle kiss in her palm, then held it against his heart. "I think it is." He looked at her soberly. "I love you, Erin."

"I know," she said, and her smile took his breath away.

* * * * *

Silhouette Intimate Moments

PARRIS AFTON BONDS
The Cowboy and The Lady

Marianna McKenna was used to bright lights, big cities and the glamorous life of a Hollywood star, so it came as quite a shock when she found herself living at the Mescalero Cattle Company, victim of a tragic mistake and a convict sentenced to work on the ranch for the next six months.

Tom Malcolm was a true cowboy, rugged and plainspoken, and he didn't have much use for hothouse flowers like Marianna McKenna. Or so he told himself, at least, though that didn't stop the yearning in his heart—or the fire in his blood.

Look for Tom and Marianna's story in *That McKenna Woman* IM#241, Book One of Parris Afton Bonds's Mescalero Trilogy, available this month only from Silhouette Intimate Moments. Then watch for Book Two, *That Malcolm Girl* (September 1988), and Book Three, *That Mescalero Man* (December 1988), to complete a trilogy as untamed and compelling as the American West itself.

IM241

MORE THAN A MIRACLE
by Kathleen Eagle

This month, let award-winning author Kathleen Eagle sweep you away with a story that proves the truth of the old adage, "Love conquers all."

Elizabeth Donnelly loved her son so deeply that she was willing to sneak back to De Colores, an island paradise to the eye, but a horror to the soul. There, with the help of Sloan McQuade, she would find the child who had been stolen from her and carry him to safety. She would also find something else, something she never would have expected, because the man who could work miracles had one more up his sleeve: love.

Enjoy Elizabeth and Sloan's story this month in *More Than A Miracle*, Intimate Moments #242. And if you like this book, you might also enjoy *Candles in the Night* (Special Edition #437), the first of Kathleen Eagle's De Colores books.

Silhouette Intimate Moments

At Dodd Memorial Hospital, Love is the Best Medicine

When temperatures are rising and pulses are racing, Dodd Memorial Hospital is the place to be. Every doctor, nurse and patient is a heart specialist, and their favorite prescription is a little romance. Next month, finish Lucy Hamilton's Dodd Memorial Hospital Trilogy with HEARTBEATS, IM #245.

Nurse Vanessa Rice thought police sergeant Clay Williams was the most annoying man she knew. Then he showed up at Dodd Memorial with a gunshot wound, and the least she could do was be friends with him—if he'd let her. But Clay was interested in something more, and Vanessa didn't want that kind of commitment. She had a career that was important to her, and there was no room in her life for any man. But Clay was determined to show her that they could have a future together—and that there are times when the patient knows best.

TALES OF THE RISING MOON
A Desire trilogy by Joyce Thies

MOON OF THE RAVEN—June

Conlan Fox was part American Indian and as tough as the Montana land he rode, but it took fragile yet strong-willed Kerry Armstrong to make his dreams come true.

REACH FOR THE MOON—August

It would take a heart of stone for Steven Armstrong to evict the woman and children living on his land. But when Steven met Samantha, eviction was the last thing on his mind!

GYPSY MOON—October

Robert Armstrong met Serena when he returned to his ancestral estate in Connecticut. Their fiery temperaments clashed from the start, but despite himself, Rob was falling under the Gypsy's spell.

Don't miss any of Joyce Thies's enchanting
TALES OF THE RISING MOON,
coming to you from Silhouette Desire.

SD 432

Silhouette Intimate Moments

COMING NEXT MONTH

#245 HEARTBEATS—Lucy Hamilton

Policeman Clay Williams wanted more than just friendship from Vanessa Rice. But when the drug gang he was after decided to get him by getting her, his campaign to win her heart became a race against time, a battle to prove they had a future together before he lost the chance—forever.

#246 MUSTANG MAN—Lee Magner

To save her father's life, Carolyn Andrews had to find a missing stallion, and only Jonathan Raider could help her. But the search threatened more than their safety. Now that she'd met Jonathan, she knew it would break her heart if they had to say goodbye.

#247 DONOVAN'S PROMISE—Dallas Schulze

Twenty years ago Donovan had promised to take care of Elizabeth forever, but now their marriage was coming to an end. He couldn't let that happen. Somehow he had to prove that his feelings hadn't changed and that the promise he had made once would never be broken.

#248 ANGEL OF MERCY—Heather Graham Pozzessere

DEA agent Brad McKenna had been shot, and he knew that only a miracle could save him. When he regained consciousness, he thought he'd gotten his miracle, for surely that was an angel bending over him. But he soon discovered that Wendy Hawk was a flesh-and-blood woman—and the feelings he had for her were very real.
